Daughter of Time

The After Cilmeri Series:

Daughter of Time (prequel)

Footsteps in Time (Book One)

Winds of Time (a novella)

Prince of Time (Book Two)

Crossroads in Time (Book Three)

The Gareth and Gwen Medieval Mysteries

The Bard's Daughter (prequel novella)

The Good Knight

The Uninvited Guest

The Last Pendragon Saga

The Last Pendragon

The Pendragon's Quest

Other Books by Sarah Woodbury

Cold My Heart: A Novel of King Arthur

Part of the *After Cilmeri* Series

DAUGHTER OF TIME

A TIME TRAVEL ROMANCE

by

SARAH WOODBURY

Daughter of Time

This is a work of fiction.

Cover image by Christine DeMaio-Rice at Flip City Books
http://flipcitybooks.com

To Brynne

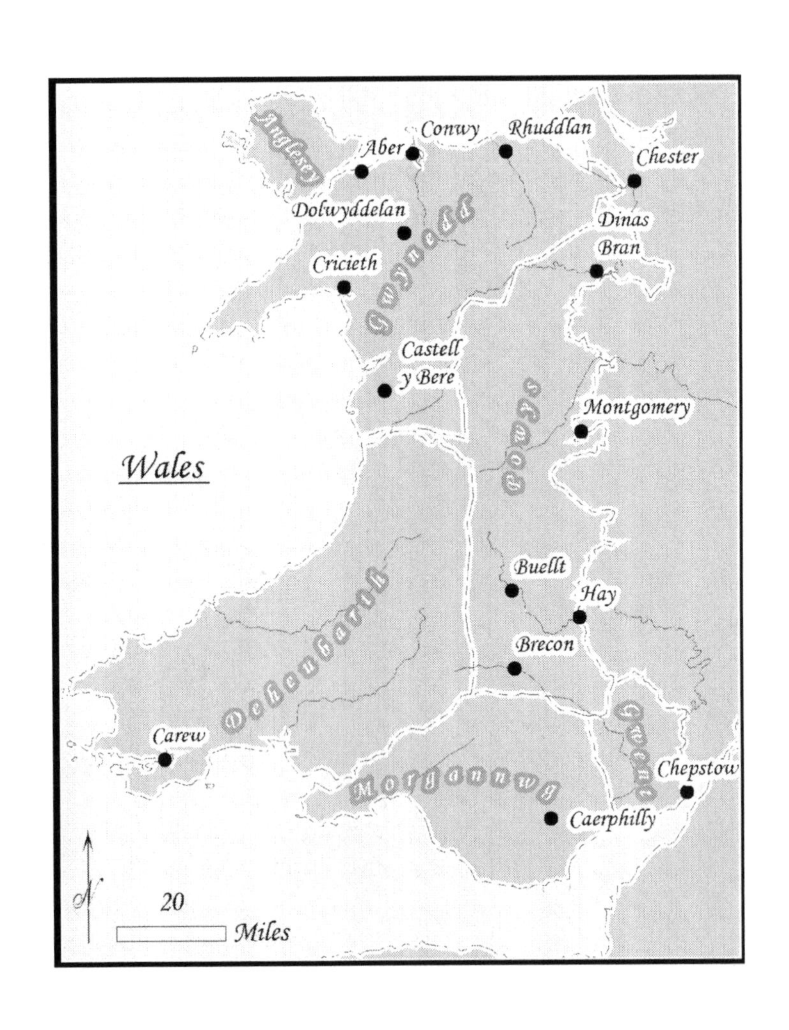
Wales
Anglesey
Aber
Conwy
Rhuddlan
Chester
Dolwyddelan
Gwynedd
Dinas
Bran
Cricieth
Castell
y Bere
Powys
Montgomery
Buellt
Hay
Brecon
Deheubarth
Carew
Gwent
Chepstow
Morgannwg
Caerphilly
N
20
Miles

A Brief Guide to Welsh Pronunciation

c a hard ‘c’ sound (Cadfael)
ch a non-English sound as in Scottish "ch" in "loch" (Fychan)
dd a buzzy ‘th’ sound, as in “there” (Ddu; Gwynedd)
f as in “of” (Cadfael)
ff as in “off” (Gruffydd)
g a hard ‘g’ sound, as in “gas” (Goronwy)
l as in "lamp" (Llywelyn)
ll a breathy “th” sound that does not occur in English (Llywelyn)
rh a breathy mix between ‘r’ and ‘rh’ that does not occur in English (Rhys)
th a softer sound than for ‘dd,’ as in "thick" (Arthur)
u a short ‘ih’ sound (Gruffydd), or a long ‘ee’ sound (Cymru—pronounced “kumree”)
w as a consonant, it’s an English ‘w’ (Llywelyn); as a vowel, an ‘oo’ sound (Bwlch)
y the only letter in which Welsh is not phonetic. It can be an ‘ih’ sound, as in “Gwyn,” is often an “uh” sound (Cymru), and at the end of the word is an “ee” sound (thus, both Cymru—the modern word for Wales—and Cymry—the word for Wales in the Dark Ages—are pronounced “kumree”)

1

Meg

My husband's body lay cold on the table in front of me. A sheet covered all but his face, but that didn't stop me from imagining the damage to his body—from the car accident and from wounds inflicted long before tonight.

The chill in the room seeped all the way through me, nearly as cold as the January air outside. The morgue was just as I'd imagined—feared—it would be. A classroom-sized box with fluorescent lights, sanitized metal tables, sinks and counters lined against one wall, with implements whose function I didn't want to know. I tried not to look anywhere but at Trev, but as I began to struggle against the rushing in my ears and the narrowing of my vision, I had to glance away, my eyes skating over the rest of the room. The police officer took my right elbow and spoke softly in my ear. "Come sit, Mrs. Lloyd. There's nothing you can do here."

I nodded, not really listening, and pulled my winter coat closer around me. The officer steered me out the door and into the hall, to an orange plastic chair next to the one in which my mother waited. It was the kind of hallway you could find in any public building: utilitarian, sterile, with off-white tile flecked with black, off-white walls, and thin, metal framed windows that wouldn't open, holding back the weather. I met my mother's eyes and we shared a look that needed no words.

What the officer didn't understand—couldn't understand—were my conflicting emotions: horror and sadness certainly, anger, but overlying all that, relief. Relief for him, having had to live for six months with increasing despair, and relief for me that he had self-medicated himself into oblivion, releasing me from living with a man I no longer loved and couldn't like.

"It's nothing to do with you," Mom said. I turned to look at her. Her face was nearly as white as her hair, but her chin jutted out as it always did when she was determined to get her point across and she thought I was being particularly stubborn.

"I know, Mom. I know that." I leaned forward and rested my head in my hands. The tears I'd controlled in the morgue finally fell, filling my eyes and seeping between my fingers.

My mother's voice came softly. "He made his choice, *cariad*. Even he could see that this was a better end."

"I know that too."

I stand on the porch of my mother's house, my hands on my hips. Anna is napping in her room and I've been enjoying a quiet hour alone. The bright sunlight of the August afternoon heats my face. I shield my eyes with one hand, wondering where I left my sunglasses, as Trev parks his car and gets out, coming around the front to stand on the sidewalk, his arms calm at his sides. I brace myself for his plea. He's going to ask me to come back to him. I'm ready to say no; strong enough now to say no as I should have been the first time he hit me.

It's been three months since I've seen him. Three months which I spent reveling in my new-found independence and planning the rest of my life, and as always, thankful that I had somewhere to go—that my mother had been willing to take us in. I've already started at the community college; I'm going to get myself back on track to the future I'd had before Trev had interrupted it.

"I need you, Meg," Trev says.

"No you don't. Or only as a punching bag."

"You don't understand," he says, taking a step forward.

I hold out one hand. "Don't come any further. You need to stay on the sidewalk or I'll call the police."

He knows now that I'll do it and takes one step back. He raises his hands, palms out, as if in supplication, except that he's never asked me for anything in his life, never stooped to saying please. This time he does.

"Please come home, Meg," he says. "I'm dying."

I gape at him. "What?"

"It's the reason I've been unstable recently. The reason I've lost so much weight."

"The reason for that is that you've stopped eating and opted only to drink straight scotch," I said. "That or bourbon."

Trev shakes his head. "It stops the ache," he says. "I've just come from the doctor. He says I have a chance to live—chemotherapy and medicines that will make me even sicker. I can't do this alone. I need you."

So I'd gone with him, out of guilt and obligation and pity. Trevor Lloyd: my husband of two years and the father of our little girl, Anna. It was for her that I'd initially stayed with him, and because of her that I'd left him. Returning because he had stage-four pancreatic cancer at twenty-three may have seemed the right thing to do at the time, but it had been a mistake, one to which the bruising from the black eye he'd given me only the night before testified. How he'd even been able to stand I didn't know, nor why I'd not been smart enough to get out of his way. That had always been my problem. I'd let him go, incapacitated as he was, strung up on who knew what cocktail of medications and alcohol, thankful that he was leaving me alone.

And now he was dead. Was that my fault?

And now he was dead and I was free.

*****

I tossed my purse on the floor of the living room, pulled off my coat, shoulders still dusted with snow from outside, and plopped myself onto the couch next to Anna and my sister, Elisa, who'd been reading her a book. Elisa, two years younger than I, was home for Christmas from her freshman year in college and would soon return to school.

It was three days since Trev's funeral; a week since he died. A week wasn't a long time to mourn, Mom said, but I'd been feeling his loss for months already, if not years, from the first time he'd slapped me across the face and sent me spinning around the kitchen table. His death had only been the final note in a long, mournful tune.

"A guy at the community college just asked me out on a date," I said.

"Really?"

I gave Elisa a glance and a half-smile. "Do I have three heads or something?" I said, and then confessed before she could answer, "I was just surprised. It's been a while since I thought about myself that way."

"Since you stopped nursing and lost some weight, you look really great, actually."

What could I do but laugh? Elisa had a way of getting straight to the point. "Well, thanks," I said. "I think. I feel more like myself. Like I'm waking up from a long sleep, or as if I've been wrapped in Styrofoam and I've finally broken through it."

"So you really are okay?" Elisa said.

"Yes. I think, finally, yes."

"No more losers," she said. "Any guy that you meet and start to date, you have to run through both Mom and me before you get serious. Bring him home and he has to submit to twenty questions before you get any further."

"That's pretty strict!" I said. "What if I just want to go to a movie with him?"

"Nope." Elisa shook her head. She was very serious. Admittedly, she was always serious but I could tell she really meant it and it touched me.

I smiled at her. "You are what I want to be. I'm so proud of you."

"Me? You're the one who's had to deal with all this stuff."

"I'm the one who chose the wrong dream to follow. Is it too late for me?"

"Of course not!" Mom bustled in. "You're going to be fine. You're only twenty."

"I'll be twenty-one soon."

Mom shook her head. "You've just made a small detour. Besides, look what we got out of it!" She leaned over the back of the couch to kiss the top of Anna's head. "*Cyn wired â'r pader.*"

Elisa and I rolled our eyes in unison. 'As true as the Lord's Prayer!' Mom had said. She knew enough Welsh to get by, as she said, and she'd diligently taught it to us. That just happened to be her favorite phrase. She'd emigrated to Pennsylvania from Wales as a girl, settling in Radnor with an aunt and uncle (long since dead). She'd grown up in Cardiff, a city in south Wales, and one anglicized enough that she'd never quite become fluent in the language.

Yet, she'd found comfort in the Pennsylvania hills that reminded her of home and in the remnants of the Welsh language that she found along the Main Line. She'd never been back to Wales, though, and Radnor, where we still lived, was as close as she'd gotten to living in a Welsh community.

After working for twenty years as a housekeeper, she married Evan Morgan. He'd been ten years older than she and delighted to find himself with a wife—and within a few years of marriage, two daughters, long after he thought himself an established bachelor. Mom had already been forty when they married so they hadn't had as long as they would have liked together; she blamed my sojourn with Trev on grief at my father's death.

Unfortunately, none of us knew any more Welsh than Mom . . . and what had Elisa and I learned in high school? *French*, and confounded our parents with our grasp of the language. Sitting on the couch with Elisa and Anna, I recalled that I used to be good in school. *A lifetime ago*. Maybe I could be again.

"Can we go, Mommy?" Anna said.

I smiled down at her and tickled her under her chin. She giggled. She had curly, dark hair, almost black, and her dark eyes looked at me with an intent expression. Her little legs stuck straight out in front of her as she held the book on her lap. She was only two and a half years old but already talking in long sentences. Sometimes I was the only one who could understand what she was saying through her little two-year-old lisp, but at least she was saying it. I didn't need her to articulate "ice cream", however, to remember my promise.

"Yes," I said. "Let's go."

"What about dinner?" Mom said. I stood to look at her, not wanting to argue in front of Anna. Mom met my eye, and then nodded. "Dessert first, then dinner. Sounds wonderful."

"Thank you, Mom." I leaned forward to put my arms around her plump waist and my head on her shoulder. "Thank you for everything."

"Dw i'n dy garu di."

"I love you too." I held out a hand to Anna. She turned over on her stomach, letting her legs dangle over the edge of the cushion, slid down from the couch, and ran to me. I bundled her into her coat, put her on my hip, and reached for my purse again. "We'll be back."

"Bye," Elisa and Mom said in unison.

Anna waved as she always did, her little fist opening and closing. "Bye."

Once in my little blue Honda, with Anna buckled into her car seat in the middle of the back seat, I allowed myself a deep breath. I leaned my head against the seat rest. *We'll be okay.* I buckled myself in, started the car, and headed away from my mother's house.

It was only four miles to the ice cream parlor. I took the turns carefully, reliving again, as I did in my dreams, what must have happened to Trev that night. Halfway there, I realized we were approaching the spot where he died. I'd been avoiding it the whole week. How could I have forgotten to take a different route this time? The intersection lay ahead of us. My stomach clenched.

I come home from my job at the library on campus. I'd been able to put Anna in bed before I left, but as I push open the kitchen door at midnight, I can see through the space between the kitchen counter and the cupboards into the living room, which is dark except for the flickering light from the television. There she is, lying on the couch with her eyes open, watching something that looks like Jaws 17. I set my books on the kitchen counter and Trev twists in his armchair. He has a beer in one hand and a lit cigarette in the other.

I just stand there, staring at him, anger, recriminations, and hatred boiling up inside me. There's a moment when I try to stop them, knowing it's pointless to complain, trying to make allowances for the crappy upbringing he had that led him to this moment. But then they spill out. "Trev," I say, trying to keep my voice down and reasonable-sounding. "I've asked you not to smoke in the house. It's bad for Anna."

"It's fucking cold out there!" he said, hitching himself higher in the chair. He's lost so much weight, his body doesn't have the mass to stay fixed in the seat anymore and keeps sliding down it. "I'll fucking die if I go out there."

"Trev," I say again. "You're smoking."

"And I'm fucking dying anyway. Shit," he says, getting angry between one instant and the next. He reaches beside him and throws the pillow in his chair across the room like a frisbee. It hits the television, which fizzles out. We've never been able to afford a better TV and in that moment, I'm glad. But Trev is mad.

He pushes out of his chair and approaches me, taking small mincing steps. He changes his voice to something whiny and high, a supposed imitation of my own. "Trev," he says. "Trev don't smoke. Trev, you're keeping Anna awake. She needs her sleep. Trev, you shouldn't be drinking while you're on your meds."

I back away, glancing at Anna to see how she's taking this. Her eyes are closed. I hope that she really is asleep, now that the glare from the television is gone, but I don't see how she could be.

"Trev," I say, one more time. "Don't."

"Don't fucking say my name!" He backhands me across the face before I can get out of the way. I fall against the kitchen table and onto the floor, and then crab-walk backward, hurrying before he can hit me again. He stumbles forward and leans down, getting right in my face, his hand fisted. "I'll do what I please in my own house!"

Then he straightens. He's breathing hard; this has taken more out of him than it used to. He staggers as he makes his way to the kitchen door and opens it. I don't say anything and neither does he as he walks away from me, into the night.

When the police officer came to the house, he told me that Trev hadn't braked at a stop sign where the road teed. Instead of turning right or left as required, he'd driven straight ahead into a tree. Facing that same junction, I eased up on the gas. My eyes blurred as we approached it and I fought back the tears, wiping at my cheeks with the back of one hand while the other clenched the steering wheel. I pressed the brake hard, as I knew he had not—but then . . . *I'm not stopping!*

"Anna!" Her name came out a shriek as the car skidded sideways on the black ice I'd not known was there. I swung the wheel, struggling to correct our course. I managed to alter it enough to avoid the tree on which Trev had lost his life, but slid instead toward the twenty-foot high roadcut to its left which was fronted by a shallow ditch. Time hung suspended during that half second before impact, stretching before me. My hands whitened on the wheel, my throat tightened from unshed tears, and Anna cried in the back seat, frightened by the panic in my voice.

Then everything speeded up as the car slid into the cut *and then through it.*

An abyss opened before me—a yawning blackness that gave me the same hollow rushing in my ears I'd felt in the morgue. A lifetime later, we were through it or across it—whatever *it* was. I registered gray-blue sky and sea before the car bounded headfirst down an incline and skidded into a marsh. It came to an abrupt halt as the world flipped forward. Instinctively, I threw up my hands to protect my head but the steering wheel rushed at my face. I tasted plastic and blood—pain, and then nothing.

2

Llywelyn

***In** the year of our Lord, twelve hundred, and sixty-eight. May God go with you.* The priest's parting invocation for the close of evening mass echoed in my head as I took the steps two at a time up to the battlements of Castell Criccieth. Darkness was coming on and I was looking forward to seeing the sun set over the water to the southwest. They say that we, the Welsh, are always caught between the mountains and the sea. On a day like today, with the wind whipping the sea into a froth and the snow-covered peak of Yr Wyddfa—Mt. Snowdon—towering above the castle, both tugged at me.

I breathed in the salty air, feeling its humid scent. In truth, I loved it all. It was as if my boots had been planted in the soil of Wales and no power in heaven or earth could move me from this spot.

My small corner of Europe had been threatened, encircled, and enslaved by kings of many nationalities since Caesar first crossed the channel into England over a thousand years before. Throughout it all, we Welsh had, in turn, fought and run, thrown ourselves upon our enemies, and hidden in our mountains. Each foreign king had eventually discovered that our resistance to his rule was as inevitable as the rain, and our place in Wales as permanent as the rock on which we stood.

And now King Henry of England knew it too. The triumph of my ascendancy was like a fire in my belly that would not go out. Every month that passed allowed me to more strongly grasp each hamlet, each pasture and village in Wales as my own.

As I stood on the battlements, the wind in my hair, the words my bard had pronounced at the New Year's feast rang again in my ears, each stanza crashing over me like the waves that hit the shore below: *There stands a lion, courageous and brave . . . Llywelyn, ruler of Wales.* Was I too proud, too full of hubris, that I heard these words in my head, long past the ending of the feast?

The sun was reddening as it lowered in the sky and I turned my back on it to look up at Yr Wyddfa, its snowy peaks now pink from the reflected light. It had been a sunny day, unusual for January, and this was a rare treat. I was just turning to look northeast again, when a—*what is that thing!*—surged out of the trees that lined the edge of the marsh abutting the seashore to the west of the castle, beacons shining from the front of it, and buried itself headfirst in the marsh.

Stunned, I couldn't move at first, but the unmistakable wail of a small child, faint at this distance, rose into the air. Afraid now that the—*thing? chariot?*—would sink into the marsh before I could reach it, I ran across the battlements to the stairs, down them, out a side door of the keep, and into the bailey. I spied Goronwy ap Heilin, my longtime counselor and friend, just coming into the castle from under the gatehouse and I strode toward him.

"My lord!" He checked his horse, concern etched in every line of his squat body. He was dressed in full armor, his torso made more bulky by its weight. His helmet hid his prematurely gray hair.

I hesitated for a heartbeat and then threw myself onto the horse behind him. Goronwy gathered his reins and chose not to argue, even though he had to know that his horse couldn't carry the two of us for long.

"We must hurry," I said.

Goronwy spurred his horse back the way he'd come, out the gate and down the causeway that led from the castle to the village. We trotted through the village and turned left, trying to reach the point where the vehicle had gone in.

While Castell Criccieth itself was built on a high rock that could be reached by a narrow passage, the marsh associated with it was legendary. The pathway fell off dangerously into a sucking swamp, fed by an unnamed underground stream that seeped its way to the sea. I'd not lost anyone in it recently and didn't want to lose anyone now, but as we came to a sudden halt along the road as it turned, I wasn't sure what to do.

The wail of the child was more evident the closer we got, though it was no longer constant but punctuated every now and then by silence. Perhaps he was tiring, too exhausted to maintain his cries. I could imagine him gasping for air between breaths as a child does, especially when he is unsure if anyone is coming to help.

"By all that is holy!" Goronwy said, seeing the vehicle for the first time. "What is it?"

"I don't know. A chariot of some kind, carrying two from the looks." It had four wheels, as wagons do, two of which spun slowly, high in the air. The vehicle had moved so fast and without any visible means of propulsion that I couldn't imagine what had thrown it out of the forest and into my marsh in the first place. It was coated in a sturdy material that wasn't wood, and was, unaccountably, blue in color.

Goronwy took in the situation in a glance and gestured to the point where the chariot had driven into the marsh. "By the trees, my lord," he said. "It looks as if the ground is more solid there."

"Yes. Keep going."

We continued on the road until it reached the trees and then along their edge until we stopped only a few yards from the chariot. The sun was nearly down now and I cursed myself for forgetting a torch. We dismounted and I took a step toward the chariot, but my foot immediately stuck a few inches into the mud. To put my weight down further would ensure the loss of my boot.

"Careful, my lord," Goronwy said.

I stepped back. "We'll find another way."

Goronwy spied several fallen logs in the woods that edged the marsh and we lugged them towards the marsh to act as a bridge between us and the chariot. Urgency filled both of us so with me in the lead, we stepped carefully across them to the chariot. I touched one of the side walls of the vehicle, hesitant, noting that it curved away from me, smooth as the water in my washing basin.

"Now what?" Goronwy said. "Do you need my help to get them out?"

Goronwy was concerned because the narrow bridge we'd built was sinking into the marsh under our combined weight. For us to stand together on one end might doom the both of us. I peered through the clear glass that separated me from the baby in the rear of the vehicle and from the woman in the front seat. The light of the setting sun reflected off the glass and I could see fingerprints smudging the window. The sight struck me as so *commonplace* that it gave me confidence.

"No. Stay where you are."

I surveyed the expanse of incredibly worked metal of which the vehicle was composed. As I studied it, I realized it was not all one piece as I'd first thought. It had been put together in sections, and then the pieces of metal attached together. Still, except for two black elongated objects aligned with each other half way down the sides, there was nothing to hold onto. I grasped one of them, hoping it was what it looked like: a latch.

I pulled on it and miraculously, the door to the chariot opened. I had to duck into the doorway since the chariot had a roof that was two feet less than my height. The girl slumped over a wheel affixed to the wall in front of her. I pulled her back into her seat and frowned at the line of blood across her forehead. Except for the one wound, I couldn't see any other injuries. Her eyes were closed, however, and she was unconscious. It surprised me, in that half a second it took to look her over, that she was an ordinary girl, admittedly dressed strangely and half my age, but there was nothing about her that told me why she would be driving this incredible chariot.

A black strap of yet another material unlike any I'd ever seen held her in her seat. I fumbled to find its ties, grateful for the bright light coming from the ceiling of the chariot. I was ready to pull my knife to cut through the straps, but almost as an after-thought, noticed the strap ended in a large red square near her waist. I pressed it. The strap released and the woman slumped sideways. I slid my arms around her back and under her knees and pulled her to me, lifting her out of the chariot. Then, carefully balancing on the logs, I cat-walked back to Goronwy and transferred her to his arms.

He had waited patiently, as if this task was the most normal thing in the world for us to be doing. He held the woman, but otherwise didn't move, since his position on the end of the log allowed me to balance near the chariot. "She's beautiful," he said, checking her from head to toe as her head lolled back on his forearm.

I gave him a quelling look, though it wasn't like I hadn't noticed. Her long hair was shot with every shade of brown imaginable and though her long lashes were down-turned in sleep so I couldn't see her eyes, I had no difficulty imagining them gazing at me. She was slender as an unwed girl, but she looked so much like the girl behind her, she had to be her mother.

"So's the little one," I said. I moved back to the chariot, sliding one foot forward and then the other, but as I did so, the pressure in the marsh shifted and a sucking sound pierced the silence. The chariot sank another foot, tipping forward so now it lay only a few degrees off vertical.

"Is there time, my lord?"

"I will not leave that child to die," I said. "I don't think the risk to me too great."

Afraid that movement near the front of the vehicle would upend it further, and at the same time worried about getting caught in the chariot's draft if it did sink into the marsh, I pulled on the latch to the rear door, which opened just as had the door in front. Although the child appeared to be in some kind of special seat designed expressly for her small size, a red circle sat in the center of her chest. Hoping that there was a system here, I pressed it and as in her mother's case, the straps released. The rear wheels were so high in the air now that the opening in the vehicle was at chest height—making it easy for me to reach into the chariot, but forcing me to lift the child from her seat with only the strength in my arms.

"Come, *cariad*," I said.

Her eyes were wide as she reached for me, but she appeared unhurt. I pulled her to me and she wrapped her arms around my neck, swiveling her head to the left and right as she took in her surroundings.

"My lord." Goronwy's voice sounded a warning behind me and I took a step back, away from the chariot, and then another, my arms clutched around the little girl.

The pounding of my heart at last began to slow as Goronwy and I backed off the logs. "How do you want to do this?" Goronwy said, the woman still in his arms. "She's not a sack of turnips, but she's heavier than one."

I set the baby on the ground, pleased she'd stopped crying and was willing to stand sturdily on her own feet. I crouched to speak to her. "Stand here. I'm going to take care of your mother."

All I caught of the girl's reply was one word, similar to Mam: *Mammy*, I surmised, though I didn't know of any children who called their mother that.

I mounted Goronwy's horse and Goronwy passed me the woman. I settled her across the horse's withers. Because the girl wore breeches, I could rest her directly in front of me, with her back leaning against my chest, and her head tucked under my chin. While her clothes were entirely too provocative, in this case I was glad she was wearing them. Otherwise I would have had to cradle her in my arms or hike her skirt up past her thighs, which might provide us with a pleasant view, but was even more immodest.

I wrapped one arm around her waist and grasped the reins with the other. Goronwy bent down for the child, who allowed him to pick her up, her little arm wrapped around his neck as she'd wrapped it around mine. She said something to Goronwy that I didn't catch and he answered in an undertone.

Then I saw his face. The look was one of pure panic, but he revealed a hitherto unknown adeptness with children and shifted her to his hip.

"I've got her, my lord," Goronwy said. "Though I'm not sure she understands the words we're saying."

"She's very young."

"She spoke to me just now in a language that was unfamiliar," Goronwy said. "I couldn't even begin to tell you what it was."

"English?"

"No," Goronwy said. "At least no sort of English I have ever heard, even lisping from the mouth of a child."

"When her mother awakes, we'll have some answers."

"We certainly have many questions. Most pointedly, *what is that vehicle?*"

"I would add, *"How did you fall into my marsh? What are those strange materials, metal, and clothes?*"

"Could they be English?" Goronwy said, leaping ahead to the most crucial question. He strode along beside me, he and the girl finding a rhythm to his walk as she continued to take in her surroundings. "Returning crusaders have brought many new discoveries to Europe from the east. When I was last at Dinas

Bran, I met such a man—he opened his own tavern, of all things—who told me of a glass through which one could see far distances. I very much would like one of those."

"I will look into it," I said. "Right now, our concern is somewhat more mundane. We need to get these two to the castle safely tonight, but come daylight, we must return to the vehicle with the woman. She has much to explain, both what it is and how it works."

I directed the horse towards the causeway, aiming for the road we'd left and anxious not to stray into the bog. Since Goronwy was unhorsed, I rode more slowly than I might have otherwise. I was never outside the castle without my guard and felt strangely vulnerable, almost naked, without them.

We'd reached the road when Goronwy suddenly stopped and spun around. I reined in, and then heard what had gained his attention: another sucking sound, louder than when we'd stood on the logs. I looked back. It was as if the vehicle were in a tipped up wheel barrow, sliding its cargo even deeper into the marsh. In three heartbeats, the light in the interior was extinguished, and then in a rush, as if a giant mouth had opened beneath it, the chariot disappeared.

It was almost a prayerful moment, though my priest certainly wouldn't have liked me saying so. Goronwy, more aptly, cursed. "By the arse of King Solomon, now we'll never discover its mysteries, beyond what the woman can tell us."

"I'm glad we weren't close to it," I said soberly, clicking my tongue to get the horse moving again.

"Any delay and the woman and her child would have died," Goronwy said.

"It was only by chance that I was on the battlements. I was thinking of other things and watching the colors change on Yr Wyddfa when it appeared."

"Chance, my lord? I think not," Goronwy said, but anything further he thought to say was cut off by shouting in the distance. A company of my men galloped out of the village and into view.

"Prince Llywelyn!" One of my captains, Hywel ap Rhys, called. Another soldier held a torch in his hand as they trotted up to me, eyes widening at the girls in our arms.

"All is well." I held up a hand to my men and Hywel closed his mouth on his questions. All of my men knew better than to disobey, but there would be no stopping some of them later. Hywel himself was a son of a noble house and believed himself all but my equal, though I was a prince and he a mere baron. Many times, I cursed the independence of the Welsh nobles, even the ones who fought by my side. Especially the ones who fought by my side.

The men fell into formation around us. We certainly formed a strange company. Goronwy and the girl continued whispering to each other and finally Goronwy spoke up. "I believe her name is Anna."

"You believe?"

"Well, it still isn't clear what language she's speaking. She appears to understand bits of what I'm saying, but I understand nothing of her words except 'Anna.' I have reassured her, to the best of my ability, that her mother will be well."

We filed through the village, quiet now that it was full-dark. A few heads poked out of doorways. Hywel nodded at the blacksmith, who stood under the eave of his shop to watch us pass. We trooped up the hill to the castle and along its circuitous road to the gatehouse.

The bailey, once we reached it, was in turmoil. "You surprised us all, my lord," Hywel said as he dismounted. He was tall, even for a Welshman, with the biggest feet any of us had ever seen. From the moment he joined the company we'd called him Boots. Half the men had probably forgotten his real name.

He reached for the woman, whom I allowed to slide off the horse. He was more than capable of bearing her weight, but when I got down myself, I quite deliberately took her back from him.

As we'd ridden up the road, I found myself going over the sudden arrival of the girl and her child, and agreeing with Goronwy that what others ascribed to chance, I was willing to view as a gift from God. Or the devil, I supposed. It wasn't something I would ever mention, not even to my closest advisors, but in the thick of the moment it wasn't always easy to tell the difference between the two.

All I knew was that I didn't *want* to let her go. The feeling was a new one, and yet, I'd learned to trust my instincts and knew myself well enough by now not to fight them. I'd had many women over the years—more than I could count, truth be told, which I'm sure had kept my confessor busier than he'd liked. But

I'd not welcomed one into my bed in several months and hadn't truly cared for any woman for much longer than that. I'd attributed my disinterest to my advanced age—and a natural evolution toward more circumspect and judicious taste.

With the girl in my arms, I strode toward the inner bailey which housed my private apartments, my men parting before me. Goronwy matched his steps to mine as we entered the great hall. Tudur, my steward, stepped toward me and bowed.

"Shall I have a room prepared for her, my lord?"

"No," I said, hearing the flatness in my voice and knowing he would obey it. "She stays with me."

3

Meg

I opened my eyes to a candle, guttering in a pottery dish on a small wooden table beside the bed on which I lay. It took only half a second for me to register that all was not as it should be.

"*Oh, my God!*" I reared up from the pillow. A man sat in a chair by the fire, reading a book the size of a coffee table dictionary. He looked up and smiled, and the smile was so disarming I just gaped at him, mouth open, knowing that nothing about him or the room was right, but unable to articulate why it wasn't.

The room was built on a grand scale. A long table surrounded by chairs sat near a closed door, twenty feet from the foot of the bed. The bed itself was a massive four-poster, with thick, crimson hangings all around. Only one side was open—the side on which I lay. The floor was comprised of wooden slats set tightly together. Rather than polished, it was faded and worn with what could only have been years of use. I took it all in, flicking my eyes from one item to the next, before returning them to the man in the chair.

He shifted and then stood to walk to a bookshelf on the other side of the room. He laid the book flat on top of several others, taking a moment to align them neatly one with another. While his back was turned, I looked around the bed, more panicked than ever because I realized that I was wearing nothing but a nightgown—and a gorgeous one at that, with embroidered lace and puffy sleeves; that my clothes were gone and my hair was braided in a long plait down my back.

By the time he turned back to me and spoke, I'd scooted up the bed until I was sitting upright, the covers pulled to my chin.

" . . ." he said.

I had no idea what he'd said. Confused because his words were completely unintelligible, even as they tugged at my ear with familiar tones, I didn't move or saying anything, just stared. He tried again. I shook my head, uncertain.

He stayed relaxed, his hands at his sides and walked toward me, speaking a little louder, as if somehow that would help. I was desperately trying to make sense of what he was saying, but as he got closer, my breath rose in my chest until it choked me. He must have seen the fear on my face because he stopped, about three feet from the bed. I finally found my voice.

"What?" The words came out as little more than a squeak. "Who are you?" I dragged my eyes from his and flashed them around the room again, seeking somewhere to run but not seeing anything but the long distance to the door and the man standing between it and me. He didn't answer my question but again tried one of his own.

"*Beth ydy'ch enw chi*?" he said.

"Meg *dw i*," I said, then gasped. I'd answered automatically. '*What is your name?*' he'd said in Welsh. *'My name is Meg.'*

I stilled myself and studied him as he stood, still calm, two paces from me. Had what he'd spoken before been in Welsh that I hadn't understood, perhaps too fast, and too complicated compared to what I'd learned from Mom? Through my foggy brain, I focused with an effort. Who is he? He still hadn't told me.

He was a large man in his late thirties, thin but muscled, nearly a foot taller than I. He wore a cream-colored shirt with a dark blue jacket, brown pants, and brown leather boots. He had a long nose and black hair, close in color to Anna's. *Anna!* Fear rose in me again and twisted to see if she was on the bed.

"She's asleep by the fire," the man said, reading my mind. He followed this statement by more unintelligible words, except for, "You say, 'Meg', but you mean, *Marged*?"

I nodded. Marged was my formal name, though I never used it. Now more afraid for Anna than afraid of him, I swung my legs to the floor and ran to where he pointed. Anna was indeed asleep in a cradle set against the far wall, with large rockers on the bottom to keep a child asleep.

Someone had changed her clothes too. She wore a white nightgown that was a match to mine and was covered by a brown woolen blanket that was incredibly soft to the touch. Though my arms ached to hold her, I was afraid to pick her up in case I needed two hands to fend off the man, and was loathe to wake her needlessly. Instead, I stroked the hair away from her face.

I sat back on my heels, still watching her. As I settled there, my surroundings seeped into my consciousness more clearly: the tapestries on the walls; the handmade chair and table between the bed and the fire; the clothes we wore. All forced me to face the no longer ignorable questions: *Where am I? What is this place?*

"Who are you?" I asked again in English, and at the man's look of puzzlement, repeated his words back to him. "*Beth ydy'ch enw chi*?"

"Llywelyn ap Gruffydd, Tywysog o Cymry," he said.

Both hands flew to my mouth. *Llywelyn ap Gruffydd, Prince of Wales*, he'd said.

Every Welsh child ever born had been told stories of Llywelyn ap Gruffydd, the last Prince of Wales, a man who'd died on a cold, snowy day in history, lured away from his companions by the treacherous English. Why was he telling me he was a thirteenth century Prince of Wales? I glanced around the room again. Had he constructed a thirteenth century house to go with his fantasies? Why had he brought Anna and me here?

"You can't be." I dropped my hands to my lap as reason reasserted itself in my brain.

"*Englisch?*" His face suddenly reddened. He took a step towards me but I hurried to forestall him, leaning forward with one hand on the floor and the other held out to stop him.

"No! No!" I said, then switched to Welsh at his fierce expression. *"Na! Na! Os gwelwch yn dda!" Please, no!*

Llywelyn stopped and I took in a shaky breath, the fear of before filling me more than ever. I knew enough of violent men to see it in him. My heart raced, but he studied me, not raising his hand or making any more threatening gestures, and gradually it slowed. I glanced at Anna, unsure if I should pick her up to keep her safe, or if it would just draw his attention to her and put us both at risk.

I dropped my hand, eased back onto my heels, and let out a steadying breath. Llywelyn took his chair, both of us more composed. My plea had diffused whatever emotion had been about to explode in the room, and for the first time I was glad I'd had Trev to deal with all those years. At times, I'd been able to say the right thing to calm him down, and weeks where I'd managed to tiptoe around him without upsetting him.

Unfortunately, there'd also been those days when Trev hadn't listened whether or not I'd held silent or begged him to stop, allowing his own inner demons to overcome him without regard to me. Now, with Llywelyn settled, I wanted to ask him more about where I was, but didn't know how to begin, and was afraid to set him off again. In a way, the fact that he was pretending to be a centuries dead Welsh prince didn't even matter.

He could think he was a purple hippopotamus for all I cared. I just wanted to get out of the room in one piece.

Llywelyn, perhaps trying to be helpful, tried again. "*Français?*"

Relief flooded through me. "*Oui!*" If he refused to speak English and I didn't know enough Welsh, at least we could communicate in some fashion. It struck me that his fantasy was remarkably consistent, in that the historical Llywelyn would also have spoken French since it was the primary language of the English court in the thirteenth century, as well as the French one.

Llywelyn smiled too. "You may not remember," he said, now in strangely accented but intelligible (to me) French, "but your chariot ran aground in the marsh below the castle. Moments after I retrieved you from the wreckage, it sank and disappeared."

"Marsh? Castle?" I said. A befuddled fog rose again to drive away my moment of clarity. "I was driving my car to buy ice cream . . ." I stopped at the look Llywelyn wore on his face—a look that said, '*your what to buy what?*'

"My vehicle," I amended, hoping that the word existed in medieval French.

Llywelyn stood abruptly. "I won't question you more tonight. You must be hungry." He strode to the door, opened it, poked his head out, and waved one hand. Immediately, a man hurried into the doorway and saluted.

"*Mau Rhi?*" the man said. *My lord?*

Llywelyn spoke words I couldn't understand, but I was only listening with half an ear anyway because this time I was staring at the man who'd just appeared. He wore mail armor, the little links catching the light with every shift of his body. Over that, a white tunic adorned by three red lions decorated his chest. He wore no helmet, and like Llywelyn, was clean shaven. He'd clearly bought into—or was humoring—Llywelyn's delusions.

I crouched next to Anna's bed, uncertain what to do. It didn't look like the door would get me very far, not with a guard outside it. I checked the room for windows. It had two, both covered with wooden shutters, though a light flashed every now and then through the chinks between the wood and the frame. In watching for it, I missed the rest of the men's conversation. Llywelyn shut the door. He returned to his chair, but not before gesturing to me to sit again on the bed.

"You must be tired," he said, back to French. "You can eat and it will make you feel better."

I couldn't bear to just obey him. Yet, I looked at my baby Anna, still sleeping, and didn't dare disobey. She lay quiet and desperately beautiful, a hostage to my good behavior. Not knowing what else to do, I stood and walked past him to the bed.

I sat on its edge, more awkward than ever. Neither of us spoke. I smoothed my nightgown over my thighs. Even as I shivered, my palms sweated. I reached behind me to tug at one of the blankets, wanting more warmth. Llywelyn leaned forward to pull the blanket over my shoulders, before settling back in his chair with a nod.

"I'll stoke the fire again before we sleep," he said.

A sickening lump formed in my stomach and it wasn't because I was hungry. A rushing in my ears threatened to overwhelm me and all I could think was *oh my God; oh my God; oh my God.* My worst fears were abruptly out in the open. I could only gape at Llywelyn without trying to contradict him, as if my mind had gotten hung up in overdrive and was revving with the clutch out and nowhere to go. He seemed so utterly unconcerned, sitting as he was with one ankle resting on the opposite knee, his hands folded across his chest. What was I going to do?

The soldier from the hallway returned with food and drink. I stared at him blindly while Llywelyn indicated that he should set the tray on the table beside the bed. Llywelyn moved the candle to the mantelpiece above the fire to give him room.

When the man left, Llywelyn gestured to the food. "It isn't much, but should tide us over until morning."

I nodded, stone-faced, the lump in my throat preventing me from speaking. Llywelyn poured two glasses of wine from the carafe and handed one to me before taking the second for himself. I didn't want to drink it, not only because I was afraid to take anything from him, but because I normally didn't drink wine at all. It had never seemed like a good idea with Trev around—either because it would tempt him or because I didn't dare lose control over myself. I also wouldn't be twenty-one until April.

I took the cup but simply sat on the bed with it in my hand. Llywelyn raised his eyebrows at me then lifted the cup as if in a toast and took a sip. "There's no poison in it, if that's what you're afraid of."

Under his curious gaze, I didn't dare refuse it any longer, even as I cursed myself for being so passive. I took a sip. It tasted bitter on my tongue—far more than the cheap, sweet wine Mom usually drank. I set the cup on the table and Llywelyn handed me a hunk of cheese and bread he'd cut with his belt knife. I drank and ate while Llywelyn watched. He seemed so *believable* in his stillness. He took the moment when my mouth was full of food to begin asking the questions he'd said he wouldn't earlier.

"Who's Anna's father?"

I took a swig of wine and swallowed hard. "He's dead," I said, glad that in this at least I could tell the truth.

Llywelyn nodded, accepting my words at face value. "And your father?"

"He's dead too," I said.

Llywelyn made a 'tsk' noise through his teeth. "I was asking their names." I didn't respond and he began work on cutting up a small apple. "My man included the apple only after I told him that you possessed all your teeth."

His words were so incongruous to the fear I'd been feeling, I choked on the next sip and barely stopped myself from spewing the wine across the floor. I coughed and then found hysterical laughter bubbling up in my throat. I could barely see him through streaming eyes as I fought it back. His mouth quirked as he started to smile too, though I didn't think he knew he'd made a joke at first—it probably hadn't been a joke to him. Then he laughed outright.

I took his half-second of inattention to lunge for the knife.

I rammed my shoulder into his arm and overbalanced him, getting my hand on his knife as he released it in surprise. I had intended to take the knife from him and hold him off with it, but instead, he spun with me, grabbing my arm as he went down and pulling me off balance too. I fell sideways, stunning myself by landing hard on my left hip and then clonking my head on the floor, my legs tangled up in my long nightgown. Llywelyn recovered more quickly than I and threw himself on top of me, pinioning each of my wrists to the floor with his big hands, the knife skittering away from me into a corner of the room.

He loomed over me, his nose only inches from mine and the full weight of his body resting on my torso, holding me down. "Who sent you?" he hissed into my face. "What devil's bargain did you make?"

I stared up at him, my vision blurring from the pain in my head as the ache from before roared back and darkened my vision around the edges. I knew what was going to happen next because it had happened once with Trev. Only once, and then I'd taken Anna and left.

"Please, don't hurt me," I said, my voice little more than a whisper. "I just want to go home. My mother will be worried about me. I wasn't going to use the knife. I wouldn't even know how."

Llywelyn studied me, the urgency in his eyes lessening, though he didn't loosen his grip on me at all. Tears welled in my eyes and trickled down the side of my face to get lost in my hair, much of which had come loose from its braid. Though his eyes never left mine, he eased away, got to his feet, and retrieved the knife. He straightened his chair and sat. When his weight came off me, I rolled onto my side, curling my knees up to my chest and pressing my face into the cool of the floor.

Llywelyn sighed. "Did you think I would force you?"

"Yes."

I lifted my head to look into his face. He rubbed his eyes with his fingers and then rested his elbows on his knees and put his chin in his hands. "I'm too old for this," he said.

Then he stood suddenly and took one stride toward me. I almost managed to hold in a shriek before he crouched beside me, got one arm under my neck and the other under my knees, and hoisted me in his arms. He brought me over to the bed and dropped me, unceremoniously, onto the spot I'd been before.

"I've never taken a woman against her will and I don't intend to start with you." He grunted as he straightened the pillow under my head. Then he grabbed a blanket from the foot of the bed and threw it over me. I curled up, cradling my head in my hands. I'd been so sure he would hurt me and that I wouldn't be able to stop him. I was having a hard time understanding he was leaving me unharmed.

"Where's your mother?" Llywelyn demanded, his feet spread wide, hands on his hips.

"R-r-r-radnor," I said.

Llywelyn's eyes narrowed. "That's days away. How did you plan on getting there?"

"I . . ." I couldn't continue, at a loss for an answer.

Llywelyn tipped his head to one side and relaxed his arms, letting them fall loose at his sides. "Where did you come from, Marged?"

It seemed like he wasn't asking for the town I lived in, or how far I'd driven today, but something else entirely; something to which I had no more answers than he did.

I shook my head. "Nothing is clear to me right now."

"I'm not surprised," he said. "How's your head? That's twice you've cracked it today."

I put my hand to my forehead where it ached, feeling a large bump where my hairline started. "It hurts to touch, and I have a bit of a headache."

"I asked also for willow bark to mix with your wine," he said. He took a twist of cloth that I hadn't noticed on the tray, and dumped it into my cup. It didn't seem possible, but it appeared as if he thought it was possible to return to a time before I attacked him, to normal interaction.

He sat on the edge of the bed, his weight making it sag, and I rolled onto my back to counter it. Once again, Llywelyn hooked his arm around my neck but this time he lifted me so I could sip the wine. I looked into the deep red liquid with little bits of bark floating in it, not liking the idea of drinking something so unfamiliar. As before, however, his will was impossible to defy and I didn't feel I had choice.

"You must sleep," he said. "We'll talk more in the morning. I swear to you that I will not hurt you."

I gazed up at him. Somehow, I believed him. "I'm sorry about the knife."

Llywelyn gave me a hard look but I was too tired to think about what he might mean by it. Mom and Elisa definitely wouldn't have approved of him. Elisa had already given me a lecture about bringing a guy home *before* I went out with him. What would she call this? A date? Not exactly. But my head hurt so badly I couldn't keep my eyes open and I couldn't fight him anymore. Even Elisa would have to agree that whatever Llywelyn was, he was unexpected.

He picked up the blanket that I'd dropped to the floor when I'd gone for the knife and tucked it around me.

"Sleep," he said.

I closed my eyes. And then I opened them again when I realized there was no way I was going to be able to sleep with Anna on the other side of the room. I sat up. Llywelyn watched me, his hands on his hips. Out of bed again, I hurried to where Anna lay and crouched to grasp the rockers. With gentle tugs, I got her bed moving across the floor.

"Marged," Llywelyn said. "Don't do that." His voice held a definite exasperation this time, but still, he nudged me aside and bent to the cradle. With a slight exhale of air, he lifted the trundle bed, his arms under the rockers, and carried it across the room.

"Please put it there," I said, pointing to a spot on the floor beside the bed. He set the cradle down and I climbed back under the covers. I reached out and found that the tips of my fingers could just touch the rail of her bed. I rocked her gently. Anna sighed and rolled onto her side. I looked up at Llywelyn. "Thank you."

He canted his head in acknowledgement, and despite my fears and uncertainties, I finally closed my eyes and slept.

* * * * *

"I must speak with the Prince!"

I swam awake, fighting through a strange fog of half-remembered dreams and conversation from the night before. Someone was pounding on the bedroom door and shouting in a confused mix of French and Welsh. Or, at least confused to me since I couldn't make out every word. The intent, however, was clear.

Abruptly, the pounding stopped and a stern voice cut through the commotion on the other side of the door. "The Prince is . . . busy."

"Stand aside! I must speak with him! Wake him for me!"

"My brother, Dafydd, is a bit intemperate."

My breath froze in my lungs. I turned my head and found myself looking into Llywelyn's face. He was lying on the bed—and admittedly it was a big bed because he was at least three feet away—with his elbow on his pillow and his head propped up on one hand, looking at me, clear amusement in his eyes. He had an almost impish expression on his face that told me he was enjoying himself enormously.

"What's happening?"

"It seems my brother seeks an audience with me. I suppose I ought to let him in before he wakes Anna."

Llywelyn's chest was bare and as he threw back the cover, *I sure hope he has something on his lower half*! had barely passed through my head before he straightened, wearing—

Oh dear God! Absolutely nothing!

I must have squeaked because Llywelyn shot me a look of amused condescension. He reached for his breeches, which he'd left at the foot of the bed, and pulled them on. Didn't medieval people wear underwear? And if they didn't, did he have to make this whole thing so authentic?

Stirrings and bangs came from the other side of the curtain and then Llywelyn appeared on my side of the bed, fully dressed, his finger to his lips. He tugged the curtain closed so it hid me. He left a little gap, however and through it, I could see Llywelyn stride to the door and open it to reveal an agitated man, his hair flattened to his head and his helmet under his arm. Despite that, he was extraordinarily handsome, younger than Llywelyn, shorter and not as lean.

"My lord," the man said. "Brother." He bowed his head.

"What is it, Dafydd?" Llywelyn said, in French. "I was sleeping."

The man dismissed his words with a shake of his head. "I've already breakfasted."

"Good for you," Llywelyn said, his voice dry.

"Not all of us are lay-a-beds," Dafydd said. This was so patently unfair I wondered that Llywelyn didn't correct his brother, but he didn't, just let the silence drag out until Dafydd filled it with his news. "Clare is on the move. He knows that Gruffydd ap Rhys has returned from Ireland with your support, and that you have plans to give Senghenydd to him, along with Castell Morgraig. Clare has begun work on a new castle at Caerphilly."

"Damn the man!" Llywelyn said. "That is my land. He knows this will bring me out. Doesn't he care?"

"Perhaps that's his plan. Perhaps he intends to thwart you with open battle or with treachery."

Llywelyn eyed his brother. "Thank you, Dafydd, for your news. I submit it could have waited until I was awake."

"Yes, brother," he said, "but then I wouldn't have had the chance to glimpse your lovely new lady." His eyes met mine through the gap in the curtain and he smirked.

"She's mine, Dafydd. Do not forget it."

"Yes, brother." Dafydd stepped back. Llywelyn shot a glance at me and then followed Dafydd into the hall, pulling the door closed behind him.

I lay there, feeling alternately horrified, sick, extremely vulnerable, and then angry. Why was this happening to me? Who were these lunatics and what were they going to do next?

The door opened and Llywelyn stalked back into the room, headed towards me. He jerked open the curtain and leaned forward, his fists resting on the bed on either side of my hips, his face only inches from mine, just as we'd been the night before.

This time, while he looked just as fierce, his eyes had a glint of something else—amusement again perhaps, or mischief.

"I must meet with my counselors," he said. "A maid will come with clothes for you and Anna. I journey south within the next two days. You must prepare, for I intend to take you with me."

"South?" I asked, feeling stupid again. "Where?"

Llywelyn didn't answer. Instead, he threaded his fingers through the hair at the back of my head, lifted me up and kissed me, hard, before letting me fall back onto the bed. "Remember what I told my brother."

Speechless again, all I could do was watch him go.

4

Llywelyn

I was in high good humor as I strode out of the bedroom. Still, I didn't want to risk my luck with a backwards glance, knowing I might find Marged glaring after me, affronted at my impudence.

Ha! The look on Marged's face when I kissed her was priceless and I found myself grinning at the intelligence and fire in her. Then my smile faded as I remembered last night's incident with the knife, and the fear plainly revealed on her face, that had driven her to attack me. She'd tried to flee, afraid I would hurt her. I'd told her who I was, and yet, my identity had meant little to her. What was behind that? I didn't know; didn't know enough of her even to ask the right questions.

And then a worse thought: had she bewitched me? Was she from the devil? With the same instinct that had prompted me to keep her in my rooms, I dismissed the notion. The priests could spend their time questioning the nature of women. Females were different from men, clearly put here for a different purpose, but I had no interest in speculating beyond that.

I fixed my thoughts on my more immediate problems, not the least of which was the very existence of my brother, Dafydd. Welsh royal brothers, my own father and uncle included, had a long history of enmity, backstabbing, and bitterness. Harmonious relations among brothers in my family were the exception, not the rule, and it was unlikely, given our past history and present course, that Dafydd and I would prove different.

"My lord!" Tudur stopped me as I entered the great hall. He was hurrying, pulling on his cloak as intercepted me. "Your brother. . ."

"He came to my room, Tudur. I've already seen him."

"I apologize, my lord, for allowing him to wake you."

"It is forgotten, Tudur. He can be very persistent."

Tudur bowed his head. "Yes, my lord."

I strode to the dais where Dafydd now sat, along with my friend, Goronwy, and Geraint, Tudur's father. He'd aged much in the last few years and had reluctantly given up the stewardship—though not his service—in favor of his son. While the other men stood as I approached, Dafydd did not. I had a momentary urge to wipe the smirk off his face with my fist in his teeth but restrained myself. Perhaps he couldn't help what he was. I only hoped he had a thought as to whom he might want to become.

Ignoring him, I said to Goronwy and Geraint, "Please join me in my office as soon as possible. Dafydd brings unwelcome news."

The two men immediately fell into step beside me. Geraint spoke in my ear as we left the hall. "Dare I say 'as always?'"

"It appears that Dafydd has the unfortunate responsibility of being the bearer of bad tidings, nothing more. This is Clare's action, not my brother's. I can't imagine otherwise at this point."

"I can imagine it." That was Goronwy, muttering under his breath. As he'd been my friend from boyhood, I let it pass.

"Your brother has already been involved in two revolts against you, my lord," Tudur said, "though he was the mastermind of neither. Do we allow him another opportunity?"

"No, we do not, friend," I said. "But he is my brother." I led them back the way I'd come, up the stairs to my office, next door to where Marged and Anna still lay. I allowed myself a moment's warmth at the thought and at Marged's unexpected spirit, and then turned to my counselors.

I had ignored their muttering, but didn't need to hear their words to know what was in their minds. While Goronwy and Tudur were of an age with me, both forty now, Dafydd was ten years younger—a different generation entirely. He'd not been involved in any of the Welsh wars under the command of our Uncle Dafydd. He'd been only two years old in 1240 when my grandfather, Llywelyn Fawr, died and Uncle Dafydd took the throne.

Nothing pleased an English king more than bickering Welsh royalty. Englishmen of the Marche—the disputed border territory between Wales and England—and of the English royal court had aided and abetted my brother Dafydd in both of his revolts against me as a matter of course, acts I could neither forgive nor forget, no matter how often the perpetrators spoke of trust and noble brotherhood.

My grandfather had been a strong man, ruling all Wales like few Princes ever had. But the stability had crumbled with his death to the point that my Uncle Dafydd had imprisoned my father and brother here at Criccieth to contain their rebellions. My mother, Senana, had gone to Shrewsbury to beg King Henry of England to intervene on their behalf with Uncle Dafydd. Henry had agreed to their release, but betrayed their agreement. He turned around and threw my entire family in the Tower of London.

Except for me.

"You cannot go back, Llywelyn!"

Goronwy grabbed my arm and pulled me around to face him. He'd come to meet me as I'd left the village for the causeway to the castle and now pulled me off the road and into the trees.

"Why ever not?" I said. "What's happened?"

"Word came this morning. King Henry has finally agreed to intercede on your father's behalf. Your family leaves for England within the hour."

I stared at him, my anger growing—not at him, but at the circumstances that had brought my family to this point. I'd never been to England and had no intention of finding refuge there. To my mind, it meant trading one captivity for another, even if my mother swore that wasn't going to be the case.

"Your mother believes King Henry will be true to his word," Goronwy said, "but I . . ." He trailed off.

"I don't believe it either, Goronwy."

I gazed up at the castle, just visible through the branches of the trees that surrounded us. Men ran back and forth in front of the gatehouse—my uncle's men for the most part, since he'd forced my father to send his away. Uncle Dafydd was the Prince of Wales, and my father might be a rightful heir, especially as the eldest son, but he was hot-tempered and injudicious, and had lost everything he owned in fighting his brother.

I nodded, finally, at my friend. "You're right. We can't return or they'll take me too. That wouldn't serve either my father or my uncle, don't you think?"

"No, my lord. I reckon not."

I turned back to the village, Goronwy beside me. I wore a bow and quiver, and my new boots my mother had given me for my sixteenth birthday. Other than that, all I possessed was what I stood up in. Sometimes, finally facing what you most fear turns out to be no more difficult than putting one foot in front of the other.

With Goronwy, I stumbled into Aber, my Uncle's seat in Gwynedd on the shores of the Irish Sea. The day could not have been more opposite from today—sunny and hot, early September instead of January. Though I'd been a favorite of my grandfather, my Uncle Dafydd had been wary of me—and me of him. He had feared that I would lay claim to Gwynedd in the name of my father.

Yet, even in my novice days, I knew to do so would be foolish; knew that I would have to earn the right to lead our people. I did learn, and learned well, everything he had to teach me, both good and ill. I was beside him when he died of that hideous, wasting disease, and was ready to stand in his stead from the moment he laid his hand in mine and passed his kingdom on to me—his father's kingdom, along with his vision of a united Wales.

In Wales, a boy legally becomes a man on his fourteenth birthday. Yet I knew, for me, it was the day I walked away, defying my parents, my Uncle Dafydd, and the King of England. Goronwy and I made our way to Aber and my uncle's court, finally putting my feet on the path to destiny.

As I faced my counselors in my office, the consequences of that day reverberated still, beyond my own thoughts and dreams. Because I'd refused imprisonment, it was I who stepped into my uncle's shoes upon his death. And while it was Dafydd who'd been most harmed by my decision to abandon my family, it was I who'd paid the price for his resentment.

Perhaps what irked me more than anything else was that Dafydd, as it stood now, was my heir. No matter how strongly I held the reins of Wales, no matter how great my power, no woman had given me a child—any child. Every hour of every day I faced the fact that my line died with me if I was unable to sire a son. I clenched my fists but then relaxed them, noting the look of curiosity on Goronwy's face. He, of all my companions, knew me best—and himself had articulated our mutual fear.

But I was only forty years old—true, most of my people died before the age of forty, but I was still vibrant and strong, my hair as dark as it had ever been, my back straight. True, I didn't look forward to sleeping on the ground amongst my men as much as in my younger days, but I could do it.

"Dafydd aside," I said, "I would like to hear your thoughts on the news he brings. I've never met this young heir to the Clare line, but I've heard that he has ambitious plans for himself. What kind of threat does he bring to us?"

"He wears his earldom well," Goronwy said. "Why do you think King Henry tried to keep it from him for so long?"

Tudur slapped his fist into his palm. He had little patience for those who couldn't keep up with his fast brain and faster tongue. "We can't allow him to build a new castle. It violates our agreement with King Henry and puts your entire rule into question. If one Marcher lord can do it, any of them can."

"They all will try," Goronwy said. "You know they will."

"It is much as it was with your uncle," Geraint added. "The moment your back is turned, each man looks to himself and his own patrimony, with no thought for the future of Wales."

"The Marcher lords have never concerned themselves with anything but their own power," Tudur said. "They are unlikely to start now."

I paced to the chair behind my desk and threw myself into it. "Gilbert de Clare assails me in the south, Humphrey de Bohun and his whelp of a grandson in Brecon, and Roger Mortimer at Montgomery. They will maintain a constant pressure, exerting just as much force as they can get away with without open war."

"Clare risks that with this castle at Caerphilly," Goronwy said.

"Henry has made it clear to all his barons long since that they can keep what they take, both from our Prince and from each other, as long as it doesn't affect him," Tudur said. "This castle is in disputed territory—territory that is only Prince Llywelyn's as long as he can hold it."

"Which I'm not doing now!" I said. "I can't be everywhere at once, can't maintain a standing army along the whole of the Marche!"

"The men of Brecon chose you as their lord," Goronwy said. "Bohun couldn't lead them now, even if he held the land. The men of Senghennydd will follow a similar course. They will fight for you and not Clare, just as in Brecon."

"We can't leave it to chance," Geraint said. "And we can't send Gruffydd ap Rhys there by himself. He wasn't able to stand up to Clare the first time; I fear he will back down the second time as well."

"He's stronger than that," Goronwy said. "The fire in him is lit. No man can be picked off like a daisy and banished from his lands without finding out where his spine is."

"Or isn't," Tudur said.

I shook my head. "Gruffydd will stand strong. With my help and the support of my men, we can put him back where he belongs. Send word to him at Dinas Bran to meet me in Brecon."

"So we go?" Tudur said.

"Yes, of course we go." I sat forward to finger the map in front of me. "We will ride south along the coast road, swinging east to come into Brecon. From there we will reconnoiter Senghennydd."

"What if Dafydd brings false news for some devious purpose of his own?" Tudur said.

I looked at him, and I could feel the mutual holding-of-breath among the other men. Tudur refused to back down and instead met my eyes. "Let it go, Tudur," I said. "This news from Clare isn't surprising. I admit Dafydd took a certain glee in its report, but I have no reason to think it false."

"And the woman?" Tudur said, pressing further.

"Excuse me?"

The three men exchanged glances. It was obvious that they had discussed this on their own before tackling me with it.

"Ahem." Tudur cleared his throat, suddenly nervous under my glare where before he'd been defiant. "Has it occurred to you that the woman arriving as she did might be part of a plot, whether Welsh or English? A spy in our midst if you will?"

I barked a laugh. "Most definitely it has. However, Marged didn't recognize Dafydd this morning, nor he her. Besides, how often does a spy bring along her baby daughter?"

"That's the point, my lord," Tudur said. "Dafydd's news on the heels of her appearance makes me suspicious."

"Your constant occupation, I know." The others smiled, relieved I hadn't lost my temper completely.

"We know nothing of her, my lord," Goronwy said. "It's not your usual practice with . . .ah . . . women."

I rested an elbow on the arm rest and my finger to my chin, studying him. "You noticed that?"

"My lord—" Goronwy said.

I cut him off. "You're right. It isn't. Be that as it may, she has my countenance and a safe haven in my house."

All three sat back in their chairs, hearing the finality in my voice. "Yes, my lord," Goronwy said.

Then I relented. They didn't know of the events of the evening before, but if they did, they would be even more concerned. Why wasn't I? My shoulders sagged. The day had begun so well, but it wasn't just my own life I risked, but all Wales.

"I ask you then, in your judgment, is it better to leave her here or to bring her and her child on this journey?" I said.

"Leave her at Criccieth," Tudur said immediately. "We are far from England and she can do little harm here. She's only a woman, after all."

Geraint glanced at his son and then brought his attention back to me. "Is Dafydd coming with us, or staying here?"

"He's staying here," I said. "He told me that he had business in the north and hoped I would relieve him of his duty to attend me. His insistence on it saved me from having to refuse him space at my side."

"Then I would bring the woman," Geraint said. "I share some of my son's concerns, but I also know that if she is innocent, she would be fair game to one such as Dafydd. You must admit his prowess with the ladies is nearing legendary status. Just to spite you, he would seek to turn her head to him, knowing that she has already shared your bed."

"That's quite an indictment," I said.

"It is," Geraint said. "I speak only because I have your best interests and that of Wales constantly in my heart."

"I will watch her, my lord." Goronwy said, suddenly more sure. "If she rides with me by day and stays with you at night, there will be no chance for her to engage in any mischief. By the time we reach Brecon, we will know her character, for good or ill."

"Is that satisfactory to you?" I said to Geraint and Tudur. Only Geraint would be riding with us. I needed Tudur to keep an eye on Dafydd. Geraint, though as crafty as ever, would have a harder time keeping up with my brother.

"Yes," Tudur said, nodding slowly. "I will hold the north for you, as always."

5

Meg

This was so not acceptable. It might be all right for Mr. Llywelyn Fantasy to live his life in the thirteenth century—and it was clear now that he must be part of some sort of intentional community in which a whole lot of people were living that dream with him—but I had to get going. Mom and Elisa would be worried sick by now. Had they called the police? If so, what would they find?

The thought nagged at me. I didn't know what had happened to my car or where I was. I remembered sliding into the embankment next to the tree on which Trev died, but nothing after that other than a gaping blackness. I concentrated, trying to recall the impact. Wasn't there a blue-gray sky? No snow, but a sea instead? How was that possible?

I lay in bed, listening hard. Sounds I'd interpreted as a fan, or the sloshing of a washing machine, or heavy breathing in and out, could easily be waves on a shore. We'd spent a summer at Cape Hatteras after my dad retired and I'd loved falling asleep to the waves rolling in and out. How far from Radnor had Llywelyn taken me? Could I be on the Jersey shore somewhere?

It was hard to believe that I'd survived the crash unscathed, except for an ache in my neck and a throbbing in my head. Anna slept on, apparently completely fine and Llywelyn himself had so far proved to be harmless, seemingly even forgiving me for trying to kill him. I rolled onto my stomach and stuck my face into the pillow, moaning at the thought. It was *stupid, stupid, stupid* of me to have tried to grab the knife as if I was some sort of karate expert.

I'd taken a self-defense class at sixteen where I'd learn to kick a guy in the balls, but had no real belief that I could do it under stress, and most of the class had consisted of role-playing games anyway, which Elisa and I had hated. Hard to imagine a role-playing game that could have effectively taught me how to respond to a man who claimed to be a thirteenth century Prince of Wales. Then again, contrary to all expectations, I hadn't needed even the tiny bit of knowledge that class had taught. Llywelyn had lain beside me in bed all night and not touched me.

It wasn't as if I thought I was irresistibly gorgeous, but I had enough experience with men to know that few individuals of the male persuasion wouldn't have at least *tried.* I'd turned guys away a time or two before Trev had tried and succeeded. Yet, Llywelyn hadn't and was offended at the very thought. At the same time, the possessiveness in his voice when he talked to his brother was unmistakable. "She's mine," he'd said. What exactly did that mean?

I rolled off the bed and stood, ready to get moving and face whatever reality Llywelyn had constructed. I walked to where Anna lay and crouched beside her bed, just to check on her. As always, my heart swelled when I looked at her, so *glad* that I had her. As Mom had said, she was the one good thing we'd gotten out of this mess.

Anna opened her eyes.

"Hey, sweetheart," I said.

"Hi, Mommy. Are you okay now? You slept a long time!" She lifted a hand and touched the wooden side of the trundle bed. She looked at it for a second before sitting up quickly, twisting her body around in a jerky motion to survey the room.

"It's okay, Anna," I said. I picked her up. She still swiveled her head to take in her surroundings.

"Is Gramma here?"

"I would like to think that she's on her way," I said. "We had an accident in the car. Do you remember?"

Anna gazed at me, her eyes solemn. "There was a man. He unbuckled my car seat."

"I imagine he did," I said. "Did he carry you here?"

She nodded.

"Was he nice?"

She nodded.

"Could you understand him when he talked to you?"

Anna shook her head. "There were two men. And a horse. And then there were more men and one of them had a big stick with fire on the end. We're in a *castle*."

Well now. Just then, someone knocked at the door and I swung around. "Come in!"

The door opened to reveal a girl a few years younger than I, dressed in brown. She was slender and short, but the most noticeable thing about her were two large buck teeth.

"Madam," the girl said, curtseying. "Are you ready for me to help you dress?" She spoke slowly in Welsh and I aligned each of her words with their modern equivalent, finding that I understood the gist of what she said.

"Yes, please." I'd made the mistake of sending her away earlier after she delivered breakfast so I could have some privacy to think—a mistake because it only took twenty seconds of contorting myself to realize I wasn't able to tie my new dress up the back. I'd opened the door to call her back, but she'd gone and I'd had to ask the guard to find her for me. Now here she was, giggling in the hall with the man, certain that I was an idiot.

We were destined for full, medieval regalia, in keeping with the fantasy: leather boots, woolen leggings, shift, petticoat, dress, and wimple, with a cloak over all of it, for both Anna and me, even though we were inside. After dressing me, the girl—Dana was her name—fixed my hair. One night and I already understood why women went to bed with their hair in a braid, because otherwise the tangles were painful to get out with only a wooden comb that pulled and caught in my hair.

With my hair finally smooth, Dana began to do something elaborate with small braids and in the end perched them on the top of my head, a cloth pinned over them. At least I wasn't being forced to wear a veil; at least the dress was blue, my favorite color. But honestly, did the fantasy have to go so far as to not allow me a shower? Or underwear? I cursed myself for not shaving my legs the previous morning. Of all days to forget . . .

Anna watched the procedure, eyes wide, taking it all in. What questions or pronouncements might I get out of her later?

I liked reading about history a lot. I liked listening to Mom's stories about Wales, but it didn't take a genius to realize that for women, living in any era but the twentieth century—the latter half of the twentieth century even—*sucked.* After the fact, I understood that I'd allowed Trev to guilt me into a subservient existence with him, but I *had* eventually left him when he hurt me, and I *knew* that occasionally I was even smart and capable. Throughout history, however, women had little say in their lives, less power, and no credit for doing anything interesting. *No, thank you.*

I took Anna's hand and she and I trailed the maid down the hall, down a flight of stairs, and through a door. I'd heard the voices from halfway down the stairs and guessed I'd find many people where she was taking me, but was still completely unprepared to step into a cavernous hall at the foot of the stairs populated by more than a hundred people. The noise level didn't really change at our entrance, but plenty of heads swiveled toward us and away again as the maid led us to an empty spot at the end of a twenty-foot table.

The room was huge—a great hall in every sense of the word. Window slits started at head height, and a fireplace took up a portion of one wall, big enough for half a dozen people to hide. Thick tapestries that looked like rugs filled in the spaces between the windows. The room smelled of smoke, unwashed bodies, roasted meat, and beer. Great. Just like that frat party Elisa took me to in October.

A smaller table stood on a dais about six feet away. Dafydd sat at it, accompanied by four men, all dressed as he was in mail armor, cloak, and boots. He raised his glass to me, the smirk thankfully absent, but I looked away and didn't return his greeting, turning instead to Anna. When in an awkward social situation, having a little girl on your lap is an excellent distraction.

"Are you ready to eat?" I asked her.

Anna nodded. The activity in the hall had struck her uncharacteristically dumb. I hugged her close and talked to her to fill the gap and put her at her ease. "It's okay. We'll have some breakfast and then maybe we can go outside and see if it's a nice day."

A serving maid brought a plate of biscuits and another of fried eggs. Next to those she laid a carafe of an unspecified liquid (mead?) and another plate of bread—flat and unleavened. I glanced surreptitiously at my neighbor to my left. He was using the flat bread as a plate.

"What's that?" Anna asked.

"A trencher," I said, without remembering where I'd heard about them.

I pulled one to me and spooned the eggs onto it. I offered Anna a biscuit with honey, which she took, moving off my lap to kneel on the bench so she could reach the table better. She wore a simple, undyed, linen dress, little boots, and cloak of her own. Her hair stuck out all over her head in a curly mass that we'd tamed with a head band. She also wore something that bore only a passing resemblance to a diaper. She'd peed in the chamber pot earlier, as she'd started waking dry more and more often at home, but I wasn't holding my breath about her being potty trained in a day. If we stayed here very long, it was I, I suspected, who was going to be trained, not her.

And then I shuddered, terrified that we might stay here longer than a day. The more I surveyed the room and these people, their total immersion in the thirteenth century became more apparent.

Did they even have a phone? Were we going to have to walk to the nearest town? Anna had mentioned horses, so maybe we could ride, not that I had any skill in that department.

"Are you okay?" I hugged Anna around the waist and gave her a kiss on the cheek.

She nodded, big eyes again. "I don't see Gramma."

"If she were here, it would be hard to spot her in this crowd," I said. "But I don't think she is. We'll see about finding her after breakfast."

Covertly, I studied my neighbors, needing to abandon this charade, get up and leave, but not sure how. No one paid me any attention, even Dafydd, who now conferred closely with a man on his right, his face turned away from me. Relieved, I slid off the bench, picked up Anna, and sidled away from the table.

I really wanted to walk out the great front double doors at the end of the hall. To do it, I'd have to cross a fifty-foot gauntlet of people, mostly men. I wasn't sure that would be the best idea. I shuddered at the memory of what could have happened last night if Llywelyn had been a different man from the one he was. Given the seriousness of these people, escape seemed ill-advised as yet. Instead, I returned to the stairs.

Thirty steps led to the second floor. Instead of stopping there and going to my room, I kept going. I climbed another twenty steps to the third floor, huffing from the effort of carrying Anna, and then twenty more before I faced a heavy wooden door, set in the wall ahead of me. I pulled the latch and stepped into a new world.

The sea air filled my lungs.

"Look at the bird!" Anna said.

The wind tossed her curls into my face. I hugged her to me and wrapped my cloak around us both, not wanting her to get chilled.

It was a seagull, exactly like the ones I might see at home. But this wasn't home—wasn't like any place I'd ever seen. We stood on the battlements of a castle, just as Anna had said. But it wasn't a picturesque castle from a fairytale. It was a working castle with stables and smoke rising from a blacksmith's forge, chickens and pigs and horses, and lots and lots of men sporting various weaponry: swords, axes, bows and arrows. Some milled below me in the courtyard of the castle and others moved purposefully from the keep, through the courtyards, and gatehouses, and back again.

Beyond the walls, the sea surrounded us on three sides and crashed on the rocks below so loudly that it wasn't any wonder that the sound had penetrated the walls. High white clouds skidded across the sky, and lower, storm clouds lay on the horizon. Gray dominated everything: the sky, the sea, the castle walls on which I stood. It didn't feel cold enough for snow, but I could believe that rain was coming. The view awed me.

Anna brought me back to reality, wiggling to get down. She ran around the inside of the circular walls once before poking her finger into a hole in the mortar between two of the stones.

"Don't be fooled by the view. The man isn't worth it." I nearly jumped in shock, and turned at the voice behind me. Dafydd stood in the doorway, one shoulder propped against the frame, his arms folded across his chest. He spoke in French, as he had with Llywelyn in the bedroom.

"Excuse me?" I said.

David pushed off the frame and walked toward me. I took a half step backward, stooping to grasp Anna's hand. I held it tightly in mine, pulling her away from the wall and toward me.

"I speak of my brother, Prince Llywelyn," he said. "War is coming. He'll be off and you'll pine for him for a while, but then you'll leave him. They always do."

"I have no idea what you're talking about."

Dafydd laughed. "Is that so? You soon will."

I took another step, trying to get away from his smile, but the tower had a diameter of twenty feet and I had nowhere to go. The cold rough stones of the battlement pressed into my back. Dafydd was very close now. He'd tied his long hair back from his face with a leather tie, revealing a sculpted face and strong jaw.

Here was a man who would have tried last night.

No doubt many women were attracted to him because of his looks alone, which of course he knew, but I saw something else in his eyes that seemed sincere, and a little vulnerable, despite the flippancy of his words.

The thought was icier than the wind. I might not be the sharpest crayon in the box, but if I needed any further evidence that the person living the fantasy just might be me, not Llywelyn, this was it. These people were real. I was out of place—and time?

I bent to Anna and swung her onto my hip. Dafydd ignored her. He put his right elbow on the top of a crenellation and stroked my left sleeve with one finger. "You're very beautiful," he said. "Why have I not seen you before?"

"I haven't been here before," I said. I scooted sideways, putting a few more inches between us. Unfortunately, Dafydd matched my movement, following me.

"My brother is very fortunate," Dafydd said. I looked away, completely at a loss. The man was flirting with me—this strange, gorgeous, armor-clad man was flirting with me on the top of a castle in God-knows where.

"Why don't you like him?" I said.

Dafydd stopped short. "He's my brother and the Prince of Wales. I would die for him."

I stared at him, completely befuddled by his statement. I hadn't thought he would tell me why, but that he would deny, with all sincerity, that he hated Llywelyn was so out of sync with his words or actions both in the past and in the future that it left me speechless.

A shadow moved below me and I turned to look down. Even from the back, I recognized Llywelyn coming down the stairs of the keep. Dafydd must have seen him too, because he straightened and pulled away from me, perhaps not so sure of himself after all. Another man had followed Llywelyn out of the keep and at his call, Llywelyn turned. In doing so, he glanced up at the battlements and saw us looking down at him. He stood, his hands on his hips, head thrown back, and met my eyes. I gave a little wave and then felt stupid to have done so, but Anna mimicked me and turned it into something cute.

"Hi!" she said.

Anna could melt any man's heart, no matter how severe, and Llywelyn was no exception. I could see his smile, even from fifty feet above him. He spoke to the other man, sketched a wave at us, and continued across the courtyard and through the enormous gatehouse that marked the entrance to another courtyard. He'd ignored Dafydd completely. Not sure what to make of that, I turned to Dafydd to try to read his expression—but he'd disappeared.

I looked to the doorway; Anna and I were alone again. I'd grown cold—and unsettled. I didn't want to stay up here alone any longer. I took one last long look at the mountains and the sea and then, with Anna on my hip, headed for the door to the stairs. Before I could reach it, however, another man came through it, the same one I'd seen talking to Llywelyn on the stairs to the keep.

"Madam," he said, with a slight bow, speaking in French. "I am Goronwy, counselor to the Prince. He asks that you come inside. Plans have changed and we will leave before the noon hour."

"Where are we going?" I felt really disoriented now.

"Brecon," he said.

A chill settled in my stomach that had nothing to do with the air around me. I knew what Brecon meant to me—a dorm at Bryn Mawr College where my sister went to school—but Goronwy meant the real thing: Brecon, Wales.

"May I ask where I am?"

"You don't know?"

I shook my head. "I don't have a good memory of last night."

"Mine is very clear. Lord Llywelyn has some questions for you on that score, but they will keep. For now, I can tell you that we are at Castell Criccieth, in Gwynedd."

I'd never heard of it. "How long will it take to get to Brecon?"

"At least a week," Goronwy said. "Lord Llywelyn wishes to depart before the rains come. If we ride inland, we can reach his manor in the forest of Coed y Brenin by evening, with a move to Castell y Bere the day after that. You will need warmer clothing."

Oh. My. God. Anna wiggled and I put her down. She crouched to point out a spider that crawled across the flagstones. Goronwy bent and spoke to her in Welsh. Watching them, I put a hand to my mouth, and a wave of hysteria rolled through me. This time I couldn't control it. My laughter began as a choke and then swelled to full-fledged giggles. I swung around to face the sea and took a stride toward the edge of the battlements. The wind caught at the cloth on my head, but I let it go, instead wrapping my arms around my waist to try to contain myself. Finally, I gave up and let the tears come.

"Madam?" Goronwy spoke from behind me. I glanced back to see him staring at me, Anna's hand in his. Anna, fortunately, was used to this sort of thing from me and was smiling too, though with no idea of the joke.

I wiped at my cheeks. "I'm fine. Let's go in."

*****

Anna toddled happily after Goronwy and he picked her up before we were half-way down the first flight of steps. That was a good plan because she took a *very* long time to navigate a set of stairs on her little legs, usually with me counting them one by one. I followed them, watching my feet as we made our way down the stairs, tears still pricking behind my eyes.

Goronwy escorted us to our room, where the same maid from before waited.

"Hello, Dana," I said. "I see we need more clothes."

She'd piled two sacks beside the door to the room. Goronwy signaled to the guard waiting outside for us that he should carry them away. Then Goronwy hesitated in the doorway, looking at me as I stood in the center of the room, my hands clasped in front of me. Dana knelt on the floor in front of Anna, helping her into an extra petticoat.

"You'll be all right, then?" he said.

I honestly didn't know, but didn't tell him that. "Thank you, Goronwy. We'll be fine."

"I'll return for you in a few minutes," he said, and closed the door. I gazed at the closed door, a cold feeling in my chest at the knowledge that I was going to have to turn off that part of me that needed to question what was happening and go with the flow of things.

Dana dressed Anna like a miniature adult, with cloak and hood like mine. On the bed lay further clothes for me. The dress split up the middle, designed for riding astride. The thick black wool cloak hung heavily on my shoulders, the clasp at the throat. It had ties up the front so I wouldn't have to keep it clutched around me while we traveled, and two slits for my hands instead of sleeves.

Goronwy knocked on our door again.

"Thank you, Dana," I said in Welsh as we left. *Diolch.*

"My pleasure, Madam."

Once in the same courtyard where I'd last seen Llywelyn, a boy stood off to the right of the stairs with a horse, waiting for us.

"Up with you," Goronwy said. I gazed up at the horse. It was huge—not that all the horses weren't huge from the ground, but this one seemed to loom over me in a most uncomfortable manner. All around us men and horses jostled each other to mount and I hugged Anna closer to me. I would be the only woman on the journey and all the men, like Goronwy, wore full armor, with long swords at their waists. At least a dozen of them also had giant bows and quivers strapped to their saddlebags.

"I'm supposed to ride this horse to Brecon? I couldn't take my eyes off the monstrous beast in front of me.

"Your chariot is sunk in the marsh," Goronwy said. He took Anna from me.

"I've been thinking," I said, stalling for time. "We're spending tonight at that place you mentioned, Coed y Brenin?"

"Yes that's right," Goronwy said.

"Isn't that where Owain Glendower was ambushed and died?"

"What did you say?" Goronwy said.

"Isn't that the place? My mother sings a song about it. He rode into a gap in the road with high hills on either side and archers attacked him and his men. He and his men fought, but they all died. It was a lot like how Llywelyn . . ." I stopped, horrified. I'd run at the mouth. I shouldn't know how Llywelyn would meet his death.

"Who was Owain Glendower?" Goronwy said.

"He—"

"We'll discuss this later."

Llywelyn had come up behind me. Without warning, he put his hands around my waist and threw me into the saddle. I plopped onto my bottom on the seat and then managed to swing my right leg over the horse to get both feet in the stirrups. I wiggled into a more comfortable position and gathered the reins, as I'd seen actors do in movies. Llywelyn handed Anna to me and she snuggled into my lap, her knees tucked inside her cloak.

"Are you sure about this?" My voice came out high. The horse stepped sideways restlessly and then swerved back to avoid another horse.

"We ride only twenty-five miles," Llywelyn said. "Was that my brother on the battlements with you?"

I looked down at him, uncertain at the quick change of subject. "Yes."

"What did you talk about?" He looked at me very intently.

"You," I said, going for honesty.

"Good." He patted my knee before walking to his horse which a groom held still a few yards away.

"I will ride with you, Madam," Goronwy said, also mounting. He made it look so easy.

"Meg," I said. "Marged *dw i.*"

"Lady Marged, then, when we speak in Welsh," he said. And then he caught me off guard with another question. "What language is it that Anna speaks? It's unknown to me, yet she has some Welsh."

I froze. There was so much to remember with all this the other-worldly craziness of what was happening to us. I was having a hard time keeping straight what I should know and what I shouldn't. In retrospect, I shouldn't have talked about Owain Glendower because he hadn't been born yet, if this was really the thirteenth century. Was I actually going to sit here and think that I'd—what?—time-traveled to medieval Wales? And then I looked around and wondered what other explanation there could be and how I could think anything else.

Goronwy still waited for my response.

I stuttered while I thought. "She speaks American," I said, in an instant coming up with an answer that wasn't even a lie and would allow me to avoid the dreaded word '*English*.'

"That language is new to me," Goronwy said. "I've never heard of it."

"No," I said. "You wouldn't have."

Goronwy looked away. "Huh."

Up ahead, Llywelyn had also mounted. He sat with a straight back. He was naturally thick through the chest and shoulders but armor had bulked him up too, just like all the men. With a sinking feeling, I acknowledged that they weren't built that way as a result of playing football or lifting weights. It was their work with swords and bows that had caused it.

"Let's move!" A man riding next to Llywelyn raised his sword and twisted it in his wrist like a baton.

With a click of his tongue on his teeth, Goronwy urged his horse forward. I shook my horse's reins and was startled when he obeyed, moving to match Goronwy's horse. Everyone paired up to ride underneath the gatehouse and onto the road that led from the castle. As we rode under the final tower, I looked back. Castell Criccieth soared above us. Two soldiers stood on the battlements at the top of the two great towers, still and silent. The wind whipped Llywelyn's flag on its pole.

The road, comprised of hard-packed dirt, led to a small village at the foot of the promontory on which the castle rested. Admittedly, it looked just as I thought a medieval village should, with a scattering of thatched-roof huts around a central green space, on which a few sheep grazed. We rode among the houses while men, women, and children came out of them to wave, a few of the children running beside the horses to keep up. As the village church came into view, a priest appeared. He stepped forward to block the road and confer with Llywelyn. They spoke, their voices low, and then the priest made the sign of the cross, blessing all of us.

Llywelyn bowed his head in answer and the priest moved aside. As I rode past him, I ducked my head and pulled my cloak over my face, not wanting to meet his gaze.

There it was. I couldn't turn aside from this no matter how I might want to deny it. Anna and I were in the Middle Ages.

6

Llywelyn

"**M**ay I ask your thoughts, my lord?" Goronwy asked. We'd stopped to water the horses at a stream and to allow men to dismount and see to their needs. Goronwy had taken the opportunity to tell me of his conversations with Marged.

"I am at sea with her," I said. "Too many things she says don't add up."

"Do you have second thoughts that she seeks to betray you? Do you believe she's lying?"

"No," I said. "No, I don't. But that doesn't make what she says true either. Yet if I'm not mistaken, she didn't believe I was the Prince of Wales when she awoke last night. She so thoroughly didn't believe me that she attacked me with a knife."

"My lord!" Goronwy said. "You didn't tell me that!"

"No, I didn't," I said, suitably chastened. "In truth, she knew so little of its use that I was never in danger. What most concerned me was her fear—particularly her fear of me."

"She rightfully feared retribution for her audacity," Goronwy said. "Many a lord who would have behaved differently, punished her certainly, and wouldn't have kept her with him after that."

I smiled. "But I am not a typical lord now, am I?"

Goronwy nodded. "Might I say, my lord, if you excuse my impertinence, that you can be confident to a fault."

"Ha!" I said. "When have I ever rebuked you for impertinence? I tried once, as I recall, when you defeated me at wrestling. Nothing ever came of it."

Goronwy smiled and I was glad to see it. He worried too much these days and it had put lines between his eyes. "There's much about her that we don't yet know," he said. "I'm most interested in the mystery of her chariot, its manner of propulsion and material."

"She has more to tell us," I said. "Not that we're going to believe it either."

Goronwy snorted a laugh. Then he checked his saddle bags and mounted his horse. I followed suit, all the while contemplating the woman in question. Throughout my conversation with Goronwy, she'd knelt on her cloak, clapping as Anna ran around the clearing. The little girl would run to one tree and then another, and then back to her mother, while Marged counted, seeing how fast the little girl could leave and return.

My men had glanced at them often, every one with an amused expression on his face. Marged was obviously genuine, obviously loved her daughter—but I wasn't sure about anything else about her. How could I be? She'd hardly sat on a horse before today, given the unprofessional nature of her seat and the stiffness in her walk when she dismounted. How had she come from Radnor? It was a six day ride in full summer for a woman, not to mention in the dead of winter with snow in the mountains and a small child to care for.

Marged gathered Anna to her and walked back to where her horse was tethered. It was the walk that got me thinking. Marged walked unlike any woman I'd ever known. I pictured her as I'd seen her striding across the bailey at Castell Criccieth. She moved along as if she were a man wearing breeches (which admittedly she *was* wearing when I found her) and not used to the hindrance of a dress around her ankles. That walk of hers was a signpost that told me there was more to Marged's differences than merely a matter of dress or of the strange vehicle in which she came to me.

It was also in the way she spoke, not only to me but to everyone. On one hand, she had yet to accord me my title, 'my lord,' in Welsh, French, or even this 'American' that Goronwy informed me was her native tongue. On the other hand, she tossed around 'please' and 'thank you' to anyone and everyone in a manner which indicated she was supremely confident in her own station, unconcerned with the station of others, or viewed every person, whether low or high, as her equal. Now that was a daunting thought.

She reminded me a bit, in fact, of my mother—not so much in later life when she was embittered by years of imprisonment and loss—but when I was a small child and it was only my brother, Owain, and me in her house. She was loving, protective, and without fear. She would stand up to anyone when we, her cubs, were threatened, even my father. When I was young, I do believe she loved me.

As I gathered the reins and led my men out of the clearing, I glanced toward the sea, eyeing the clouds that moved closer with every breath. At noon when we'd left Criccieth, they were still distant. I'd allowed only this one short rest at mid-afternoon because the clouds were beginning to crowd the space between the sea and the sky and I didn't think we had much longer before the rain hit.

"Reminds me of when your Uncle died," Geraint said, tipping his head to the western sky.

Dark clouds had gathered in the east that day, which we'd taken as a sign of trouble to come. Trouble always came from the east, though the weather almost never did. The storm had broken, with cacophony of hail and crashing rain, unusual for Wales at any time of year, where the wet was generally steady and unrelenting, but quiet.

"Uncle Dafydd liked to describe England as a looming storm, biding its time before it struck, downing us without warning with lightening and thunder," I said. Twenty years later, the menace was less evident, yet the only difference was that I was older, and that the men of Wales had rallied around my masthead, more prepared to weather any storm England could inflict upon us.

"But we should only have snow today, praise be to God." Geraint's body swayed with the easy walk of the horse. "We need to reach the manor before the sun sets."

Watching him clutch his cloak around himself, I had a pang of regret that I'd brought him on this journey. I valued his advice and selfishly wanted him with me, but if I needed extra cushions on the road, he needed a bed. God willing, we wouldn't spend any night on the open road. The mountains between us and Brecon formed a barrier that was only thirty miles across—forty miles if we took the old Roman road from Llanio—but in a blizzard, forty miles could be four hundred for all the difference it would make.

I looked back to find Marged. She'd tucked Anna inside her own cloak, so only the little girl's head showed from between two of the ties. Marged noticed me watching and grinned. That was another difference between her and any other woman . . . how many women would have come on this journey without complaint, and then had the stamina to grin at me?

Of all the women who'd shared my bed in recent years, I'd always known, even through the blindness of lust, that they were with me *because* I was the Prince of Wales. Either they or their fathers put them in my path because they wanted the prestige it could give them. But as always, none had born me a child, and eventually I'd urged each of them to marry someone else.

Goronwy noted my attention and trotted up beside me. "We're approaching Coedwig Gap," he said. "It's the perfect place for an ambush if Marged's memory is correct, whoever this Owain Glendower might be."

Hywel reined in close on the other side. "Should we prepare, my lord?"

"Yes," I said. "At worst, the exercise will wake everybody up. It's easy to become complacent when the challenges have become fewer or farther between."

Hywel nodded. "If this is a trap, I have no intention of going in unprepared." Putting his weight on his stirrups, he stood in them and raised his sword to gain the attention of the men.

"Find someone to take charge of Marged, Goronwy," I said, keeping my voice low underneath Hywel's call. "I need you if there's to be a fight."

"Yes, my lord."

We rode on, in better formation and more watchful. Another quarter of a mile and we crested a rise that gave us a view of the land around us, though not the road ahead as it bent and was obscured by trees. Goronwy checked his horse, looking southeast. I followed his gaze, only to grimace at the sight: smoke rose towards the sky in billowing clouds. It was too much for daily activity in any village, not to mention the small one that crouched in the valley below, separated from us by expansive fields and stands of trees.

Hywel had seen it too. "Is that the trap?"

"Hard to know until we enter it," Goronwy said.

"I don't know of whom Marged speaks," I said. "But whoever this Owain Glendower was, he should have known better than to ride through Coedwig Gap without precautions."

"We should divide the company," Goronwy said.

"Do it," I said. "Take Marged and half the men along the road and the rest of us will ride across the fields. That leaves both of us with twenty-five men—still a formidable force."

I pulled my horse out of line. "Come!" Hywel and I led our men off the road, urging our horses across the fields that separated us from the unnamed village. The men were on high alert; those with bows strung them, the rest of us had unsheathed our swords, riding with the bare blade ready for use.

"I don't like it," Hywel said. "If it looks like a trap and smells like a trap, it's probably a trap."

We slowed our horses as we reached the summit of the last hill before the village. It lay before us, quiet in the sunshine. Nothing stirred except the three scouts I'd sent ahead. They worked their way from hut to hut, looking for survivors. It was a village of twenty thatched huts, all burning, with a small green. It was the green that drew our attention. The possessions of the villagers had been piled in its center, ten feet on a side and another fifteen feet high, and lit. The entire wealth of the village was going up in flames.

"Mother of Christ!" Hywel breathed. "We don't have time for this."

"Only goods, not bodies," I said. I wheeled my horse around. "A trap, but not for us! To Coedwig Gap!"

The company flowed into formation behind us as Hywel and I hit the track heading west at speed, back to where our companions rode. We knew these roads, had ridden them many times before; a path ahead led to the back side of the hill that overlooked the road at Coedwig Gap. The view from above would give us the opportunity to assess the situation without falling into a trap ourselves.

"Goronwy would not have been surprised easily," Hywel said, through teeth gritted in concentration.

"He shouldn't have been surprised at all," I said. "It's the possible numbers he faces that worries me."

Spying the path, Hywel signaled with his sword and the men followed us up the trail. It was steep on this side but our horses were bred for the Welsh mountains and didn't falter. We came out of the trees on the crest of the hill and looked down onto the road below, a heavily treed hollow with hills that rose sharply on either side.

Hywel cursed beside me. "*S'mae cwd!*"

My twenty-five men were in brutal hand-to-hand combat with a company of men who hadn't the honor to wear the colors of their lord. A few had managed to keep their seats, but Goronwy was unhorsed, feet planted, astride the body of another man. I didn't see Marged.

I gave Hywel a quick assessing glance and raised my sword. "*Am Cymry!*"

The men cheered and spurred their horses. We surged down the hill in a massed cavalry charge, that even with two dozen men, implied overwhelming force. The enemy, whoever they were, were unprepared to be hit from behind.

As always in the face of battle, my insides turned cold and my hearing dulled, even as my vision sharpened. Slicing through the arm of one man, I caught the neck of another on the upswing. I registered the cries and calls of pain, but they didn't disrupt my focus. I reached the edge of the road, having passed through the main body of the men and checked my horse in front of Goronwy. While a few survivors raced north from the battle, in less than two minutes, my men had driven through the intruders. Their bodies lay strewn across the road and hillside. It was a sight I'd seen many times, and always hoped never to see again.

Hywel breathed hard beside me. "We'll get after them, my lord."

He pointed his sword and a rush of men chased after the remainders. One of my men pursued and overtook a man on foot and cut him down from behind. I turned away.

The power drained from me, more quickly than when I was a younger man. I dismounted and rested my head against my horse's neck. I closed my eyes and whispered my thanks and encouragement to her, before straightening and gazing at the carnage. Goronwy knelt next to the man whose life he'd guarded with his own. It was Geraint.

Not Geraint.

"He's alive but perhaps not for long," Goronwy said in an undertone as I crouched beside him.

"Damn those bastards to hell," I said.

Goronwy ignored my profanity. "He has a head wound and a gash in his side that has bled heavily."

"Where's Marged?"

Goronwy pointed with his chin back down the road to the north. "In the trees. I should have left Geraint beside her, but he insisted on riding with us."

"Fool," I said, though my throat closed on the word, and I was angry at myself for not ordering my old friend to stay behind. *Sweet Mother of God, he would have obeyed me.*

Hywel planted himself stiffly in front of me. I read in his face the bad news he carried, and stood so as to give his report the honor it deserved.

"We've lost eight men and three more are grievously wounded," he said. "Several others are less so. All of the men who rode from the village are alive, with few injuries. We caught them completely by surprise."

"We did exactly as they should have expected, Boots," I said. "Why weren't they prepared?"

Hywel shrugged. "Perhaps they assumed we'd see the village but ride to it along the road. If our thoughts were fixed on the village, we would have been unprepared for an assault here, at the Gap."

"Possible," I said. "And they wouldn't have known we had warning. The real question now, is who knew we would come this way this morning and had the wherewithal to set a trap?"

"Someone at Criccieth," Hywel said.

I was grateful he didn't give voice to what he thought—what every one of my advisors would think after a single heartbeat of contemplation: *Dafydd.* He'd not come with us, and we'd only taken this road with such urgency because of his news.

And then there was Marged.

"Haul these men off the road. I don't want to leave them in the way," I said, damping down my anger but knowing that my words had come out stiff and pointed. "For the rest, I want a survivor I can question."

"Yes, my lord," Hywel said. He bowed and strode away.

"We must send to that village for help," Goronwy said. He eased Geraint's helmet off his head and threw it across the road. It rolled away and came to rest in the ditch among the fallen leaves. "Geraint needs a healer."

"The village is destroyed and her people absent," I said. "Whether dead or missing I don't know."

Goronwy absorbed this news without speaking but tightened his grip on Geraint's hand. "We have bandages in a pack on Marged's horse."

"I will find her," I said.

7

Meg

Goronwy directed the men forward as we approached the gap. At this location, the road ran through a narrow crevasse, which Goronwy informed me led ultimately to the ford across the Eden. A young man named Bevyn who wasn't even old enough to shave remained beside me. He focused his eyes ahead, however, and I could tell he resented the duty of riding with me if it was going to keep him from the forefront of a fight.

As the hills rose up on either side, Goronwy suddenly signaled a stop. He glanced back at me and Bevyn and tipped his head.

"We must stay here, my lady," Bevyn said. "Get well back into the trees."

He and I dismounted and led our horses away from the road, Anna still high in the saddle, clutching the pommel with both hands. I could hardly believe how well she'd done these long hours of riding, but she seemed unfazed.

Bevyn tethered my horse to a tree but kept the reins of his horse, prepared to launch out of the woods to save his companions if he had to. With Anna on my hip, she and I found a higher spot from which to watch the road. The trees were bare of leaves, making hiding difficult but allowing me a better view of the road.

At first, our soldiers moved easily, though their shoulders were tense, waiting—for what, none of us know.

"This is the worst part," Bevyn said. "Before it happens."

"You've been in battle before?" I asked.

He turned to look at me before returning his gaze to the road below. "My father tells me this."

Then, a roar broke the silence, coming from the trees on our side of the road, but further south. Bevyn shoved me to my knees and I put out a hand to stop myself from toppling with Anna to the ground. The road became the definition of chaos, arrows flying at Goronwy's men and them struggling to return fire.

Goronwy's horse reared and he cursed. He managed to stay on her, while at the same time swinging his shield around to block any further arrows. A dozen of Goronwy's men turned towards the wood, urging their horses forward, but at the same instant, a host of men charged out of them, aided by the terrain which gave them the higher ground.

The two lines of horses crashed into each other and men on both sides went down. Beside me, Bevyn had mounted his horse, hardly able to contain himself. I pressed Anna's face against my shoulder while she cried at the noise and at my fear.

"Awn! Awn!" I said. *Go! Go!*

He went, crashing through the bracken and spurring his horse out of the trees and onto the road. He raised his sword arm sliced through one attacker and then another, neither of whom even had time to turn. He cut down one man who pressed on Goronwy, who'd lost his horse and now stood astride the body of another man.

I watched only Bevyn, too frightened to look away, praying with everything in me that he stayed upright; that he lived through this. His sword developed a coating of blood and it flashed as he moved it up and down, killing every enemy within reach.

And then Llywelyn came.

I couldn't see his face from this far away, but I could imagine his grimace, that teeth-bared look all the men had as he and Hywel galloped full-speed side-by-side down the opposite slope. Bevyn broke off from what he was doing and flowed into formation behind Llywelyn. The soldiers moved as a unit and I understood then that that was what Bevyn meant, more than the daily practice with wooden swords that I'd always imagined was standard for knights-in-training. It was the ability to work as a team, to trust that you didn't have to block that enemy's sword because the man beside you had already done it.

They moved fluidly through the opposition. I didn't know how they avoided their own soldiers but they did. I barely had time to catch my breath before it was over. So many men were dead or injured. But I couldn't see them, through the tears that poured down my cheeks.

I stared at the battlefield, unseeing, until I caught sight of Llywelyn pacing north along the road towards me. By the time, he glimpsed me among the trees, I could tell he was angry. His focus was such that I could practically see the blood thundering in his ears and that his vision had narrowed to a red haze.

Just like Trev.

He burst into the space in front of me, grabbed my arms, and pulled me to him. He brought his nose to within inches of mine.

"Tell me how you knew!"

"I . . I . ."

"Are you the traitor? Are you a spy for the English?"

"No! No!" I said.

"Who did you tell that we were coming this way?"

"Nobody! I didn't tell anyone! I didn't even know until just before we left!"

"You knew they'd attack us here!"

"I only knew that at one time someone had! Would I have told you about it if I planned to betray you?"

He stared down into my face while I gazed up at him, my face white and my eyes wide. He'd gripped my upper arms so tightly it was going to leave marks. Then my words finally penetrated and Llywelyn's vision cleared. He relaxed his hands and set me on my feet. Anna had been asleep on a blanket but sat up, her eyes wide, looking at us. Llywelyn's face fell and he put his forehead into mine.

"I didn't mean to scare you or her." He ran his hands up and down my arms. "Last night, I promised you I wouldn't hurt you, and here I've already broken that promise. I can't fix it. I'm sorry, Marged."

"I didn't betray you, Llywelyn," I said.

"I know that now," he said. "But there's too much about you that is unfamiliar and unusual. I haven't had time to hear your story, but you can't evade my questions any longer. I will not abide another day in ignorance."

"I know no more than you, Llywelyn," I said. "I don't know how I came to be here, or why, only that Anna and I are here."

Llywelyn eased back from me further. "Perhaps you are a gift from God," he said, in Welsh. "Perhaps he sent you so I wouldn't die at Coedwig Gap today."

"How many are dead?" I said, in French, not letting him know I understood him. His comment had been for himself alone.

"Too many."

"I saw the battle. I saw men fall, but many, surely, survived."

"And they need help," Llywelyn said. He stepped around me to my horse. "We need the bandages you carry."

"Is there someone who can stay with Anna? Perhaps I can assist. I took a first aid class last quarter."

He glanced at me. "You know something of healing?"

"Yes," I said. "I do.

Okay, so by twentieth century standards I knew nothing about healing, but I figured if this really was the Middle Ages, the people here knew less than nothing and I might actually be useful.

In addition to that first aid class, which I should have known not to mention to Llywelyn since he couldn't possibly know what 'first aid' was, I'd had a baby. I'd doctored Anna's knees countless times. I'd even held Elisa together when as a child she'd run into a barbed wire fence without seeing it. Our parents hadn't been home and in the first frantic minutes, I'd staunched the blood, cleaned her wounds, and plastered her with bandaids before calling my neighbor for help.

"We'll need clean water and alcohol," I said as Llywelyn tugged the saddlebag off the horse and lugged it toward the road. I grabbed Anna's hand and hung back, not wanting her to see what was in front of us. I'd followed the battle as best I could from my hiding place. Men had died, many of them.

"Rhodri!" Llywelyn called to a young man hauling a man by his feet off the road. Helmetless but unhurt, he trotted over to Llywelyn.

"Yes, my lord," he said, a little breathlessly. His face was whiter than the usual Celtic pallor.

"I want you to stay with the little girl, here," Llywelyn said. "Marged has some healing skill that we need."

"Yes, my lord," Rhodri said. "I've six younger brothers and sisters. I know how to look after little ones." He crouched in front of Anna. "Would you like to walk with me and look for bugs?"

I thought the chances of finding any bugs in the middle of a leafless, January woods in Wales slim to none, but he had the right idea. I bent to her and spoke in English. "Will you go with him? Mommy's going to be right over there, helping some people who got hurt. Rhodri wants to know if you'd like to look for bugs with him?"

Anna nodded and transferred her hand from mine to Rhodri's. They set off slowly toward the woods, away from the road, Rhodri modifying his gate to a loose-hipped walk to match her tiny steps.

"Okay," I said, looking after them for another few seconds, and then turning the other way. I didn't know if I was traumatizing Anna for life by all she'd seen and heard in the last twenty-four hours, but she'd been making friends among Llywelyn's company during our ride, so I hoped she was okay with Rhodri—and more importantly, okay inside.

The scene in the gap hit me like a punch in the stomach. Dead men and horses lay strewn across the ground, although Llywelyn's men were attempting to clear the road. I'd carelessly mentioned the possibility of ambush, but the reality was far worse than I could have ever imagined. There was blood everywhere. The *Middle Ages. Dear God, I'm in the Middle Ages.* I walked faster, hustling to keep up with Llywelyn's long legs.

When we reached Geraint, Goronwy shifted out of the way and I fell onto my knees beside the wounded man. Llywelyn crouched beside me, his hand resting gently on the small of my back.

"Oh, my Lord," I breathed. "What's to be done?" The sight of his bloody shirt lessened my hope that I could help him or anyone.

Llywelyn ripped open Geraint's shirt so we could see the extent of the damage. "That's the first time you've used my title," he said. His voice was low so I wasn't even sure I heard him correctly.

I glanced at him, confused, and then realized that he thought I meant *him*, not God. It made me want to laugh, that hysteria from this morning bubbling to the surface yet again, but one look at Geraint and I sobered. I lifted the cloth that Goronwy held to the old man's side and revealed a three-inch hole. "He's just bleeding out on the road," I said.

"Can you help him?" Llywelyn said.

I thought back to my basic biology from high school. There weren't very many organs on the left side of the body, but it was a *huge* hole and I couldn't imagine that his intestines weren't punctured. At least the site wasn't full of dirt, as the sword had ripped through layers of mail and cloth to reach Geraint's skin, but who knew where that sword had been.

"Do you have some strong alcohol?" I asked Goronwy, who'd been waiting nearby, in French. "Not to drink but to pour on the wound. It's the best way to clean it right now."

"I'll find some."

"Hurry," Llywelyn said.

I sat back on my heels as Llywelyn pressed at the wound again, trying to staunch the flow of blood. During the minute it took for Goronwy to run to one of the horses and back, the bleeding gradually slowed. Llywelyn looked up and met my eyes.

"I'm sorry," I said. I couldn't take my eyes off Geraint's face. I'd seen death before—of course I had—but never like this. I'd never held someone's hand as his life left his body, both of you knowing that it's over. In the last second, Geraint's eyes had widened, as if he'd really *seen* me, and I met his gaze. There had been acceptance there, but something else that looked like despair. I ached for him and didn't want to move or have anything to do with all the others who lay as he did, dead or injured in the road.

Llywelyn closed Geraint's eyes, then cleared his throat. "Others aren't as bad off."

"Yes, Llywelyn," I said. "I'll see what I can do."

Llywelyn straightened and stared down at his friend, long lines drawn in his face. *How old is he?* I didn't know; didn't even know what year this was. Llywelyn helped me to my feet just as Goronwy reached us, having slowed to walking pace at the sight of us. We didn't need to tell him the news.

"Here," he said, handing me a flask. "Others have need of it."

Llywelyn led me to a young man who sat on a stump a few feet off the road. He hung his head and his right hand pressed on his left forearm as blood seeped between his fingers. I knelt in front of him and gently nudged his hand away to see his wound. Thankfully, a sword hadn't slashed through a vein at his wrist, but across the top of his forearm—more like a laceration than a cut.

"My bracers protected my arms," the boy said, "but the blow was so strong I can't even feel my hand."

"*Brifo,* Cadoc," Llywelyn said, his hand on the young man's shoulder. "This is going to hurt."

I struggled to control the shaking in my hands as I mopped at the blood with a wet cloth. I poured a small measure of the woody-scented alcohol on the wound, grimacing for the boy as I did so. He jerked as the first drop hit, and swore, but then the only indication of pain was the slow tears leaking from his eyes. I wrapped the wound in strips of cloth and tied it, then looked for Llywelyn again. He must have been watching me, at least part of the time, because he broke off his conversation with Hywel and came over.

"If he gets the cloth dirty or he changes the bandages, he needs to put more alcohol on the wound," I said in French, my entire Welsh vocabulary having apparently evaporated from my brain. "Otherwise it will get infected. It still might."

"What's this, 'infected'?" Llywelyn asked.

I searched for the proper word. "Festering?" I suggested. "Full of evil vapors?"

Llywelyn nodded as if that explained anything and he sent me to the next man. All told, I worked on five men like Cadoc, each one with a wound caused by the hacking of a sword at limbs that should never have been near a sharp object in the first place.

"I thought armor was supposed to prevent this kind of damage," I said as I tied the last knot on the last man.

Llywelyn glanced at me, surprise showing on his face. "If not for the armor, they would have lost their limbs entirely. These are minor wounds compared to what they would have experienced unprotected."

And that was certainly something I should have known, if I were a thirteenth century woman. I put a hand to my head and bent forward, feeling all of a sudden the dizziness that I'd been holding back for the last hour as I worked on the men.

"Sorry," I said.

Llywelyn put his hand on the back of my neck and pushed me down, so that my head rested on my knees. "Breathe," he said. "You've done very well." He called something in Welsh that I didn't understand and could barely hear anyway as the rushing in my ears was so loud. Then a new pair of boots appeared by my knee. It was Goronwy.

"My lady," he said, "Can I help?"

I shook my head, just trying to regain control. This always happened to me once the danger was over. I just hoped I wouldn't pass out. After a few minutes, breathing came more easily and I looked up. Llywelyn had left me to confer with someone whose name I didn't know. In the time I'd been working on the wounded, order had set in. The dead enemy had been stacked in the ditch on the far side of the road and our dead had been wrapped in blankets, laid out in a line near where Llywelyn stood. Several men helped to heave the bodies onto horse's backs for the rest of the journey to the manor.

"Your color returns," Goronwy said. "If you can ride, we need to move. The sun will fall behind the trees at any moment."

He helped me up. Though I swayed, I managed to stay on my feet.

"Do we know what happened?" I asked him. "We left Castell Criccieth on very short notice. Someone must have been working very quickly to ambush us here."

Goronwy's face grew more grim. "It's someone we trust," he said. "Someone knew that we might come, had men ready for that possibility, and sent word ahead. A rider alone could have arrived here before us easily. The question is who that rider was. I recognize some of the men we killed, but no faces leap out as having been at Criccieth. Most were men of Powys, Gruffydd ap Gwenwynwyn's men."

"*Whose* men?" I'd never heard such a bizarre name, even in Welsh.

Goronwy glanced at me, a hint of a smile on his face. "Gwenwynwyn. He and Prince Llywelyn are at peace, but in the past, Gruffydd has been a staunch ally of Prince Dafydd, Lord Llywelyn's brother, and of King Henry. I'm disappointed to think that he is involved in this attack. Regardless, neither he nor any of his men were at Criccieth."

"So who's the traitor?" I asked. "Does Llywelyn suspect his brother? I'm not sure that I liked him very much."

For the first time since I'd met him, Goronwy looked amused. "The Prince has asked that we don't speak of him for now. He will not countenance unfounded suspicions. If Prince

Dafydd has betrayed his brother, his actions would be unforgivable."

I wasn't too sure about that. Our library hadn't carried any Welsh history books to speak of, but Mom loved to tell stories. Growing up, it was Mom's stories that gave me a sense of Wales, but I wasn't sure how many of them were myth and how many were true.

But one thing I did remember: Dafydd never got punished much for anything he did. He'd even tried to assassinate Llywelyn once. He'd fled to England afterwards and the King of England took him in—and then later forced Llywelyn to take him back. It looked to me like a classic case of a coddled rich boy who'd gotten as far as he had on some innate intelligence, good looks, and charm. That's certainly how Dafydd had acted with me.

The sun disappeared and the men lit torches. Rhodri reappeared with Anna, who seemed no worse for wear. "Look, Mommy," she said, as she came up to me. "We collected leaves!"

I bent to admire them, marveling at how simple life could be if only we could live it. "They're pretty sweetheart," I said.

"She's very curious," Rhodri said. "I taught her some Welsh and she was able to repeat them back to me."

"*Diolch*," I said. *Thank you.*

Llywelyn finally returned and handed me a wet cloth to wipe my hands. I took it, noticing for the first time the blood on my clothing. I turned towards him, shocked. "Llywelyn," I breathed. "Anna shouldn't see me like this."

He leaned down so his mouth was only inches from my ear. "She won't notice if you don't call attention to it. She's only a child and will see what she expects to see."

He put his hands around my waist and boosted me onto my horse. Rhodri then bent to pick up Anna and handed her to me. I bundled her underneath the cloak, wincing at the blood again, but Llywelyn was right. It had dried and blended in with the blackness of my cloak.

Rhodri took the reins from me and pulled the horse forward, leading us. "Is your horse . . ." I stopped, afraid to ask anything more.

"He's alive," he said. "We've lost too many, though, and a dead companion rides him instead of me."

I nodded and it was a somber company that traveled the last three miles to Llywelyn's manor in the forest.

By the time we reached it, Anna had fallen asleep and I was numb from head to toe, physically and mentally. I found myself reliving the fight and its aftermath over and over again. I didn't know what Llywelyn would find when he questioned one of his prisoners, but I know what *I* saw, and would never forget . . .

I couldn't imagine living another day in this world. I wanted to go home.

8

Llywelyn

I poked my nose into my bedroom. Marged slept on the big bed, curled around Anna, whose raven locks I could just make out above the blankets they'd pulled nearly over their heads. *I can appreciate that. A day like today makes me want to hide too.* I had many questions for Marged but at least I'd settled the most important one. Whatever her origins, I would no longer consider the notion that she was a spy.

Her face, when she looked at me over the body of Geraint, had been so full of pity and understanding that I'd come close to weeping. She'd seen that too, seen the effort to contain it and saved me by speaking to Goronwy herself to give me a chance to find composure.

We lost, and lost, and lost again, and I could never find my heart so hard that it didn't rip me apart inside with each death. At least Geraint had been an old man, bent with years of age and care. He died knowing he'd left his lands and lord—his life's work—in the capable hands of his son, Tudur. The others we'd lost had been young, one only sixteen, and we could only raise our fists and curse at the utter, bloody waste of it.

The mood of all the men was dark, taking out the despair at death with anger at the men who'd done this. But as much as I wanted to start pulling out our prisoners' fingernails, I refrained. Now if I had Gruffydd ap Gwenwynwyn under my nose, Goronwy would be hard pressed to hold me back. Too bad he hid behind King Henry's skirts where I couldn't touch him.

I closed the door to the bedroom and turned toward the stairs that led to the kitchens. Even though it was nearly midnight, servants were still awake, preparing food and drink for those of my men who couldn't sleep after the day's work. The morning would come all too soon for everyone. I pushed open the door to the courtyard and strode towards the stables where Goronwy had put our two surviving prisoners.

"One's no older than my man-at-arms who'd died," Goronwy said in an undertone as I walked in. "Perhaps like him too, this was his first mission for his lord."

"He will be the one you break first," I said.

"His face is white and he's near in tears," Goronwy said. "Third stall from the right."

"Not much longer now, my lord," Hywel said.

He leaned back in a straight-back chair, his giant feet up on a trough. Lanterns blazed from hooks along the walls, sending light into the darkest corners. The stables had room for more than fifty horses, as was necessary given the number of men I often brought with me in my travels or for a day's hunting in the forest. The manor house itself barely deserved the name, however. It had a large hall and rear kitchen, but only three rooms above stairs. And no dungeons, which is why Goronwy was using two stalls for our prisoners instead of the usual horses.

I scuffed at the floor with my boot, glad to see that attention to detail of the stable boys, even in my absence. With only fire for light, even protected within a lantern, they had to be constantly vigilant about loose hay tracked across the floor.

"Shall I bring him out, my lord?" Goronwy said.

"It's your decision, Goronwy," I said. "I stand by your assessment."

Goronwy signaled to the two guards who stood on either side of the boy's stall. One of the guards was the man, Bevyn, whose charge it had been to care for Marged. She told me she'd ordered him to leave her, but I wasn't satisfied, even if he'd saved Goronwy's life. It was my orders that he needed to obey; neither his nor Marged's judgment had yet been proved, even if today's escapade had ended well for them. It might not have.

The guards disappeared inside the stall and came out leading the boy, his hands tied behind his back. Bevyn pushed him to his knees in front of Goronwy. The boy was older than Goronwy had implied, nearer to twenty than fifteen, of middle height and thin, with reddish hair and a pointed beak of a nose.

"Your name," Goronwy said.

The boy squared his shoulders, raising his chin in a manner that matched the fine cut of his cloak. "Humphrey de Bohun, Lord of Brecon and the Marche!"

"Ho!" Goronwy said. "Not quite yet, I don't think."

"I grant your family has held lands in the Marche since your ancestors came to Wales," I said, "but Brecon Castle belongs to me, unless you have further unwelcome news?"

"No, sir," Humphrey said. "I do not."

I had to admire his courage and panache. He could have denied his antecedents, but then he was probably hoping I'd ransom him, as was customary among the nobility, rather than kill him, as he might have deserved. The boy didn't appear as close to breaking as Goronwy and Hywel had thought, but then, they hadn't known who he was before either.

"Your grandfather lives?" Goronwy said, keeping to the main point. Humphrey's grandfather was also Humphrey de Bohun, the Earl of Hereford and one of my most formidable opponents in controlling the Marche. Humphrey's father had died at Evesham fighting for my ally, Simon de Montfort, *against* King Henry. The shifting loyalties of the English nobility were often hard to keep straight.

Humphrey nodded. "He is well. He will pay for my release."

"I bet he will," Hywel said.

The boy's directed a sharp look at Hywel, who gazed back at him, his face blank.

"His Welsh is better than I would have expected," Goronwy said, in aside to me, "but perhaps it would be better to speak in French."

At my nod, Goronwy pointed his chin at the boy. "*Français,* then?"

A look of relief passed through Humphrey's eyes before he mastered it. "Thank you," he said. "I expect you to return me to my grandfather's house immediately."

Hywel snorted. I smiled at that and shook my head. Goronwy needed to break through Humphrey's upright equanimity. However much I distrusted the boy's grandsire, I respected him, and could see his training in the grandson.

"What in the name of heaven were you doing at Coedwig Gap, involved in such a cowardly and ill-favored venture?" I said.

Humphrey's chin quivered. Then he visibly steeled himself. The look was one I'd seen before, most recently in Marged's eyes. Did he expect a backhand across the face? I found my temper growing hot at the thought that any man had hit her. I forced it down. Humphrey was not Marged.

"For the time being, it seems you are my guest," I said, "provided you explain your participation in the events of today."

"May I stand?" Humphrey asked.

"I think not," Goronwy said. "The quicker you talk, the sooner you can get off your knees. I'm sure they've started to ache on this hard floor."

No torture indeed. I smirked, remembering my Latin master forcing me to recite verbs on my knees over and over again until I got them right. The pain certainly sharpened *my* mind. We'd see what it did for Humphrey.

Humphrey swallowed hard. "It started out as a lark, really. Gruffydd ap Gwenwynwyn's son, Owain, proposed venturing into Gwynedd to probe your defenses and see how far we could penetrate. It was easy; the roads are nearly deserted this time of year and the snowpack sparse, even in the mountains. Two days ago, Owain received a message that called him away. He left me in charge of the men. We had camped at the foot of Rhobell Fawr when one of the men who'd left with Owain returned to camp with word that you had left Castell Criccieth."

"So you prepared the ambush?" Goronwy said.

"Owain left the rider with instructions as to what to do."

"And the village?" Goronwy said.

I nodded. I'd not forgotten the odd absence of people there, and our uncertainty as to their fate.

"If they're dead, it wasn't our doing!" Humphrey said. "We came upon the empty village the day before Owain left. In his note, Owain suggested burning the village as a distraction. We did *not* kill anyone."

"Just my men," Hywel said.

"As to that," Humphrey said, "from our end, it was worth the cost if we could take you, my lord Prince, as a prize. Our intent was not to kill you. Owain said that you would be a valuable hostage."

Goronwy glanced at me. I raised my eyebrows, willing to take the boy at his word, for now. If the villagers had left of their own accord, we didn't need to add their deaths to his list of crimes.

But Goronwy wasn't done. "Owain said? Why is that all that I have heard from your mouth? What Bohun hides behind another man, no matter who he is, unable to think for himself? I would have expected more from you. So would your grandfather."

Humphrey blinked. His face was impassive still, but a bit of doubt had crept into his eyes.

"And where is Owain now?" I said. "Obviously not here."

"No," Humphrey said, his voice curt. "He is not."

"He found it convenient to have you do his dirty work," Hywel said.

"And how do you feel about that ignoble fact?" Goronwy said. "To your grandfather, a man is one who stands up for all his actions, whether for good or ill. It is why you chose not to lie about who you are, isn't it. You've learned something from your grandfather anyway."

And why the boy might become a formidable enemy for me when he came into his inheritance. "Does your grandfather know where you are?" I said.

Humphrey didn't answer at first. He stared at Goronwy, and then me, his jaw clenched and stiff. Then the fight went out of him. His shoulders sagged. "No. You could kill me now and put out that I fell in the battle. None would be the wiser."

"Is that what Owain would do?" Goronwy said, not willing to make this easy on him.

Humphrey looked down at the ground, shifting uncomfortably. "I think he would."

"One measure of a man," Hywel said, "is with whom he associates. You might consider your choices more closely in future."

"Are you going to kill me?" Humphrey squared his shoulders, aiming for an authority and manhood he'd just discovered he hadn't quite achieved.

"We could," I said. "But we won't."

Humphrey gazed at me, hope etched in his face.

Hywel's eyes showed resigned contempt, but he stood and held out a hand to help the boy to his feet.

"Do you swear not to attempt an escape?" Goronwy said.

"I swear it," Humphrey said. "On my honor as a Bohun."

Goronwy nodded. "And perhaps you've suddenly discovered what that means, and you care more about it than you thought you did. You may sleep in the hall with the other men."

"Who is your companion in the other stall?" Hywel said.

I'd forgotten him.

"He's one of Owain's men, one Dai ap Maredudd."

"He'll keep, then. He will make a good messenger to your grandfather," Hywel said.

*****

We were into the early hours of the morning before I managed to escape my duties and find my bed. With no maid to assist her in undressing, it looked as if Marged had fallen asleep in what she stood up in. I made a note to myself to remedy that in the morning. There had to be a local girl Goronwy could conscript. It was unseemly that she was unattended. I watched her breathe slowly in and out before blowing out the candle and crawling into bed beside her. Or rather, beside Anna. The thought made me smile and for the moment put away the concerns of the day.

I'd decided that we would stay in the lodge for several days, hoping for the recovery of some of my men and for reinforcements from Criccieth and Castell y Bere. We needed to spread a wide net in hopes of picking up Owain ap Gruffydd Gwenwynwyn and the men who remained with him, and to quickly determine what had happened to the inhabitants of the village. Why had they left their homes in the dead of winter? It could be for a dozen reasons—disease, famine, marauders—any one of which would require keeping a close eye on the events in the surrounding countryside.

It seemed I'd hardly closed my eyes before I woke to sunlight trickling through a crack between the wooden shutter and the frame. Anna still slept, but Marged was awake, her eyes open, studying me.

"Did you sleep well?" I asked in French. Goronwy had informed me that her Welsh had improved over the course of the ride from Criccieth—as if she were remembering something she'd merely forgotten instead of learning it from scratch—but she was more comfortable in French and I wanted precise answers this morning.

"Well enough," she said. "I don't know that I really expected to, after yesterday."

"It was your first battle," I said. "One hopes that it will be your last."

"The older man who died was your friend. I'm sorry." She fingered the embroidery on the pillowcase, not looking at me, and then glanced up to check my face.

"He was my seneschal," I said. "My steward. His father served my grandfather and my Uncle Dafydd, and then when he died, Geraint took his place."

"I'm sorry I couldn't help him," she said.

"I know. But you helped the others."

"I hope so," Marged said. "As you say, I've never seen a battle before, never even imagined it would be anything like that, despite what is shown in movies."

There it was again. That difference. "What was that word? *Movies*?"

She didn't answer, chewing on her lower lip as she thought. "I don't think I can explain," she said. "I don't understand how I came to be here. I've been with you for two nights and a day, and already my life before coming here seems impossibly far away."

"And where is that life? That land that speaks *American*?"

"You won't believe me."

"You're sure of that?"

"Yes," Marged said. "I wouldn't believe it myself if I weren't living it."

"Tell me," I said. "Nothing can be as bad as you imagine. Push through your fears and just say it."

Anna stirred. Marged smiled down at her, still stalling I thought, and swept a handful of curls out of the little girl's face and tucked the blanket more firmly under her chin. "The bards speak of Madoc ap Owain Gwynedd," Marged said, finally capitulating. "Nearly one hundred years ago, he sailed from Wales to a new land, a new world nobody had ever seen before."

"Yes, of course. I know the tale well. I am a descendant of Owain Gwynedd, Madoc's father," I said. "Madoc sailed away to escape the infighting among his brothers at his father's death. He returned, but then left again. He died in that land across the sea."

Marged took in a deep breath and eased it out. I waited, not wanting to stop her now that she'd started.

"I think the easiest way to explain who I am is to say that I am a descendant of Madoc's people," Marged said. "I am from the land that he discovered. We call it America."

I gazed at her, lips pursed, not quite able to marshal my thoughts for an adequate reponse. It wasn't that she'd surprised me, though she had, but . . . "I entertained a dozen notions of who you might be, and from where you might have come, but this never occurred to me," I said.

"How could you? How could anyone?"

"In one sentence, you have upended all expectation," I said. "My family has wondered for generations what became of Madoc. We looked for him, trust that we did, but his sails never appeared on the horizon again. I'm glad to hear that he survived to produce descendants."

"America has many people in it."

"If he'd stayed in Wales," I said, "his line may have ended, given the fratricide that followed Owain Gwynedd's death. My grandfather was one of the few who survived it."

Marged bit her lip and I watched her warily, since that couldn't be all she had to say. The vehicle, for instance, remained unexplained.

"And . . ."

"The explanation gets a little more complicated after that," she said.

"Hmm," I said. "I imagine it might." We lay silent, me still studying her and Marged gently curling a lock of Anna's hair around one finger.

"Are you ready for the rest?" she said, once the silence had grown awkward. "It's a bit harder to hear."

"Are you going to tell me that your mother doesn't really live in Radnor?" I said.

"No. She does." Now, a waver entered Marged's voice for the first time. She swallowed it. "I haven't lied to you. Not once. I don't want to start, either. It's that . . . well . . . the Welsh settlers who came to America named towns for places in Wales that they loved and remembered."

I smiled at that, just for a second, until the questions began to pile up in my mind again. "So . . ." But Marged cut in before I could properly formulate a question.

"I know what you're thinking. I can see it in your eyes. You're noting that I didn't arrive in the marsh at Criccieth from a boat. You're wondering about my vehicle—how it was made—how I brought it here."

"Yes," I said. "I was wondering exactly that."

Marged took another breath. "You absorbed the first part of my explanation without too much difficulty, but the next part is harder. Please remember, when you stop believing me, that I said it was complicated."

"I am the Prince of Wales. My life is nothing if not complicated."

"Okay," she said. (There was that word again, which seemed to mean everything and nothing*)* "I'll tell you straight out: I'm not only from that other land but from another time."

I stared at her. "I'm not understanding you. What do you mean—another time?"

"Please, Llywelyn," she said. "Please tell me what year this is I've fallen into."

"It is the year of our Lord, one thousand, twelve hundred and sixty-eight."

"Oh, my lord," Marged said. She eased back from Anna who seemed more deeply asleep now, and turned her head to bury her face in the pillow.

"That's the second time you called me by my title," I said. "You're improving."

Marged twisted back. Her hair had fallen over her face and she pushed it away. Her voice, when she spoke, had tears in it.

"How can you laugh? Two days ago, I was living in the year of our Lord, one thousand, nine hundred, and ninety-six. I was born in America, seven hundred years from now."

The smile faded from my face. For once, I was lost for words. How could that be true? She obviously believed it, and yet. . . .

Marged huddled under the covers with her hands over her ears as if a storm were raging outside instead of the clear blue winter sky. I wanted to put my arms around her and comfort her, but didn't want to scare her.

"Marged," I said instead, aiming for reasonableness. "Why are you telling me this? Surely you can come up with a far simpler explanation for your appearance at Criccieth without *this*."

"I knew you wouldn't believe me. I didn't want to tell you," she said, her face back in the pillow, her words muffled by the down, "but there's no other way to explain who I am and why I know what I know."

"You're telling me that this is why you knew about the ambush in advance? Because you are from a future time where the events we are living now have already happened? That's not possible, Marged."

Marged lifted her head. "Yes and no. I knew there had been an ambush in this forest, but I still don't remember it being an attack on *you*."

"Ah yes," I said. "You spoke to Goronwy of this 'Owain Glendower'."

"Owain Glyndŵr, really," Meg said. "Glendower is how the English say his name."

"And who was he?"

Marged sighed. "He was a man who attempted to unite Wales under his banner about two hundred years from now. I believe he was a descendant of one of your brothers, but I can't remember which one. Not Dafydd. Do you have one whose name begins with *R*?"

"Rhodri," I said, speaking automatically as I processed what she was saying, which appeared both more and less absurd as she added detail. "You say attempted? You know my future, then? You know what becomes of me, of Wales?"

Now Marged rolled onto her back, her fingers plucking at the blanket. "Yes," she said. "I do. At least, I know what did happen, before I came here."

"Now I'm lost again. Speak plainly."

"In my century, traveling through time is talked about, speculated upon, in books and among scientists." She tipped her head to look at me. "I don't know what you call them in this age. Philosophers? Physicians? People who study the world and how it works."

"Ah," I said. "Like Aristotle."

"Oh, yes!" Marged said. "Exactly like that. I have traveled to your world, in a fashion completely outside the range of explanation. What changes will your world incur because this happened? In the future that I left, neither books nor myth about medieval Wales mention me. Does that mean I've already changed history enough to make the future that I came from different? What changes will you make now in your life because I came here—or will it make no difference at all?—was I destined to come here and are we making the same choices we always made?"

"None of what you've just said makes any sense, Marged."

"Tell me about it." She lay on her back, one wrist across her eyes, completely still.

"So this is why you were afraid of me—was it only last night?" I said. "You didn't believe me when I said I was the Prince of Wales."

"No," Marged said. "I didn't. It didn't even occur to me that you could be telling me the truth."

"And why is that? Is there no Prince of Wales in your world?"

Meg stillness deepened. "There is, but he isn't Welsh. He's English . . . well . . . of German descent even, I think. His mother is the Queen of England."

"What is this leading to, Marged? What do you need to say to me that you're not saying? If I accept your proposition that you are from the future, than you do, indeed, believe you know mine. You believe there is a future for me that I'm not going to like, isn't there?"

Marged flipped the blanket over her face but her voice came through it, strong and steady. "In late November, 1282, you travel south, out of Gwynedd. On December 11th, you are lured away from your men by a false promise of allegiance and killed.

With your death, King Edward . . ." she pulled the covers down again and glanced at me. "He's not king yet, is he?"

"No," I said. "It's his father, Henry."

She nodded. "Edward subjugates Wales so completely that it's two hundred years before any Welshman attempts to claim the title *Prince of Wales.* Even in my day, Wales is subsumed into England. With your death, Wales ceases to exist as a separate country. Though," she amended, "the Welsh have never forgiven or forgotten their subjugation. And they've never forgotten you. You are a symbol to them of all that is Welsh. A martyr, even."

I absorbed this news with more equanimity than I would have thought possible ten minutes ago. Fourteen years. She thought I had fourteen more years. There was a freedom in that that perhaps Marged had not considered.

"Who betrayed me?"

"Roger something and his brother. I can't remember the name . . . Morgan? No, that's not right because the traitors were Marcher lords, not Welshmen."

It was my turn to roll onto my back and fling my own arm over my eyes. "Mortimer," I said. "You're telling me that I plan to meet the Mortimers and instead meet my death? Why would I do such an crazed thing? Why would I think I could trust them?"

"I don't know," Marged said. "The English found a paper on your body addressed to you. It was from one of these Mortimers and indicated he might be willing to switch allegiance. Maybe you thought that sounded credible at the time?"

"And my heir?" he said. "Do I have one?"

"Before your death, you marry someone," Marged said. "I can't remember who, though, and have a daughter. I'm sorry to say that your wife dies in childbirth. That's in 1282 also."

"Not a very good year for me, then, it doesn't sound," I said.

Marged rolled over to face me, astonishment written all over her face. "Again, you laugh at this? How can you laugh?"

"How can I not?" I said. "You fell into my life two days ago, saved my life yesterday, only to warn me that I will lose it, at some future date. How is this not ridiculous? How can I not laugh?"

"You believe me, then?"

I gazed at her, taking in her features and her beauty. "I don't know. The fate you describe sounds . . . complicated, as you said. Roger Mortimer's father married my aunt, making him my cousin. In turn, Mortimer's wife has two sisters. One married my Uncle Dafydd and was Princess of Wales. The other is the mother of one Humphrey de Bohun, who is sleeping in the hall below us as we speak and was one of the men who orchestrated the attack on us yesterday."

"So you are murdered by your own family?" Marged gasped. "That's . . . that's . . . terrible!"

I smiled, warmed by her outrage on my behalf, but rueful. "Roger and I have been enemies in recent years, but I find it hard to believe he would lure me to his castle to kill me."

"I don't think it was actually him," Meg said. "I think it was his sons."

"Oh, well then. Perhaps that's more credible," I said. "That's the nature of politics in the Marche."

"So what does this mean to you, right now? What are you going to do with Anna and me?" Her voice was suddenly very small. "I would go home but I don't know how."

I twisted a long lock of her hair around my finger. "This changes everything, and nothing," I said. "The most important thing for you to know is that unless you have a different home to go to, you're going to stay with me."

"You mean that? I'm sorry to have to even ask this, but why do . . . do . . do you want me?" Marged stumbled over the question, more uncertain than she'd been even when she was telling me her fabulous tale.

"How can I let you loose in the world? You would be a danger to yourself and everyone around you. Besides," I paused, considering my own certainty in the matter, "I've grown fond of seeing you—and even Anna—in my bed."

"B-b-but," Marged said, stuttering again. "You don't know me. Not at all."

"Don't I?" I said. "I think I've learned quite a lot about you in the short time we've been together. And I expect to learn quite a bit more in the coming days." I took her chin in my hand. "Being the Prince of Wales has its advantages, every now and then, apart from dying for my people, that is. Occasionally, I get to do what I like."

I kissed her forehead and released her. Her eyes were as wide as Anna's sometimes were, watching me. I got out of bed and dressed quickly in the cold room. "Llywelyn—" she said, but I shushed her.

"Get some sleep, while you can," I said. And for once, she had the grace to obey.

9

Meg

I stood at the washbasin and peered through a crack in the shutter, trying to get some sense of what it was like outside. Then someone knocked on the bedroom door.

"Come in," I said, and turned.

The door opened to reveal a short, lean woman, significantly older than I, her brown hair streaked with gray.

"You're ready to get up, then," she said in Welsh. As two different people—Llywelyn included—had prevented me from doing so earlier, I could hardly be blamed for staying in bed. She came into the room, her arms full of clothes. "My name is Angharad. The Prince asked that I help you while you're here."

Pleased that I'd understood all of her words, I nodded and then looked ruefully down at what I'd worn to bed. "I couldn't get out of these clothes last night so I'm a little worse for wear."

"It was a difficult day yesterday," Angharad said. "I'm sorry that I wasn't here to assist you when you arrived."

"Thank you for coming to help me now," I said. "I didn't expect it."

"Well, you should, a fine lady like you," Angharad said. "My husband is one of the Prince's men-at-arms but no longer rides with him," she said. "He serves as caretaker for the manor and I run the household."

"I don't know that I am such a fine lady. I'm sure you are very busy without having to worry about me."

"Never mind," Angharad said, waving her hand. "It's a pleasure to get out of the kitchen."

She tsk'ed over me, looking me up and down, and then noticed Anna. I'd allowed her to wander off with a maid earlier, but she'd come back, checking in with me as she always did, as if we shared an invisible cord that reeled her in every once in a while.

"What a beautiful child!" Angharad said. She came closer as Anna, who was standing on the bed and holding onto my arm, peered around me. "What is your name?"

"Anna *dw i*," Anna said.

I gaped at my daughter.

"She speaks very well," Angharad said, obviously pleased. "I'd heard that she didn't have any Welsh; that you spoke only the French language, but it's not true. She's very small to be speaking at all."

"Anna has just spoken her first words in Welsh." I said.

"Well, good for her," Angharad said.

"I speak only a little Welsh," I added, "though I understand more than I speak, provided you talk slowly."

"I will do my best," Angharad said, speaking much more slowly—over-exaggerating now, which wasn't really what I wanted either.

We muddled through, however and the rest of the morning was taken up with dressing and caring for Anna, eating breakfast, and a little exploration of the grounds. It had turned colder in the night and I didn't want to spend too much time out of doors without something more substantial for warmth. Like a parka.

The manor house was a two-story affair, surrounded by a wooden palisade. Goronwy said that it wouldn't stand up to a concerted assault, but would protect us for the time it took to organize a defense and give us walls for archers to hide behind. I didn't enter the long, low building that was the stables; Goronwy asked us to avoid it as he was keeping a prisoner, Dai, inside, though he'd allowed Humphrey de Bohun, as a nobleman, out. Anna and I were standing on the steps to the manor, in fact, when Llywelyn and Humphrey walked down them to meet Hywel, who led Dai and a horse across the courtyard, ready for release. At Llywelyn's nod, Hywel stepped behind Dai and severed his bonds with his belt knife.

"You understand the importance of your charge?" Humphrey said.

"I'm a free man of Wales and no servant of yours," Dai said, in Welsh, the sneer evident in his voice and on his face. "I ride with Lord Owain of Powys, not with English bastards."

Humphrey stepped towards him, his face flushed, but before he could get farther, Hywel had the man up against the stone wall of the manor, moving so fast it had barely registered that he'd moved at all.

"Do you know who this is?" He tipped his head to Llywelyn. His voice was low and urgent, but carried no anger, just a dark intent that any fool should recognize.

"The Usur—"

Before he could finish his sentence, Hywel cut him off with a shake, choking the words out of him. He tightened his grip on Dai's tunic and knocked his head against the stones. Dai coughed and sputtered—and when he quieted, Hywel spoke again, his teeth gritted, every ounce of power in his large frame directed at overpowering the man.

"He is the Prince of Wales, and Gruffydd ap Gwenwynwyn's liege lord," Hywel said. "You do understand what that means?"

Dai didn't answer, trying to get his breath through the constriction around his throat.

Hywel didn't seem to expect a response and answered for him. "It means that you obey him or so help me God I will hunt you down and personally see that your head is removed from your body. Is that clear?"

The man coughed again and nodded. Hywel released him and stepped back. Dai slumped to his knees, his hands around his neck, pulling at his collar to help him breathe.

"Apologize," Hywel said. He kicked Dai in the thigh. Dai straightened, using the wall for support and looking a little green, he levered himself to his feet.

"My lords Llywelyn, Humphrey," the man bowed. "I beg your forgiveness. I am prepared to carry your message if you would be so good as to give it to me."

Llywelyn, who'd been watching the proceedings with an impassive expression, didn't answer. It was Goronwy who spoke.

"Tell Lord Bohun that Prince Llywelyn sends his greetings and wishes to discuss with his lordship his grandson's activities in Wales. You are to assure the Earl that Humphrey is unharmed and being treated as befits his station."

"Yes, my lord," the man said, bowing again. His held his shoulders stiff and limped to his horse. He scrambled onto it while we watched, nobody making a move to assist him.

"See that you complete your charge," Hywel said.

Dai saluted, turned his horse's head, and rode out the gate of the manor.

"See that he takes the road to England," Llywelyn said to three of his men who'd sat in the saddle, waiting for Dai to mount.

They obeyed and Anna and I watched them go, still silent.

Llywelyn put a hand on my shoulder before turning back inside. "You are well?"

"Yes, Llywelyn," I said.

"Good. If you need anything, let me know."

"I will."

What I didn't immediately say was that I didn't feel I'd needed to see that little drama in the courtyard. Anna *really* hadn't needed to see it. I didn't tell him that what I needed was a shower, which he couldn't help me with, or at a minimum, a good book to read. I was really glad I'd told him I was from the future, though. My heart had been in my mouth the whole time, but it cleared the air between us. He might not believe me—or might not be able to believe me, more to the point—but I wasn't keeping secrets from him or living a lie, and I could live with that.

"And the ransom?" Humphrey said, matching Llywelyn stride for stride as they took the stairs two at a time back up to the manor house. "What are you asking in exchange for me?"

"I'm leaving that up to your grandfather," Llywelyn said. "We will see what he feels you're worth."

Humphrey's face fell. It was a scary thought—to assert a monetary or territorial value on a person, and have that person know what it was. Goronwy stayed behind a moment with Anna and me. Anna had found a stick with which to draw in the dirt.

"I'm sorry you had to see that," he said.

"Dai was going to say 'Usurper'," I said. "What did he mean by that?"

Goronwy's mouth tightened. "Owain and his father are Prince Dafydd's allies. They believe Prince Llywelyn has denied his brothers their proper place as rulers of Wales. Owain, at least, is Prince Llywelyn's elder brother and feels he should have primacy."

"I did realize that," I said. "But—"

Goronwy didn't let me finish. "It might be better if you stayed inside. It's Boots' job to see to the obedience of the men—whether they are his own men-at-arms or another's."

"I understand," I said, and I guessed I did. To obey one's superior, to place oneself in line in the social strata, was the natural order of things in the thirteenth century. I wasn't too sure about it for myself, however, obedience never having been my strong suit, as my relationship with Trev could attest.

"We'll be here a few days," Goronwy said. "The weather is due to turn colder."

"Thank you, sir," I said.

Goronwy waited, watching me. At first I didn't know what he was waiting for, and then I realized he meant I was to start obeying *now*.

I picked up Anna and we went inside. But there wasn't anything to do. Within a few hours boredom set in to the point that my back teeth ached with it. My Welsh wasn't as good as Angharad seemed to think, especially in the hall when it was crowded with people and the general noise drowned out individual sounds. During daylight hours, few men stayed there, as they rode on patrol (or hunted to feed us) most of the day and returned, sweaty and hungry as dusk fell. They'd not found any sign of Humphrey's former companions, nor any clue as to what had happened at the village.

"Or what has become of Owain," Goronwy said over dinner. "The man is a well-heeled snake, much like his father."

"No," Llywelyn said, "his father is much more predictable. He wants land and power and fights me for it. Owain appears to do what he does out of spite."

"Or arrogance," said Hywel.

"And leaves others to pay the price," Goronwy said, with a glance at Humphrey. They'd been speaking in Welsh and Humphrey gave no indication that he could understand. Like me, however, he probably understood more than he could speak.

"I will speak to Owain's father of it the next time I see him," Llywelyn said, "but that might not be for some time."

"He can come to Brecon," Goronwy said. "He will hate the time spent away from his lands and view it wasted, but it will do him good to see you exert your authority in a tangible way."

"What Gruffydd needs to do is keep a tighter rein on his rule—and on his heir, if he expects to keep hold of what he has," Llywelyn said.

I was pretty sure that Gruffydd wouldn't be too pleased to hear that either.

*****

The days passed, one much the same as the next, which was kind of remarkable in itself, given where and with whom I was. It wasn't that life was the same as at home—not in the slightest—but Anna and I fell into a routine, just as we had at home: get up, dress, eat, play with a toy or two, eat again, sleep. The worst thing was that I had no books to read, either to her or for me, and I was going to have to do something about that if we stayed here much longer.

Perhaps of most immediate concern to me—and the most disconcerting—was that Llywelyn and I slept together every night and spoke of the events of the day, but he never touched me, not even a repeat of that fierce kiss from the first morning at Criccieth. I hadn't a clue why, didn't dare ask, and was reluctant to admit to myself, even for one second, that I *wanted* him to kiss me. He was just so . . . *damn compelling*, and I found myself watching him during the day, waiting for him to come to bed before I myself could sleep, and measuring the tempo of the day by what he was doing.

Given the disconnect between my twentieth century reality and his thirteenth century life, I wasn't sure I wanted to know what was happening between him and me; which is why Angharad's comments the morning of the fourth day at the manor proved so enlightening.

"You've started your courses, then," Angharad said.

"Excuse me?" I asked, and then twisted around. She showed me the blood on my nightgown.

"Oh," I said, nonplussed.

"I'll inform the Prince. Where are your cloths?"

My what? You'll do what? "You're going to tell Llywelyn?"

Angharad gave me a look that clearly said *how can you be so clueless?* "He has to know," she said.

"Why?"

Angharad let out a forceful burst of air that told me she didn't want to explain this. Since I wasn't getting it, I couldn't help her. Finally, she took the plunge. "He must know if any child you carry is his."

I gaped at her, at a loss for words. Llywelyn wasn't being thoughtful or romantic. He hadn't touched me because he was worried I could be pregnant by someone else and pass the child off as his. The color rose in my face, along with my temper and I was marshalling some kind of horrified response when Angharad cut into my thoughts to explain further and make me reconsider.

"The Prince has no children, you see," she said.

"No sons, you mean," I said, getting a grip on reason. "No heir."

"No," Angharad said. "He has no children at all. No one knows why. The physicians cannot provide an answer for him. The people whisper that it is a curse against him; that he is bewitched, or he has a traitor among his household who poisons the womb of all the women who've lain with him."

Angharad nodded, almost talking to herself rather than to me. "That's why he hasn't married, and why the women have become fewer and far between in recent years. Each one must belong to him alone, so that any child she bears must be conclusively his, or no one will believe it. His childlessness has gone on too long and is known by too many people. Even King Henry has been known to mention it, thankful as he is for his own son, Edward."

"Llywelyn hasn't said anything to me . . ." I stopped again, my brain refusing to function properly.

Angharad patted my hand. "You're so fortunate," she said. "Perhaps you will be the lucky one."

Holy crap! And then I thought again and realized that he assumed I knew all about this. Just like he assumed I wouldn't fear him when he told me at Criccieth that he was the Prince of Wales. He was a forty year old Prince who had no heir, and the entire world mocked him for it.

Yet I knew, and now he knew because I'd told him, that he did have at least one child with a wife he had yet to find. I didn't know how that changed anything, but maybe it would relieve some of the pressure on him to produce a child *now*. Of course, the child was a girl and his wife died giving birth to her. I thought back to our conversation. *Yeah, I'd mentioned that.*

I had less than a week to figure out what I was going to do about this, if anything, and how I was going to respond to Llywelyn, when and if he asked for more from me than friendship. I gazed at the wall above Angharad's head as she got my clothes together. Going home never seemed less possible and more necessary.

We'd awoken that morning to snow—a lot of it—and only a handful of men stood sentry or left the gatehouse. It wasn't so cold in our bedroom I could see my breath, but these rooms were hard to heat in winter, and unless you were standing right next to the fire, they were often chilly. Since Llywelyn's bedrooms were always large, the fireplace tended to do a poor job.

Nobody was allowed to go anywhere and Llywelyn's questions about the ambush remained unanswered. From what I gathered, the assumption was that if we couldn't see anything in this weather, nobody else could either. But by that afternoon, I was thoroughly sick of myself and everyone else.

Anna and I hid in a corner of the great hall, Anna playing with a doll Angharad had given her. I was beginning to think that learning to sew might be a viable option—appalling notion that it was. To stave off such dreadful thoughts, I began to look through the wooden boxes that were positioned along the wall opposite the fireplace.

Most were full of clothing and blankets but I opened one to find a set of musical instruments, which included a simple flute, a tambourine, a small drum, and, unbelievably, a six-string guitar. Learning guitar had been my small musical defiance when every other girl played the flute or the clarinet, and my eventual answer to the symphonic hell that was middle school band. I hadn't know they had guitars in the Middle Ages.

I pulled it out and one of the strings twanged. Instantly, the hall fell into such a complete silence, you'd have thought they'd never heard an instrument before. I straightened and found every face turned towards me, looking expectant.

Goronwy spoke from his seat by the fire. "Can you play that?"

"I . . . I think so," I said. "It needs tuning."

"We'll wait," he said.

Huh. My fingers slipped on the strings, sweaty from nerves. Thankfully for me, since there was no way I'd have been comfortable playing with him there, Llywelyn was absent, probably laboring in his office. Goronwy brought a stool for me to sit on and I plucked through the strings. They hadn't been tuned to the standard 'E A D G B E,' but I fiddled with them a bit and finally got them right. It seemed likely that my playing would be totally different from what the men were used to, but I didn't actually know. The man-at-arms who doubled as a bard had died at the Gap and except for some drunken bellowing after dinner, no one had sung since we'd been at the manor.

As I tuned the guitar, my stomach roiled because every one the songs I could think of was in English—or rather, American. Plus, I didn't think R.E.M. was going to go over well with this crowd.

I met Goronwy's eyes. "Are you sure about this?" I said, my voice low. The men had returned to their conversations while I tuned the guitar, but I could feel their glances as they waited for me to get ready.

He nodded. "Please play for us," he said. "We will enjoy whatever you feel like singing. Take your time."

I allowed myself a relaxing breath and thought again. I did know some folk music; maybe a few simple songs would do to start. It only took one strum for the hall to quiet, and another for everyone's heads to turn to me again. From the interest in the men's faces, I knew I had my audience.

"Three score and ten, boys and men were lost from Grimsby Town . . ."

Since the Welsh were morbid a lot of the time, I hoped an English sailing song was appropriate and the sentiment carried, even if nobody but me understood the lyrics and it had been written six hundred years from now. With the second time through the chorus, the men began to nod their heads and keep time with their feet. When I finished that song, I went on to a jig, a ballad, two drinking songs and a couple of anti-English Irish folk songs which everyone would have appreciated if they'd understood the words. I was willing to bet there were plenty of anti-English Welsh folk songs I could learn to play later.

A servant brought me a cup of water and I stopped playing to drink it—and to give myself time to come up with something else.

"More!" Someone at one of the tables shouted, followed by a chorus from several others and some nodding of heads.

I looked over the rim of the cup at Goronwy, who now had Anna on his lap with a rattle she'd been shaking to an approximation of the beat.

"Please," Goronwy said.

"Okay," I said. "Tell me when to stop."

"We won't," he said. But he was smiling when he said it.

I strummed another chord, and with it, remembered that I did know one Welsh ballad. I had no idea what the words actually meant, but Mom was always humming it. I gave Goronwy an assessing look, had a moment's panic that the song had something to do with Llywelyn's death, and launched into it:

Afallen peren per ychageu.
Puwaur maur weirrauc enwauc invev.
In diffrin machavuy merchyrdit crev.
Gorvolet y gimry goruaur gadev.

To my astonishment, I'd barely finished the first line before the men began to join in. Their pronunciation was different from mine and I still had no idea of the meaning of the words they were singing, but when I hesitated at the end of the first verse, Goronwy twirled his finger, telling me to keep going. So I went around again. And again. The song was about, from the bit I could translate, apples, and somewhere there in the first verse, a pig.

In the middle of the third verse, Llywelyn appeared in the doorway. His eyes met mine from all the way across the hall, and though my fingers still played, they stiffened. Still the men sang. Llywelyn tipped his head and smiled.

The song came to an end and my fingers came off the strings. In the silence that followed, Llywelyn moved closer, his footsteps ringing hollowly on the wood floor, and came to rest with one shoulder propped against the wall a few feet away from where I sat.

"One more?"

I nodded. Mom had another song, one she'd sung occasionally when I was a child, but then more often after my father died. It was a slow lullaby, not a raucous tavern song like most of the others, and I understood the words. I sang in Welsh, translating in my head as I went along for my own benefit. Halfway through, however, my fingers skipped a note. I'd forgotten the ending. Though Mom had sung this as a lullaby, it wasn't really. It was a love song—and I was singing it to Llywelyn:

Walk with me, under star-strewn skies,,
Your hand warm in mine.
Until the dawn, I'll dream of you,
Good night, my love. Good night.

All the while, Llywelyn watched me, his arms folded across his chest, a small smile playing around his lips.

10

Llywelyn

"**M**y lord!"

The young soldier, Bevyn, trotted across the hall to the high table where I sat in a moment of idleness, watching Marged play chess with Goronwy. Marged claimed only a passing knowledge of the game but I thought I'd let Goronwy have a go at her before I tried, just in case. I could stand to lose, but I'd like to see it happen to someone else first.

The boy came to a halt in front of us. He bowed to me, but then turned to Goronwy.

"Yes, Bevyn," Goronwy said, still focused on his game. "I'm busy."

"Busy losing, looks like," he said, "if you don't mind my saying so."

"I do mind, young man," Goronwy said, looking up, "but I forgive you if you give me an excuse to bow out of the game. What is it?"

"It's the village, sir," Bevyn said. "Sir Hywel requests your presence there. They've returned."

"The villagers have returned?" I asked. "All of them?"

"They're back in their homes, not happy to be lacking possessions, but taking up their lives again," Bevyn said.

"Did they say what happened?"

"I don't know," Bevyn said. "Sir Hywel sent me to you straight away."

"We'll come." I turned to Marged. "Sorry to postpone the drubbing, Marged, but we're off. Kiss Anna for me when she wakes."

Marged's face went suddenly blank, and then cleared. "Yes, Llywelyn," she said.

I nodded and stepped of the dais, though Marged's look had taken me aback. *What was wrong?* I put it away. Either she'd tell me or she wouldn't and I didn't have time to draw it out of her.

It was only three miles to the village; I took ten men with me, plus Goronwy. We didn't cross through the Gap, but all of us gave the road ahead an extra look before turning onto the track that headed east to the village just before we reached the ambush site.

"A bad business, my lord," Goronwy said.

"Indeed," I said, thinking of Geraint's funeral the day before. It had been cold enough outside that we could wait to bury him until Tudur arrived. He'd ridden in on the first clear day after the snowstorm, bringing another twenty men with him. I'd sent him with Hywel today, thinking that it would do him good to get his mind off his father's death. Now I wasn't so sure.

We rode onto the village green, now cleared of debris. The grass had blackened where the fire had burned, while the snow around the edges of the village had melted off into a frozen mud that cracked as we walked across it. I checked the sky. Geraint would have told me a thaw was in the offing. *Damn, I miss him.*

Hywel was off his horse, talking to a peasant in a ragged brown cloak. Tudur had been watching for us. I caught his eye and he came over as I dismounted.

"What's the story?" I said.

"They were paid, my lord," Tudur said.

"Paid?" Goronwy said from behind me.

"The headman says a nobleman came to them, one Rhys ap Gruffydd," Tudur said. "Rhys had a dozen men with him. He sat on his horse, threw the headman a sack full of coins and told him they had two hours to get out of the village.

Goronwy scoffed at that. "Rhys ap Gruffydd? Who's that? One of Gwenwynwyn's bastards?"

"I find it hard to believe a man would give up his home so easily," I said.

"For coin?" Tudur said. "Many a man will do far more for less."

"What did he look like?" I said. "Surely the headman can describe him."

"Of medium height, medium brown hair, rich clothes."

"Now that's a helpful description," Goronwy said.

"I suspect they were paid not to say more, too," Tudur said, "but we have no means of proving it and I can't get anything more out of the headman."

"String him up by his ankles if you have to." I turned to Goronwy. "Where's Humphrey, perhaps he can help us?"

"I'll get him." Goronwy headed to where Humphrey stood next to Hywel, listening to their conversation while surveying the burned green and the devastated huts surrounding it, all of which were undergoing restoration. Goronwy returned with both men a moment later.

"What do you think of the headman's tale?" I said to Humphrey.

"I cannot say," Humphrey said. "I told you all I know. The village was deserted; we burned it."

"On Owain's suggestion," Tudur said.

"Yes." Once again, Humphrey's chin firmed at Owain's name. "There is nothing more that I can tell you."

I turned to Tudur. "How devious do we think Owain is? Enough to get rid of the villagers so Humphrey could burn their village to the ground?"

"Maybe he just wanted them out of the area so they couldn't report his activities to you or anyone else," Hywel said.

"Then when Owain heard you were coming, he took his opportunity to set the trap."

"Owain isn't that smart," Humphrey said. "He is too impulsive for such forethought."

"I said 'devious,' not 'smart,'" I said.

"Devious can take you a long way down the road to smart, particularly if you're lucky as well," Tudur said.

"If it matters," Humphrey added, "the headman's description, such as it is, fits Owain."

I sighed. "It matters and it doesn't. I wish that he were here right now, but as it is, he's beyond my reach. I will task Owain's father with his behavior just as soon as I am able."

"Over here!"

The five of us spun to face the eastern woods. Goronwy put a hand on my arm to check me as the other three ran forward. "Wait, my lord. Not until we know what is happening."

He'd become more protective of me as we'd grown older. I understood Goronwy's concern but chafed at it. I didn't *feel* that much older, but ever since I'd gained King Henry's blessing as the Prince of Wales, Goronwy's caution had increased.

"My lord," Bevyn said, Glewdra's reins in his hand.

I pulled myself into the saddle, more comfortable now that I was in a position of strength and could see the whole area.

Humphrey returned at a run. "There is something you should see, my lord," he said.

I trotted Glewdra through the trees that formed a barrier at the eastern edge of the village and into a small clearing, fifteen feet on a side, fifty yards in. In the middle of the clearing, a horse cropped the grass—what he could find of it—next to the body of a man. Hywel crouched beside the body and looked up as I approached.

"He's dead, my lord," he said, "for some days from the looks. He's near frozen solid."

"At least he doesn't smell," Bevyn said.

I glanced at him, wondering if I should slap him down or encourage him. I had need of men with courage and brains and even though Bevyn was only seventeen, he was already well supplied with both. He'd made me laugh more than once and I was growing accustomed to his dry sense of humor.

Hywel rolled the man over and the cause of death became obvious: a sharp slice to the throat. "Killed from behind, by my guess," said Hywel.

"Mine too," I said. It was hard to argue with that kind of evidence.

Humphrey spoke. "He was one of our men. I didn't see him after the ambush, but he was with us before it."

"Was he the messenger Owain sent to you?"

"No," Humphrey said.

I returned my gaze to the dead man, digesting the evidence. Meanwhile, Tudur went through the horse's saddle bags. He froze, glanced at me, and then looked down again to an object in his hand. Taking this as a cue that I should pay attention, I urged Glewdra nearer. "What is it?"

Tudur shifted his shoulders to block the view of the other men, who'd begun to disperse to look for any more clues as to what had happened here. He opened his hand to show me its contents.

My heart grew cold at the sight of the signet ring he held. "That was my father's," I said.

"I remember it, my lord," Tudur said.

I held out my hand. Tudur dropped it into my palm and I clenched my fist around it. I looked up to see Goronwy watching me. I canted my head and he nodded, understanding that I would share the find with him later. I didn't want to think what the discovery of my father's signet meant, but for my own safety—and that of my country—I had no choice but to find out.

"Keep an eye out for anything else that's out of place, Tudur," I said. "I need to know who I'm dealing with."

"Yes, my lord."

My men wrapped the body in a blanket and threw it over the horse's back and we returned to the manor, more silent than when we'd left.

Marged greeted me as I entered the hall, her upturned face searching mine. "You have news?"

I hesitated, remembering the blank look that she'd given me earlier, as if she'd been disturbed that she had to remain behind. "You may listen provided you keep to a corner and hold yourself quiet until we're finished."

"Thank you." She trailed after me up the stairs and into my study. She settled herself on a cushion under the window, and if the others were surprised to see her there when they entered, they didn't show it.

With Hywel, Tudur, and Goronwy arrayed before me in front of my desk, I cleared a space and dropped the ring onto the center of the desk. Goronwy put out a hand and fingered it.

"It's your father's, Llywelyn," Goronwy said.

"I know," I said.

"I found it among the dead man's bags," Tudur said. "But with no letter, no other indication of who gave it to him or why."

"Who inherited it when your father died, my lord?" Hywel asked.

"My older brother, Owain," I said. "I don't recall it being among his possessions when I put him in Dolbadarn Castle, but . . ."

"We should find out if he had it," Goronwy said, meeting my eyes, "and if not him, if he gave it to one of his sons, his wife . . ." his voice trailed off.

"Or his brother," Hywel said.

"See to it," I said, a growl forming in my throat, threatening to close it off entirely.

"I'll go," Tudur said abruptly. "It's not far to Dolbadarn. He might not tell me who has it, but then again, he might if I offered to give it back to him."

I clenched my fists at my sides and then relaxed them. "I would prefer to keep it."

"With your permission, my lord," Tudur said, bowing, "I will offer the ring only as a last resort."

"I'm sorry, Llywelyn." Marged's voice piped up from the corner. "Could someone please explain what's happening?"

I turned to her, finding myself angry—not so much at her, though she would be an easy target given her impertinence—but at the situation. Goronwy forestalled me, however, by waving one hand airily and dropping into a chair.

"It's like this, Meg. Pretend the ring is a child's ball, bouncing from one person to the next across Wales instead of the floor. Where does it come to rest? Why do we find it here, outside the village that Humphrey destroyed—at the urging of men who do not ally with us? What was the message he carried, for why carry a signet if not to prove to another who his master was?"

"So," Marged said. "You're saying that one of Llywelyn's family members has betrayed him."

"Yes," Goronwy said. "Probably."

"That's a surprise," she said.

I stared at her. She was making a jest. Goronwy glanced at me, and then grinned at Marged. "Go on."

Marged shifted in her seat. "It seems to me you have multiple issues to address, some more important than others." She stumbled a bit over her words but then became more assured as she realized she had our full attention. "You know that Humphrey leagued with Owain of Powys to ambush you at the Gap. You know that one of your family members isn't loyal. What you don't know is one, who told them you were leaving Criccieth; two, who paid off the villagers; three, where the messenger was going with the signet ring; and four, who killed him? It's that final point that concerns me now, because that man is still out there, and he's dangerous." She'd ticked these points off on her fingers as she spoke, but now stopped as silence fell on the room. I studied her. The others, of course, were waiting for me to say something; waiting for me, perhaps, to put her in her place.

"I agree, Marged," I said. "The presence of the ring distracted me from the main point."

"And then there's issue number five," Goronwy said. "Given that the mind behind this isn't Bohun's—or Owain's, is someone else waiting for us on the other side of the forest of Coed y Brenin?"

Hywel rocked back on his heels. "We've been facing the wrong way. Backwards instead of forwards. The danger isn't behind us, it's ahead."

"But it always is, isn't it," Marged said. "You live with that threat every day—every time you leave your castle, you face that. You have so many enemies it's impossible to keep track of them all. It almost doesn't matter who's behind any of this. You can't trust anyone."

"But he has to, don't you see?" Tudur said. "His men, his counselors, you . . . he has to trust because no Prince can govern alone."

Marged met my eyes. "We both know who sent that ring, Llywelyn. Don't we?"

I let out a breath, but didn't answer her. Such was honor. Such were my obligations to my title and myself. Instead I turned to Goronwy. "Have we reached our full complement of men for the journey south?"

"We're at fifty once again, my lord."

Tudur and Hywel nodded. "We've enough. Our enemies become bolder, my lord," Hywel said. "There appears to be little they will not attempt, and no depths too low for them to sink."

"Then we must think faster than they, and always remain two steps ahead," I said.

"Easier said than done, my lord," Tudur said.

"Then don't say it; do it."

Their faces had a somber cast as they filed out the door.

11

Meg

"You didn't do as I asked, Marged," Llywelyn said after everyone else had left the room. He sat behind his desk, his long legs stretched out in front of him, his ankles crossed and his hands folded on his belly. It appeared to be one of his favorite postures, and I could understand since every chair I'd sat in so far had been nothing if not uncomfortable.

"I'm not sure what you mean," I said. "What didn't I do?"

"Keep quiet; hold yourself still until we were finished."

"Oh," I said. "I didn't realize that you meant *quiet*, as in, *don't talk at all.*"

"I was very clear when I spoke to you in the hall," Llywelyn said.

"Yes, but . . ."

"What part of what I said didn't you understand?"

His words brought me out of my seat. "You're really mad about this aren't you?"

"Mad?" Llywelyn said. "I don't know that I'm mad; more confused and disappointed, perhaps even irritated at how disrespectful you are to me at times."

"I have no idea what you are talking about." I folded my arms across my chest, irritated myself that I sounded just like the sulky child Llywelyn thought me. "Why does it make sense for me to sit there quiet? If I knew what you were talking about, I might have an idea which could help. And I did."

Llywelyn's brow furrowed. "We seem to be having a problem with communication, Marged, so let me be a bit more clear." He pulled in his feet, stood, and walked to me. Putting a hand on each of my shoulders, he bent to look directly in my eyes. "As long as you are with me, Marged, you do as I say."

"What if I have some contribution to make, like today? What if I have a thought or idea that might make a difference?"

"Then you tell me afterwards, when my men have left," he said. "And you will call me *my lord*, at least in public, if you can't manage it in private."

"It would be easier if you just didn't give me orders at all. That way I wouldn't feel I needed to disobey them."

"I can't believe we're having this conversation," Llywelyn said, a half-laugh in his voice, though the exasperation was even more evident. "Are we really arguing about whether or not you're going to obey me? What kind of land are you from? Do women there not obey their men?"

"Not—" I stopped. "Not like this. Besides, I don't see why it's such a big deal. I helped, didn't I?"

Llywelyn flexed his big hands around my shoulders once and then put his nose only inches from mine. "When you disobey me in front of others, you undermine my authority," he said, articulating each word clearly. "Now, you may not care much about Wales, or its rule, but I care about both very much. It matters little to me if you don't like it, don't want to, or think that you shouldn't have to. But I am the captain of this ship and as long as you are on it, you will obey me."

"Okay, okay, I get it," I said. "I just don't know if I can do it. I don't know that anyone has ever used the word *obey* in my presence before—ever. In my world, some parents feel that their children should obey them, I suppose, but we never talked about it that way in my family, and women—wives, mistresses, whatever—certainly don't *obey* their men. We're equals."

"I can't imagine how that might actually work, Marged," Llywelyn said. "But in any case, it isn't just women. It's everyone. Look a little closer and you'll see it and maybe start to understand. In the meantime . . ." he put an arm around my shoulders pulled me into his arms, "I expect you to try."

"Yes."

Llywelyn laughed as he steered me to the door. "See. That wasn't so hard. Now if you can just tack 'my lord' on there at the end, we'll be all right."

*****

I tried to pay attention to what Llywelyn was talking about, and he did begin, ever so incrementally, to treat me a little differently—more like a friend and less like a possession. That, I appreciated, but it didn't make me any more certain of him. If anything, it confused me more.

The thing that irked me most about this new twist was that I really liked Llywelyn—was undoubtedly starry-eyed over him. He was such a contrast to Trev that I was consistently amazed that such a man as Llywelyn could even exist. It wasn't just that he was a prince, but that men appeared to follow him because of *how* he was on the inside, rather than *who* he was on the outside. He didn't have to make up stuff to prove what kind of man he was. He didn't have to pretend to be something other than what he was, because he *was* amazing.

From our conversations, I'd gotten a glimpse of what it must have been like when he was younger—the struggles and the uncertainty and the endless striving for the impossible. He didn't become the Prince of Wales only because of who his father was. He became the Prince of Wales because he got down in the trenches—whether in warfare or politically—and made himself worthy of it, sometimes through sheer willpower and against incredible odds.

All the while, he carried in his heart his grandfather's dream of a united Wales, and all the while, every other noble, including his own brothers, were working to undermine his vision because if he became the Prince of Wales, they would have less power than they thought they deserved. Hard to argue with that, actually; hard not to feel sorry for them. In an age when democracy was unheard of, it was tough to be born in a time when only the fittest survived and you weren't one of them.

Llywelyn's biggest flaw, it seemed to me, was that pride of his. If anything, he was arrogant to a fault and the people he treated least well were those he deemed to be foolish. I'd seen him publically dress down one of his men and I was glad that when he'd chastised me, at least we'd been alone.

At the same time, he'd saved Humphrey when he didn't have to. He was playful with Anna, and had taken to carrying her around on his shoulders or playing horse between dinner and bedtime. He was courteous to servants, even, and that was important. I remembered reading somewhere that it was how a man treated his inferiors that was a true measure of him.

Well, everyone is inferior to Llywelyn. Except, perhaps, for me. Even if he doesn't know it.

*****

"Tell me about your husband," Llywelyn said. "Was he a good man?"

We were riding at the head of Llywelyn's host of men, finally heading towards Castell y Bere, his primary castle in south Gwynedd, built by his grandfather as many of his castles had been.

"No," I said. "He wasn't."

"Why did your father choose him, then? Or is this another matter where you weren't required to obey, hmmm?"

I refused to rise to the bait. "My father died when I was seventeen so he wasn't there to help me choose."

Llywelyn's expression turned grave. "I'm sorry. I was sixteen when my father died." He paused. "We were not close."

"I gathered that," I said. "I loved my father. I think I'm only now recovering from his death, three years on."

"But you chose a husband of whom he wouldn't have approved."

I ducked my head. I didn't know why he was pushing this line of questioning, and felt the pressure of a correct response. "I went a little crazy, I think, when my father died. I made some poor choices."

"You had no uncle to step in? No brother?"

"Where I grew up, women choose their own husbands."

"Humph. And look where it got you. Your husband beat you, didn't he?" Llywelyn asked, sending the conversation into a new, and even more unwelcome, direction.

I turned to face him, though for once he wasn't looking at me.

"Yes."

"And Anna?"

"I left him because of her," I said.

Llywelyn grunted again at that and released some of the tension in his shoulders. "The man was a fool to treat you thus," he said, finally looking at me. "In Wales, under the law of Hywel Dda, a husband may beat his wife for laying with another man, for mistreating his possessions, or for maligning him in public."

"I didn't do any of those things. What happens to wives like me?"

"They can ask for a divorce," Llywelyn said.

"Well I was working on that when he died," I said.

"Just how did he die? In battle?"

"Battles are few and far between in Radnor," I said. "No, he was dying of a disease we couldn't cure and was drinking too much alcohol at the pain of it. He drove his vehicle into a tree."

"Madam."

I started and turned to find Humphrey moving his horse closer.

"I couldn't help overhearing your last words," Humphrey said. "My nanny died of such a disease. It's a terrible end and I'm sorry for your loss."

"Thank you, Humphrey." I glanced at Llywelyn and shared a rueful look with him. We needed to be more careful about our conversations if there was a chance that someone else could overhear. We hadn't said anything too terrible or obviously out of place, but I was so comfortable talking with Llywelyn now, I could easily have done so.

It was fewer than twenty miles from the hunting lodge to Castell y Bere. The road wasn't as well maintained in this section as nearer to Criccieth, but even so, we made good time. By noon, we approached a significant river and could see Castell y Bere in the distance, standing guard over its valley. Whether through a trick of the light, or just because the sun chose that moment to come out from behind a cloud, it seemed to be shining above us, the sun reflecting off the whitewashed stones.

"A beacon, isn't it?" Llywelyn said. "Guiding us home."

Clearly, the other men thought so too because our pace quickened and we came in a rush to the river's bank. Unfortunately, there wasn't much of a ford.

"It's in flood, my lord!" Hywel shouted over the roar of the water.

"If I'd not seen it myself, I wouldn't have believed the snow could melt so quickly," Humphrey said. "It's become so warm, I can hardly believe we're only a week into February."

"What are we going to do?" I said.

Humphrey shrugged, while Llywelyn pondered the river. I wasn't at all happy at the idea of crossing it on the back of a horse, especially not with Anna on my lap.

"There's really a ford here?" Humphrey said.

Goronwy turned to glare at him. "You will not take advantage of the generosity of my lord to work against him."

"What was that?" I said.

Humphrey shook his head. "The location of fords are open secrets among the common folk, but to betray such knowledge to an enemy is worthy of death. Lord Goronwy doesn't care for the fact that I will know the location of this ford. It's too close to the castle for comfort."

One of Llywelyn's men had dismounted to probe the water with a stick. He took a step, determined how deep the next step was, and then hopped forward through the water as he found a path. He reached the other side without mishap. "It's five feet deep at the most, my lord," he called to Llywelyn across the water.

"We will cross," Llywelyn said. "Castell y Bere isn't far and it's worth a little wet and cold to reach it today."

Llywelyn sent two men into the water together. Their horses didn't even balk, which surprised me, but they were extremely well-trained. The men had reached the middle of the river when one of the horses suddenly sank another foot into the water.

"Careful!" Hywel shouted.

"I'm all right!" The man said, and his horse managed to right itself on the next step.

Goronwy came back to me. "I'll take Anna," he said. "You may need both hands on the reins."

"Okay," I said, and passed her over, glad she was content with the arrangement. She liked Goronwy.

Goronwy directed his horse into water, with two men-at-arms on either side. Anna's head swiveled right and left, as curious as always about what was going on around her. All three horses avoided the potholes in the ford and soon they were at the opposite bank and trotting up and out of the river. Anna didn't even get wet. Goronwy turned back to the river and Anna waved to me from her seat on his lap.

I still didn't want to cross, balked at it far more than any horse, but then Humphrey pulled up beside me. "We'll go together. I'll cross downstream from you, so that if you fall, I can catch you."

I thought that was very noble of him, and with no more excuse for cowardice, urged my mare into the river. I pulled my knees higher, not wanting to get my feet wet. The water quickly rose almost to his withers. We'd taken care to avoid the hole that the first rider had hit, but all the same, half-way across, my luck failed. Unfortunately, Humphrey's did too. At the same instant, our horses' right forefeet sank. I fell sideways, clutching at the reins and trying to keep my seat. I tried to grab the mane of Humphrey's horse, but his horse had overbalanced more than mine and foundered.

We went into the water together and it was so cold my heart froze in my chest. I came up sputtering.

"My lady!" Humphrey reached for me but within half a second, he'd sailed three feet further downstream from me. Voices behind us at the ford rang out above the roar of the rushing river, but it took only another second for both of us to plunge out of reach.

"Llywelyn!" I caught a glimpse of him, urging his horse into the water after us, and a flash of Goronwy clutching Anna to him before I spun around a bend and lost sight of anyone but Humphrey.

The rough river swamped me. I swallowed a gulp of water, choking on it as it went down. I wasn't a strong swimmer under the best of circumstances, and the heavy cloak, petticoats, and boots I wore weighed me down and made it hard for me to keep my head above water. I pulled up my knees to try to work my boots from my feet, but my fingers were already so stiff from the icy water they didn't want to move.

I manage to kick the boots off, however, as well as unpin the broach that held the cloak around my neck. Further on, Humphrey fought the force of the water, trying to swim toward me, but in vain. The river swept us downstream and further apart with every second that passed. Then, our river met another and spun us into a larger channel twice as big as the first. Debris sailed past me and I tried to grab onto something that would keep me afloat.

I was fighting my way to the bank when Humphrey cursed. He hung in the water twenty yards ahead of me and though I couldn't see what he'd hit, it was big enough to hold him steady in midstream. In the half a second I had to think about it, I braced myself for the impact.

A thick branch projected out from the northern bank and I slammed into it further into the stream than Humphrey. Much of the year, it might have hung above the waterline, but with the heavy rains and flooding, the river had risen to meet it. Humphrey and I hung on, bent at the waist and exhausted, with the water flowing over and around us, undeterred. The impact had forced the air from my lungs and I struggled and spit, glad to have stopped moving but aching from the cold and the effort of holding on.

Humphrey grabbed my arm. "This way. We have to get you out of the water." He tugged on my arm to get me moving.

Slowly we edged our way along the log to the northern bank of the river. Humphrey grasped a low-hanging tree branch and pulled himself out of the water. He fell forward on his hands and knees on the muddy bank in relief. I wasn't far behind him, standing to the waist in the swirling river, but was still having trouble moving my legs with my dress wrapped around my ankles.

"My lord," Humphrey said and coughed. "Help her."

I looked up to see Llywelyn's brother, Dafydd, standing on the log beside me. He hung onto a branch above him to keep himself upright, and reached with the other hand towards me. And grinned.

I stared at Dafydd—and at his hand, which he held out to me—and refused it. I turned away, thinking that throwing myself back into the water was a better option than accepting rescue from him. Humphrey, not understanding my sudden fear, lunged back to me and caught my arm before I could slip away. Dafydd, in turn, grasped me around the waist and heaved me onto the bank.

"My lady!" Humphrey said, his breath coming in gasps, still thinking that Dafydd had saved us. "Are you all right?"

I lifted my eyes to his and he closed his mouth. I don't know what he saw in my eyes that silenced him. I only know that I shivered as much from fear as from the cold of the river. I was afraid of Dafydd—of what he might do out of mischief and amorality. Though it wasn't for myself that I feared so much as for Anna, who couldn't possibly understand where I was, except that I wasn't with her.

Dafydd, still grinning, scooped me off the bank and tossed me onto his horse. Again, it appeared that my sole function these days was to act as a dead weight or useless object for men to throw this way and that and use as they pleased. He swung onto his horse behind me, leaving Humphrey on his knees in the muddy leaves and dirt beside the river. Humphrey scrambled to his feet but we were away before he could counter Dafydd.

"Did you miss me?" Dafydd said, his voice an erotic whisper in my ear.

I shuddered. Unfortunately, he interpreted the motion as a request for warmth. He more snuggly wrapped his cloak around me and pulled me to his chest.

"Please let me go. I don't want to be with you."

"You will," Dafydd said, all confidence.

I didn't want to mention Anna, afraid that he would use her in some way against me later. I refused to speak to him and the hour's ride to the sea passed in a blur of cold and fear, and growing numbness, both physically and mentally. With the sight of the beach, however, the horror came back in full force. Boats had been pulled onto the shore and we made for them.

"You see," Dafydd said. "We came prepared."

"You couldn't have planned this," I said. "You couldn't have known I would fall at the ford."

"It wasn't you that I was prepared for," Dafydd said. "I confess I'd put you from my mind entirely. Owain wanted to rescue Humphrey, but I know that tight-assed youth better than he does and told him he wouldn't come, not even if we asked. It was Llywelyn we wanted."

"You think you could have taken him?" I said. "How?"

Dafydd smirked. "Never you mind."

He dismounted and pulled me from my seat on the horse. I fell into his arms, wobbly again, but in that instant, I knew I couldn't go quietly with him. My feeble attempt at gaining an advantage over Llywelyn that first night in Wales had been a failure, but I told myself I wouldn't enter that boat with Dafydd under any circumstances.

I twisted out of Dafydd's arms and the second my feet hit the sand, I ran. The long emersion in the cold water, however, coupled by the hour-long ride on the back of a horse, had tightened my muscles so that they refused to move like I wanted them to. I stumbled along the shore, moving as fast as I could but not fast enough.

"Get her!" Dafydd said.

I looked back. The rider Dafydd had directed to chase me gained on me with every thud of his horse's hooves. I swerved up the beach, cursing myself for running in a straight line like the idiots always did in movies, but I'd come to my senses too late. The rider leaned down, grasped me around the waist, and lifted me off my feet. He carried me back to Dafydd like the sack of potatoes I'd become (or turnips, here, since they didn't have potatoes yet), and dumped me into one of the boats.

"Swine!"

Dafydd laughed. He actually laughed.

"I love a woman with some spirit in her," he said.

Then he tugged at my arm and pulled me onto a bench away from the feet of the oarsmen on either side of me. I sagged against him, purposefully giving him the impression that I'd given up, but he took it wrong and grabbed my chin. He kissed me and I let him, recoiling inside all the while.

Smirking, he released me. My shudder should have been apparent to the blindest man but he didn't see it.

"See, gentlemen," he said when I slumped on the seat. "So much more effective than the back of my hand. Women just need some attention every now and then."

I said nothing and lowered my eyes to stare at the bottom of the boat. The men began to row and Dafydd sat beside me, content. I shivered, even in his cloak.

Laughing again, he thrust it off me in a careless move and began to untie the laces at the back of my dress.

"You need to get out of these wet clothes," he said.

A choke caught in my throat and I glared at him, but he merely smirked again. He was right, however, that the heavy fabric only made me colder and at his urging I pulled my arms out of the sleeves and wiggled out of the dress. It left me in only my shift.

I hated it that Dafydd watched me the whole time, even if the majority of his men averted their eyes. Then he threw his cloak over me as he had during the ride from the river. I huddled on my seat in the boat, sodden, sick, and angry. I hated men. Every single bloody last one of them.

12

Llywelyn

"**H**oly Mother of God!" The sight of Marged, spinning down the Cadair River behind Humphrey de Bohun nearly had me diving in after her. Thankfully, she'd let go of the horse's reins and allowed the water to take her, rather than struggling against it along with her horse. Instead, one of my men dove into the river after the horse, but Marged was already too far away to reach.

"After them!" Goronwy pointed at men who hadn't yet crossed.

But he needn't have said anything, as half a dozen men-at-arms, including Hywel, already raced away. By the time I'd turned Glewdra in the swift current, Goronwy had spurred his horse into the water. Anna held on to the horse's mane, her eyes wide, but not crying.

"They'll find her," Goronwy said, tipping his chin towards the way the men had gone.

I grunted noncommittal agreement. I could depend on them to find her if she were possible to find. As boys, we'd spent many hours in this river and we both knew the dangers, both from the more northern Cadair, and the Dysynni, which flowed from the south and merged with it a dozen yards downstream.

We skirted the trees that grew close together on the bank and pushed our horses down a track that ran along the fields that lay on our side of the river. We rode as hard as we could, but the trail was a rough one and I didn't want to lose Glewdra to a gopher hole. That would slow us down more than caution now. Then a shout came from up ahead.

"Quickly!" Goronwy and I crashed through the bushes to our left and trotted into a small clearing near the river. Humphrey stood in the middle of it, white-faced and sopping wet but otherwise unharmed. He held a spear-length stick in his right hand and leaned on it like a crutch. His shoulders sagged when he saw me. I reined in sharply.

"Where's Marged?"

"The whoresons took her, my lord! I tried to stop them, but without my sword, I was no match for them."

"*Who* took her?" Goronwy said.

"Owain, my lord, with ten of his men," Humphrey said. "And your brother, Dafydd."

"What?" I'd been about to charge out of the clearing, but checked Glewdra at his last words. "Did you say that Dafydd was among them?"

"Yes, my lord," Humphrey said. "Lady Marged and I managed to reach the bank just over there. He was waiting to help us out of the water. I accepted his help, assuming he meant well."

"He took Marged?" That he had was obvious, since she wasn't here, but my mind was struggling to keep up with the magnitude of what he was saying.

"I thought he meant to help us, but as soon as Marged came out of the river, he dragged her away from me, mounted them both on his horse, and raced away. I tried to stop them, but without a horse of my own . . . it . . . I couldn't . . ." Humphrey looked down at his toes. I caught the word *hopeless*.

It wasn't his fault but my anger was making it difficult for me to see reason. I couldn't stand to look at him. Even so, he appeared to be telling the truth. "Where will they go?" I said to Goronwy.

"They can't cross the Dysynni River today. Lady Marged is wet through; she'll need warm clothes soon if they expect her to live."

"Perhaps they'll head north, then, back to the manor?" Hywel said.

"Neither of them know this country well," Goronwy said. "I wonder if they might, perhaps, head to the sea?"

Jesus wept.

"Before you reached us, I sent men in pairs in every direction," Hywel said. "They'll find her."

By now all of my men had arrived at the clearing, including the man leading Humphrey's horse. He recognized it and without a by-your-leave, ran to it, stripping off his shirt as he did so.

"This is my fault, my lord," he said, his teeth chattering as he opened his saddlebags. The leather had protected his belongings for the most part so he could pull off the rest of his clothes and redress in ones that were merely damp instead of soaking. "I must come with you."

"Keep up, then," I said. I turned to my men. "Owain of Powys and my brother, Dafydd, have taken Marged. We don't know in what direction, but they travel with twelve horses, one of which is carrying two. Goronwy suggests they are riding to the sea, but we can't assume that."

"Dane returns, my lord!" Hywel pointed west.

"My lord!" Dane said, pulling up in front of me. "Bevyn continues along the trail, but I've returned to lead you. The riders head southwest, following the river. They could be aiming for where the Dysynni empties into the sea at Tywyn."

"We go," I said. "We can't allow them to put to sea, if that's their intent."

As the crow flies, it was fewer than ten miles to the sea, but we had many more than that to travel as the river twisted and turned and the trail that ran beside it twisted with it. This region of Wales was cut through with dozens of streams, flowing out of a series of hills that ended abruptly at the sandy spit that met the sea at the mouth of the Dysinni. I hoped that we would gain ground, since we didn't have to follow the river as precisely as Dafydd and

Owain. We all knew where it emptied, and didn't need to ride around every twist and turn as they might to make sure we were traveling in the correct direction.

In all the years of discord with Dafydd, through all the accusations that he'd directed at me over the years—my unfairness, my arrogance, my usurpation of his birthright—he'd never acknowledged that his familiarity with all-things Welsh was limited. Although it wasn't his fault, being a small child when our father was imprisoned in the Tower of London, he'd grown up in England. He spoke French more easily than Welsh, and his playmates, rather than staunch advocates of a free Wales like Goronwy and Tudur, had been English—even Edward himself, King Henry's son.

Growing up, Dafydd and Edward had egged each other on as to which of them could behave more recklessly. Their bravado had been celebrated and encouraged by my mother, and King Henry. Edward, however, under the tutelage of the finest scholars and warriors in England, had tempered that recklessness into an adult boldness that was both intelligent and forceful. A careful planner, he saw openings where others balked. Dafydd, on the other hand, had only become foolhardy, using his uncommon good looks to slip through holes that didn't exist, never disciplining himself to any one endeavor or any one allegiance—other than to himself.

It was Goronwy who articulated my thoughts. "What is your brother thinking, Llywelyn? This is reckless in the extreme. He can't hope to get away with it."

"He doesn't think, Goronwy," I said. "Or only about himself, his desires, and his concerns."

"Yes, but . . ." Goronwy couldn't find the words to properly express his outrage.

"Who knows? He could view this as simply a lark; the same lark that convinced Humphrey to venture into Wales with Owain of Powys."

"He might also think we distrust our young Humphrey more than we do," Goronwy said, "and him us. Perhaps he thinks Humphrey will protect him, or that we will disbelieve him no matter what Humphrey tells us. As Dafydd has no honor himself, he may not recognize it in those who do."

Less than an hour later, we crested a rise overlooking Tywyn, half a mile away. Four boats hovered near the beach, two in the water, oarmen already pulling away from the shore, and two others still on the sand. The long and lean boats had been built to ride onto beaches with almost no keel, and yet carry men, horses and cargo.

The few men remaining on the beach spun around to look at us—and at Bevyn, who had outpaced us and was coming on fast.

"Go! Go! Go!"

A small figure that might have been Marged stood up in one of the boats that was already in the water. And then I was sure it was she because the man beside grabbed her arm and tugged her back down. I didn't need to see that smirk on Dafydd's face to know it was there. If I never saw it again, it would be too soon.

The remaining men threw themselves into the boats and started rowing fast. Ten heartbeats later, Bevyn was off his horse, had thrown his boots in the sand, and was in the water. We spurred our horses, but in my heart, I knew we wouldn't be able to stop the boats. We cascaded down the beach anyway and pulled up just short of the water's edge. Hywel checked his horse beside me, breathing hard.

"Shall I have the archers fire upon them?"

"No, Hywel," I said. "We don't want to hit Marged."

Then a splash came from one of the boats, at least a hundred yards off shore, and a chorus of shouts. I strained to see what was happening but my distance vision was not as sharp as it once was. Two boats turned in the water, but after more shouting and splashing, straightened again and continued west, away from us.

"My lord, look!" Goronwy pointed out to sea. He still had one arm wrapped firmly around Anna, who stood on the saddle to see better, her head level with Goronwy's. And it was Anna who understood what she was seeing.

"Mommy!"

Bevyn had swum hard to the boats, but now returned, a small figure struggling beside him. *Meg*. They rested and swam, rested and swam, and were boosted in the end by the strong waves that pushed them to the beach.

They were crawling by the time I reached Marged, thrown onto their knees in the shallow water. I pulled her into my arms, aware of how light she was and how exhausted. She wore only her linen shift and her teeth chattered loud enough to hear. I tried to wrap my cloak around both of us, but Humphrey hurried up with a spare cloak and laid it over her.

"I'm so sorry, my lord," he said. "I failed you."

I couldn't speak.

"Events were beyond your control, Humphrey," Goronwy said, striding up the beach with him and saving me from having to answer and losing my temper completely. "If you hadn't chosen to ride beside her, and fallen with her, we might never have found her at all."

"Goronwy is right, Humphrey," Marged said. Shivering uncontrollably, she'd pressed her face into my chest and the words came out muffled. "If this was anyone's fault it's Dafydd's."

"Or mine," I said.

"How can you say that, Llywelyn?" She lifted her face to look into mine.

"Because I allowed him back into my country," I said.

"And if you hadn't, my lord," Goronwy said, "King Henry wouldn't have agreed to the treaty and acknowledged you Prince of Wales. You had no choice."

"There's always a choice," I said.

Actions have consequences far beyond what we can ever foresee, and most of the time, we're just struggling to stay upright as the surf pounds us to our knees.

*****

"I'm fine, Llywelyn," Marged said, as I loaded her onto my horse. "I'm warm enough."

"You're not, *cariad*. For Anna's sake, if not mine, you will listen to me."

She might not like it, but for once obeyed. I'd dressed her in one of my men's spare clothes—he was only a little taller than she, though twice as wide—and she'd grinned at me through blue lips at the sight of the breeches. Now, she hugged Anna for just a moment before relinquishing her to Goronwy once again. Anna seemed content with that, but I'd observed enough of Marged's mothering to know how few circumstances there were in which she would ask Anna to sit in another's arms if hers were available.

"I don't know why you feel the need to pretend otherwise. Any one of my men would be unwell if they'd experienced the day you've had. We need to get you warm and into a bed, but we've at least an hour's ride before we'll reach Castell y Bere."

Marged pushed her hair out of her face with one hand. The careful style had long since come down and lay a sopping mass around her shoulders. "Yes, Llywelyn," she said.

"I've sent men ahead to warn the castellan that we're coming, and in what condition," Hywel said.

"We're short a horse," Humphrey said. "Yours shouldn't carry two that distance. I'll walk. It's no matter to me."

"You will do no such thing!" Goronwy said. "Although you were far too arrogant before, contrite doesn't suit you either. We won't allow the grandson of the Earl of Hereford to walk ten miles home!"

"Yes, sir," Humphrey said, still looking sheepish.

"Come to think of it," I said, "you may ride Glewdra behind Marged. She's strong enough to carry you both. I'll ride your horse. That way, none must be left behind."

"As you wish, my lord," Hywel said.

Though I didn't think much of Humphrey's arms around Marged, either in principle or fact, I wasn't concerned about some upstart English youth usurping me. She'd thrown herself out of Dafydd's boat, risking death, rather than sail off with him. Dafydd, who'd never failed to charm any woman he wanted, when he wanted, and none ever seemed to regret the experience. Except Marged.

"Can you tell me what happened, Marged?" Half a dozen men had donated their blankets and she was so bundled up that all I could see of her was her white face, poking out from the blankets. Her cheeks had turned pink, a much a healthier color, and from the cold outside, not within.

"Humphrey must have told you what happened at the river, right?" Marged said. She twisted in her seat to look at him.

"Some," I said.

"Dafydd was there to pull us out of the water," Humphrey said. "I have no idea why. But I suppose after our days at your hunting lodge, it would have been easy enough to get here ahead of us. He must have known where we were headed."

"He knew," I said.

"So your brother leagues with Powys," Humphrey said. "Not for the first time, either."

"Nor the last," Marged said under her breath. I gave her a sharp glance, but Humphrey didn't indicate he'd heard her.

"Go on," I said. "Tell me the rest."

"Dafydd picked Marged out of the water, threw her onto his horse, and off they went," Humphrey said. "That's all I know."

Marged picked up the story. "We rode to the sea shore with its waiting boats."

"What luck that you were so easy to take," I said. "I would have thought they'd come to rescue Humphrey."

"I guess not," Marged said. "From the little Dafydd said it was you, my lord, that he wanted, not me."

"Me? Are you sure?"

"So he said."

"But he settled for you because you're my woman."

"Apparently."

"Because he's concocted yet another nefarious plot that we don't really want to know about," Goronwy said. "That Owain went along with it is astonishing. I thought he'd have better sense."

"Dafydd hasn't any," Humphrey said. "He should have taken me with him or killed me in the clearing."

"And why didn't he?" Marged asked.

Humphrey had the answer. "Because he thinks I'm still on his side, on Owain's side. They left me to be a spy in your camp."

I deliberately didn't look at Humphrey. I wasn't sure he realized what he'd just admitted.

"And now that we that we know of his perfidy, what do we do about it?" Goronwy said, smoothing over the sudden silence. "Dafydd has sailed away, free and unhindered, as usual. The next time we see him, no doubt he'll try to brazen it out, either denying or laughing off his actions."

"We could run him out of Wales," Hywel said, his voice almost a growl. "He's no soldier."

"Right into Henry's arms again," I said. "Not a plan that I would favor, all things considered."

"My grandfather would support you," Humphrey said. "He and I would tell the truth to the king."

"And I appreciate that," I said. "At the same time, as a future lord of the Marche, you should appreciate my desire to keep the events of Wales, within Wales, without disturbing the King of England with them."

Humphrey snorted. "Disturbing is right."

He knew what I meant, but even in friendly company, was too cautious to say any more.

Although my—and my grandfather's—disputes with the lords of the Marche were legendary, both they and I would do almost anything to avoid entangling our politics with England's. Henry's power and resources were so much greater, his men so much more numerous, that England was always favored in any battle. I had won the right to rule Wales as its Prince, not because

King Henry had lacked the power to defeat me, but because he lacked the will.

Given my conversations with Marged, I wasn't confident I would get the same half-hearted response from Edward when he succeeded to the throne of England. I studied her as she leaned back against Humphrey, eyes closed. *She'd called me 'my lord'.* Once. It pleased me, far out of proportion to what was probably reasonable. At last, maybe I was getting somewhere with her.

Humphrey had wrapped his right arm around Marged's waist, held the reins with his left, and was instructing Glewdra with his knees. At eighteen, he was already a skilled horseman and would be as skilled a warrior as his grandfather when he grew into his man's frame: a fine addition to the Bohun legacy.

Humphrey looked as if he might become a man I could respect, possibly even work with. And for that reason, I would let him return home unhindered, despite the danger in doing so. In time, he might forget what he owed me. The necessities of rule—and the tutelage of his grandfather—might well insure that he would try me for many years to come.

13

Meg

"**I**'m so cold, Llywelyn," I said. We'd finally made it to the castle hill and wended our way up and around the long road to the castle gate.

"I know, *cariad,*" he said.

Humphrey stopped the horse and Llywelyn, dismounting in an instant, plucked me off of her. I'd been shivering badly for the last fifteen minutes, my limbs numb. I stuffed my hands between my thighs to warm them but because my legs were so cold, it didn't help. With Goronwy carrying Anna and Llywelyn carrying me, we crossed the crooked and slanted bailey to a tower.

Upon entering the hall, a wave of warmth swamped us. I wanted to crawl right into the massive fireplace near the high table, but Llywelyn whisked me through the great hall and down the stairs to the kitchen level—a similar arrangement to both Criccieth and the manor we'd stayed in. I didn't see much of the great hall, as I was fighting tears now. My muscles had relaxed in the warmth and I was losing the tight control I'd kept on my emotions during the last hours of fear, captivity, and rescue.

A fire blazed in the grate of the chamber to which Llywelyn brought me. I was stunned to see that it was a genuine *bath* room. A giant wooden tub, full of water, sat in the center of the room. The men Llywelyn had sent ahead had done their job. They'd warned the castellan that we were coming and explained what we needed.

Llywelyn pulled at the blankets, walked to the tub, and set me down. Dismissing, the servants, he stripped off my breeches and jersey before I could protest and dropped me into the tub. I didn't have the energy to be horrified and instead allowed the warmth of the water to seep through me. I leaned my head back and took in a long, deep breath.

"Where's Mommy?"

I peeked over the edge of the tub. "Here, Sweetie. Mommy's going to have a bath."

"Don't forget to wash behind your ears," Anna said, and I found myself smiling and fighting tears at the same time at the seriousness in her voice.

"Excuse me, my lord," Goronwy said from the doorway. He bowed and took Anna's hand. I leaned back in the tub again with a sigh, and then the latch to the door closed with a click.

Llywelyn walked back over to me. "Close your eyes."

I watched through eyes at half-mast as he settled himself on a stool and rested his arms across the rail of the tub, and then closed them completely. "I knew you'd follow. But I didn't see how you could reach the shore in time," I said.

"We didn't," Llywelyn said. "I feared that we wouldn't, and when I realized that we were too late, when Dafydd's men pushed off and started rowing, I felt my own impotence. I could have strangled my brother with my bare hands."

"He's not a nice man," I said. I turned my head to look at Llywelyn, who had his chin on his hands and was watching me too.

"He's a dangerous child," Llywelyn said. "As a prince of Wales, even a discredited one, men follow him because of his father, and because I have not noised far and wide how much I distrust him."

"And now? What will you do?"

Llywelyn pursed his lips. I waited for his answer, too tired now to really even care. "I don't know," he said, finally. "I will have to discuss it with my counselors."

"I'm safe. He'll argue there's no harm done."

"You are safe," Llywelyn said, "by your own efforts and no thanks to him. But good men died at the Gap and that I cannot forgive."

"Do you think he really meant you to die?"

"What do you think?"

I thought back to my encounters with Dafydd, including his assertion of loyalty at Criccieth. "Dafydd says one thing and does another. I think he wouldn't do the deed himself, but he wouldn't grieve at your loss and he wouldn't be above conspiring with someone else to ensure your death."

"Do you know a man by his words or by his actions?" Llywelyn said. "The priests say that a man can't reach heaven by good deeds alone, but I would say that even if that's true, evil deeds will lead a man to hell."

"*Cyn wired â'r pader*," I said.

"As true as the Lord's prayer," Llywelyn repeated. He reached out a hand to me and I brought mine from the water to give it to him. He gazed at me steadily. "The water is warm, Meg, and I'm tempted."

He never called me that, preferring the Welsh *Marged*. I met his eyes, feeling a little panicked. I'd as good as admitted I was his. He had to know it. He stood to loom over me and slid his hand behind my neck so he could kiss me. I could have drowned in him, more than in the sea.

He released me. "But it wouldn't be right today. I'll send a woman to help you."

"Anna," I said, though without urgency. Goronwy had her. Within minutes she would have made herself the castle pet.

"I'll see to her. Don't you worry." He kissed the top of my head and strode from the room.

Thinking that I was warm enough, and a little restless after that kiss, truth be told, I pushed up to get out of the tub but my legs wouldn't hold me. Dizzy, nauseous, and breathing hard, I sank back into the water and closed my eyes.

We move out from the shore: ten yards, twenty, thirty. And then my heart catches in my throat. Llywelyn and his men have crested the hill beyond the dunes. I bounce off my seat but Dafydd pulls me down and pumps his fist at his brother. In the same instant that Bevyn enters the sea, one of the horses in the boat, perhaps not as tightly tethered as the others, shifts. Dafydd staggers sideways; I throw off his cloak and dive over the side.

I stay under as long as I can but finally bob up, twenty yards from the boat. Dafydd shakes his fist at me and shouts: "You have chosen the wrong brother!"

Dafydd hadn't understood it at all. It wasn't that I'd chosen Llywelyn. I didn't think it was possible to choose Llywelyn. Llywelyn chose whom he liked, and the woman either went along with it or she didn't.

What I'd done, rather, was recognize that I couldn't passively sit by and allow myself to be carried off by Dafydd. Even if I didn't have Llywelyn a hundred yards away on the beach, Dafydd was a man it was easy for me to say no to. Dafydd was too much like Trev for me not to recognize it.

*****

All I wanted to do was sleep. I woke the first time to find Llywelyn sitting silently beside my bed, but another time it was someone else—a woman I didn't know—and twice Anna came to me, rubbed her nose gently against mine, and curled up in my arms. When that happened I wrapped my arms around her and slept deeply, waking again only when the sun lit the room and a young woman came to take her away.

I dozed in and out all the next day, feeling a fever rise and fall within me. People in the doorway spoke in whispers that were too low for me to hear and I could sense their unhappiness. A woman put a poultice on my forehead and someone lifted me to tip water into my mouth. Alternating hot and cold, I lost track of time. Another day passed, and then another.

I opened my eyes, finally, with only the usual low candle providing a light for the room. The blankets had come off my shoulder and I tugged on them but they didn't release. I turned and found Llywelyn stretched out on his back, fully dressed, on top of the covers. And on top of him, her head on his chest, with a loose blanket thrown over both of them, was Anna, sound asleep. My breath hitched and emotion tickled the base of my breastbone.

I studied them, sprawled and intertwined, Anna with her arms wide about him, one hand tucked underneath Llywelyn's left arm, the other hidden under the hair on his right shoulder. He'd braced his elbows on the bed and placed his hands on either side of her to keep her secure. I lay back down, now facing them, and slipped my right hand under his right shoulder, just to touch him as he slept.

As I did so, I realized I hadn't ever touched him before, not on purpose—not since I tried to take the knife from him. He slept on; I closed my eyes. I wasn't sure if anyone in this world would know what love was—not on my twentieth century terms. The tales of romantic love and chivalry were starting to come out of

France about now, but that wasn't love either, as far as I was concerned. Did I care that he didn't love me? Yes and no. But it wasn't hard to see that he loved my daughter. Trev hadn't loved her and he'd never held her this way.

Llywelyn had an inner core that was so solid, he gave the impression that he didn't need anyone, emotionally least of all. He did need people to do his bidding, and they all did—out of loyalty, or perhaps self-preservation, or even love. He was an easy man to love, in fact, because he was so obviously *there*. He believed in Truth, Justice and the Welsh Way—in all capital letters. He was slow to anger, unlike Trev, whose temper always simmered just below the surface, waiting to lash out.

What he might not be was an easy man to live with—not for me, and maybe not for anyone. It wasn't that he wasn't honest, because he was. He told everyone straight out what he wanted from them and what he expected of them, and then he expected everyone to do exactly that. He was so sure of his own *rightness* that it didn't leave a lot of room—or any room, for that matter—for anyone else's insecurities. He held himself so tightly, I wasn't sure that he had any emotions at all. And yet, he held Anna now, and I'd seen his eyes when he'd lost Geraint at the Gap, when he'd picked me out of the surf, and when we were quiet together. There was more inside than he let on.

Many hours later, I awoke and wondered if I'd dreamed Llywelyn's presence. From the light coming through the window, it was getting on towards evening. I was alone in the room again. Perhaps they knew, as I suddenly did, that I was well.

I slipped out of bed, shivering as my feet touched the cold floor, and dipped my hand into the water in the basin beside my bed. It was lukewarm, which meant that the maid had brought it recently. She'd also stoked the fire. I looked for a robe to wear over my nightgown and found a blue one hanging over the back of a chair. I put it on. It was Llywelyn's. It made a grand train behind me as I walked and the sleeves hung nearly to the floor. I belted it at the waist and my stomach growled. How many days had I been ill? I didn't even know.

Hoping for some sustenance, I poked my nose out the door and looked into the hallway. It was empty. All I wanted was to sneak into the kitchen for food without anyone making a fuss over me. Or sending me back to bed. I tiptoed into the hall, and then continued towards the stairs at the far end. Halfway along the hall, I flitted past an open door. Just as I crossed the opening, I realized whose room it was, and that I probably wasn't going to get away without being recognized.

"Meg."

Llywelyn growled at me from inside the room. Resigned to capture, I peered around the frame of the door into Llywelyn's office.

"Hi," I said.

He stood next to a table near the door, polishing his sword. "What do you think you're doing?"

"Getting up," I said. "I don't need to sleep anymore."

"Hmm." He carefully scraped oil down the length of the blade and back up the other side. He glanced at me and then back to his sword. "This was my grandfather's weapon. My squire polishes my armor but I allow no one else to touch the sword."

"It's beautiful," I said. I entered the room and reached out to touch the crosspiece with one finger. Silver and gold threads had been worked into the steel, though no gems adorned it. Perhaps they were used only in ornamental swords.

Llywelyn set the sword in its rest, carefully laying it crosswise in a padded cradle. He wiped his hands on a cloth and then reached for me. I allowed him to pull me in front of him, hands at my sides, a little stiff. He rubbed my arms up and down, studying me all the while with an enigmatic smile on his face. Then he nodded, as if he'd just completed a conversation with himself, and kicked the door to the room closed.

"Now that you are well," he said, as the door clicked into place, "I wanted to talk to you."

"What about?"

He hesitated, and then smiled again. "'What about?' she asks, as if she doesn't know."

"Llywelyn," I said, as confused by him talking to me—or maybe it was to himself—in the third person, as I'd been by his smile.

He was standing so close to me that I would have stepped away had the table with his sword on it not been right at my back. I was almost afraid to look at him and he appeared to sense it because he put his finger under my chin and tipped my face up so he could see my eyes.

Oh. About that.

"I'm not prepared to lose you," he said.

I wasn't sure how to answer that. "I . . . I'd rather not be lost."

Llywelyn didn't seem to notice how terribly lame that sounded. "You were very brave. When you dove out of the boat and started swimming to shore, I couldn't believe what I was seeing."

"Things have happened to me here that I never could have imagined in a million years," I said. "Where I grew up, I would never have fallen into a river—I would never even have been on a horse. Did you know we don't even use horses anymore in my world?"

Llywelyn's fingers found mine and he laced his through them. "Do you think about your world all the time?"

"Yes," I said. "Sometimes it feels like this is a dream that I'll wake up from at any moment. There were times over the last few days when I was sure I would find myself in my own bed in Radnor when I opened my eyes."

"I'm not a dream," Llywelyn said.

"I noticed that," I said. "Truly." He was so close to me now I was having trouble speaking and my breath caught in my throat.

"Would you return if you could? You and Anna?"

I opened my mouth to answer, and then lowered my eyes, not wanting to hurt his feelings. *You have no idea, Llywelyn. You have no idea what it's like.* "So many terrible things have happened since I came here. I wasn't prepared for any of it."

He gave a half-laugh. "I take that as a yes, then," he said.

"Is the question so important Llywelyn? I've no way back. Whatever door I opened when I came here has closed. This is real and Radnor is just a dream."

"So you'll make the best of a bad job, is that it?" Llywelyn laughed again, without humor, and then sobered. "Does that include me?" His voice had gone soft. "Can I make up for some of what you've lost?"

"Oh," I said, and forced myself to look into his face. "I think so, yes."

"You do have a choice," he said.

"Are you giving me one?"

"Yes," Llywelyn said. "I am. I won't keep you like a selkie who only stays with her man because he's stolen her true self and hidden it in a chest. I won't keep you here if the door to your world opens and you want to walk through it. I thought about this as I sat by your side these last few days, with you fevered, afraid I would lose you before I really made you mine. I decided that I'm quite selfish enough to bind you to me, but not against your will."

I was trying to keep up, to figure out where this was going. "Bind me to you?"

"I'm forty years old, Meg," he said. "I've never married. Do you know why?"

"Angharad said something to me about it," I said. "But I'd rather hear it from you."

"I've not dared marry anyone. There is danger in tying myself to one woman if she cannot give me an heir," he said. "I've loved women in the past, but never committed to taking that last step with them."

"But you can't with me either," I said.

Llywelyn studied me. "Perhaps I can."

"Llywelyn," I said. "I'm a nobody, a commoner."

"Who says?"

"Everybody!"

"Is that so?" Llywelyn said, back to the half-smile. "You've heard people speak of it?

"Well, no. Actually, I haven't. I just assumed it to be the case."

"I have chosen you," Llywelyn said. "And that should be enough for everyone, including you. It is certainly enough for me."

"So . . ." I felt more and more at sea. "What are you saying?"

"I believe God has put you in my path and swept you along with me for a reason. I will not turn my back on what He has given me." His voice had lowered and I began to believe what he was saying. "At the same time, I must warn you that I can't marry you in the eyes of the Church. The Pope must approve any royal marriage, to prevent relationships with close kin. I can't produce any bloodlines for you that would satisfy the Pope unless you can tell me different."

"No." The hysterical laughter that came at the most inopportune times rose in my chest. "Not exactly. And especially not if I claim kinship with Madoc ap Owain Gwynedd."

"The Pope has threatened me with excommunication in the past, and I well remember the long years of the interdict placed on my grandfather. The candles were extinguished in all the churches in Wales because of his actions. My grandfather refused to bow to King John of England, as I have at times to King Henry. As you tell me I will to Edward when he takes the throne. If I must, I will risk my own soul, but I prefer not to risk the souls of my people unless the need is very great."

Llywelyn's face held such earnestness, I couldn't look away. "I'm not sure where you're going with this. I don't understand what you're asking of me."

"I'm asking you to marry me," he said. "Right here, right now. As God is our witness."

"Llywelyn." I couldn't speak above a whisper. "I don't know what to say. You can't mean it."

"I do mean it, Meg."

The laughter caught in my throat. "What if I'm the same as all those other women? What if I can't give you a son?"

Llywelyn laughed too—and this time it was genuine. "You could never be the same as any other woman! I can't imagine such a thing." Then he sobered, watching me, and waiting.

"And Anna?"

"I love Anna as my own daughter."

Silence. I couldn't think.

"Say yes," he said. "Say you love me. You do, don't you?" A sliver of worry appeared in his eyes at that last question, perhaps not as sure of himself as he wanted to be.

"I'm not sure that's entirely the point."

"So you do," he said, self-satisfied. "I want to hear you say it. Say you love me."

The abyss opened before my feet and this time it was one of my own making. "I love you, Llywelyn."

Llywelyn grinned. He moved his hands to my waist and pulled me closer. "You've been married before. What are the vows you say in your time?"

"Llywelyn," I said, trying to be rational through the fog in my brain. "What do you think you're doing?"

"I'm trying," he said, tucking me under his chin, "to do the right thing. I'm trying to give you my heart."

"Oh." I stepped forward over the edge and accepted that I was falling and that I would find no bottom.

> *"I, Marged ferch Evan, take thee, Llywelyn ap Gruffydd, to be my husband; to have and to hold, from this day forward, for better, for worse, for richer, for poorer, in sickness or in health, to love and to cherish, until death do us part."*

Llywelyn bent to touch his forehead to mine. "I don't like that last bit," he said. "What is death to part us? It's *time* I'm worried about."

"We can leave it off, then."

He nodded. "Among the common folk, when there is no priest to hand, we say:

For as long as there is wind in the mountains; for as long as there's salt in the sea; for as long as rain falls on these green hills; I will stand with thee. Marged ferch Evan, I claim thee as my wife."

He brought his hands forward and clasped mine to his chest, one of my hands in each of his, and we stood there, pressed close and breathing each other in, for a long time.

14

Llywelyn

"You seem inordinately pleased with yourself this morning," Goronwy said sourly as we met over my desk the next morning. He'd spent the previous evening going through the castle accounts with Castell y Bere's steward. Goronwy had trained this man well, but sometimes two heads were better than one.

I smiled at Goronwy. "I am."

I'd just left Meg sleeping in our bed and was looking forward to breakfast with her later. I'd been reluctant to leave her warmth and the inviting curve of her hip, outlined under the blanket, but the duties of the day called. I found myself changed, in no more time than it took to turn a page in a book. Finally being acknowledged the Prince of Wales in the eyes of King Henry was like the closing of one chapter, and Meg's coming into my life the beginning of another.

Goronwy rolled his eyes. He was slumped in his chair, his hair mussed, having run his hands through it time and again as he wrestled with the numbers on the pages. A scholar Goronwy was not, but of all my advisors, I most trusted him.

"We've lost a dozen men to death and injury," he said, "we've progressed only a few days from Criccieth in nearly two weeks, and are no closer to deterring Clare's despoiling of your land."

"It's winter," I said. "Clare couldn't have laid more than a few stones this week. The intrigue we've uncovered is more important; not only is Dafydd ricocheting around my lands wreaking havoc, but he's in league with Owain of Powys, whose father claims loyalty to me. We must determine if Dafydd's disloyalty has spread further than this."

"To Powys, then, as we initially planned?"

"To Powys. We will summon Gruffydd to us at Brecon," I said. "He must account for his son's actions, even if he doesn't countenance them."

"And the boy, Humphrey?"

"We will escort him to his grandfather's lands, or allow his grandfather to come get him. That is one young man I hate to let go, for he could become a great enemy some day. It's my hope that our treatment of him will outweigh that danger, at least for now."

"And ransom?"

"As I told the boy—no ransom," I said. "I prefer that the senior Bohun is beholden to us."

"He would prefer to pay ransom, I'm sure," Goronwy said. "He will hate that you return Humphrey for free."

"I look forward to greeting him in what was once his own hall," I said. Then I stood abruptly, shut the door to the office, and pulled up a chair next to Goronwy, whose eyes turned wary. "I have something to tell you, old friend."

He straightened, the gloom in his face lifting with the intensity in my voice. "What is it?"

"It's about Meg," I said.

Goronwy lifted his brows. He may not like numbers, but he was good with people. She'd impressed him on this journey, and he adored Anna, who'd attached herself to him whenever he was available. If I was going to tell anyone who they were, it was he.

"What do you make of her strangeness?" I said, by way of easing into the truth.

"We should simply call her Morgane and be done with it," he said.

That made me sit up. "What makes you say that?"

"She comes from a faraway land, she's a healer, and she's bewitched the Prince of Wales. She even sings of apples."

I laughed. "Everyone knows that song. No, the truth is strange enough without bringing Arthur into it." I stopped.

"What is it, my lord?"

"She has come to us from a future time, Goronwy. Thus, her sudden appearance and the strange vehicle."

Goronwy studied me, his gaze neither quizzical nor skeptical, just waiting. "What do you want me to say, my lord? I saw her chariot, so I can't say what is and is not impossible, but I can't see how what you say could be true."

"I didn't either, at first," I said. "But after some reflection, and the more she spoke of the future we face, the more credible her story seems. On top of which, why would she lie about this? How could she invent such a story?"

"My lord, you know it can't be true. The priests speak of a beginning and an end. There is no possibility of returning to a time once we've passed through it."

"She gives me fourteen years, Goronwy," I said, getting to the heart of the matter. "I am betrayed on a snowy hill at Cilmeri by the Mortimer boys, who profess to be seeking an alliance with me against Edward."

"Ho," Goronwy said, sitting back in his chair. "That is a tale."

"She also says that if Edward troubles us now, it's nothing compared to the difficulties he will present when he becomes king."

"That I can believe," Goronwy said. "I've observed the man and he's come into his own since Evesham. He awaits the day of his father's death with impatience. He seeks to grasp the reins of England and ride her where he wishes. That day will not be a good one for Wales."

"So Meg says."

Goronwy looked thoughtful. "That a young woman such as she should expend her energies thinking of such things is best testimony to their truth, but surely, you can't really believe she's from the future?"

"I'm beginning to, Goronwy."

"Perhaps she's a throwback to an earlier time as I said before—that time of Morgane when a woman might see the future in a scrying bowl?" Goronwy said. "The world has changed from those days and perhaps she denies what is in herself for fear of retribution. Such a one would not be welcome in a church—or in a prince's bed." Goronwy lowered his voice to match the depth of his concern.

"I love her, Goronwy," I said. "Whoever she is, she's in my bed and there she will remain."

Goronwy nodded. "Yes, my lord. If magic swirls around your castle, better it work for you than against."

I was glad he accepted that, but wasn't entirely satisfied. Goronwy didn't believe me. But then, he hadn't heard the tale from Meg herself. At this point, acceptance was perhaps more than I had any right to hope, from him or anyone.

"Find your breakfast, Goronwy. I will finish here."

He stood, understanding that it wasn't the work I wanted, but to be alone. I stared at the documents, not seeing them, and after a moment, found myself too restless to remain inside. I followed him down the stairs and into the great hall. Goronwy sat at one of the tables, but I simply held up one hand to him and continued into the bailey. The air had remained warm and the young men were out in force, working on their sword practice. On a clear day it was possible to see the peak of Cadair Idris towering above us, but today was muggy and overcast, threatening more rain to melt the rest of the winter snows.

Humphrey was working with the squires in the bailey. He was stripped to the waist, sweat glistening off him as he stretched and lunged, blocking the sword of the youngster he was fighting. His opponent was outclassed, but Humphrey didn't press his advantage as much as he could have.

That Humphrey was clearly winning was obvious to me, but the other boy appeared not to realize it, so careful was Humphrey not to reveal the extent of his skill. He kept himself controlled, thinking and moving just enough ahead of the other boy, keeping his feet steady on the uneven ground of the bailey, just as if he were standing on the more even floor of a great hall polished from years of use.

"My lord!" One of the guards at the top of the gatehouse tower shouted to me. "A rider approaches! He wears the Hereford colors!"

The shouting distracted Humphrey's opponent, rather than Humphrey who could have been forgiven for it. Humphrey took the opportunity to relieve him of his sword. It clattered to the rocky ground. Humphrey looked almost apologetic, but turned to me.

"I would greet whoever has ridden here, my lord," he said.

"Come," I said.

Humphrey handed his wooden sword to the boy he'd been fighting, who took it with something like reverence, and caught up his shirt and cloak. Like many of my castles, Castell y Bere was built on a narrow spur, overlooking a valley. Two summers ago, I'd commenced work on a second, more secure keep to the south of the present one, and last year I'd reinforced the entrance with a new gatehouse and curtain wall.

Thus, I led the way past the cistern and the round tower on which the guard stood, to the old gate below, now much more protected than before. A man could reach it only by riding across the drawbridge, through the new, guarded outer gate, up a flight of stairs, into the barbican, and then through the inner gate. Humphrey and I walked quickly down the steps to the outer gatehouse and then up through the tower, so we could peer down at our visitor from above.

The man rode alone, and as the guard had said, wore the red and gold of the Earl of Hereford, Humphrey's grandfather. I watched Humphrey closely, but even so, almost missed the flash of recognition, hope—and then dismay—on Humphrey's face before he mastered it. The recognition and hope I expected, but the dismay was a surprise.

I switched my gaze to the rider my guards admitted. Though he would be seeking an audience with me, I allowed him to go on without me. I wasn't quite finished with Humphrey yet. "The fight was well done," I said, catching him in the act of putting on his shirt.

He stopped, the shirt half over his head, and then pulled it down smoothly. "Thank you, my lord. I was focused on the fight and thus unaware of your presence. Otherwise, I would have greeted you when you entered the bailey."

"You had a task to complete," I said, and then spoke again quickly, trying to catch him off-guard. "Who's the rider?"

Humphrey's face went blank. "One of my grandfather's men."

"As I would expect. What I didn't expect is your uncertainty in seeing him here."

Humphrey glanced at me and then looked away. "We've had dealings in the past," he said. "It's of no importance."

"He has come a long way from England to see you," I said, still watching Humphrey closely, but he controlled his expression and gave nothing away.

We returned to the keep. The messenger stood in the center of the hall with Goronwy, who leaned against one of the tables, his arms folded across his chest, mouth pursed, and Hywel, who sat languidly in a chair behind the high table. They all turned to look at our approach.

"My lord Prince," the stranger said, and bowed. "I am John de Lacey, riding from Huntington."

I nodded. "You have news for me?"

"Lord Humphrey de Bohun, First Earl of Essex, Second Earl of Hereford and Constable of England sends you greetings and asks word of his grandson."

I canted my head to where Humphrey stood, clearly in the best of health. "You can see for yourself that he is unharmed."

"My lord was concerned at the . . ." John hesitated.

I raised my eyebrows at his attempt at diplomacy.

" . . . the time it was taking to return him."

"These weeks have been eventful," I said. "When a prince's life is threatened, he has the right to be cautious."

John bowed again, but not before shooting a look at Humphrey, who stood impassive beside me. "I ask on behalf of the Earl for the return of Lord Humphrey."

"No," I said. "Not yet."

A general sigh eased around the room. "My lord asks that you consider an exchange," John said, not giving up. He held out his hand in entreaty. "Not a ransom, my lord, but a gift of information, in memory of his son who died at Evesham."

Ah. So that's the way of it? "Perhaps we should talk in private," I said.

John barely waited for the door to my office to close and his rear to hit the seat in front of my desk before he started speaking, obviously barely able to contain his news. "First, the Earl would like to say that he had no foreknowledge of his grandson's misadventure."

"So I gathered." I glanced at Humphrey whose expression hadn't changed and had assumed the same guarded position as in the hall. Perhaps his insides churned at being treated like a child—not undeservedly so, since he'd behaved like one—but he didn't allow it to show. "Humphrey made that clear."

"My lord has sent word of the attack on you and the identities of the perpetrators to Gruffydd ap Gwenwynwyn. He too was unaware of the activities of his heir, Owain, and pledges to take him in hand."

"If Owain treats his father as he does me, it will serve little purpose," I said. "Both Owain and my brother are grown men and not subject to the rule of any man, other than me."

John's eyes widened at this. "Your brother! Prince Dafydd was also involved?"

I grimaced. "I understand the nature of the trade," I said. "I'm sure your lord will be very interested in your report when you return."

"What my lord is most interested in is avoiding, shall we say, *royal entanglements*," John said. "He too wants to be sure that news of the activities of Owain, Humphrey, and your brother remain within Wales and the Marche."

"He has reason to believe that others might be interested? Or are already involved?"

"He does." We sat and thought about that for a minute.

"Edward, then," I said. The name fell into the silence like dropped crockery on a stone floor.

John nodded his head ever so slightly. "As you say, my lord."

"I don't like it," Goronwy said. "Are you saying that Edward's hand is to be found guiding these other men?"

"I . . . I wouldn't want to go that far," John said.

"Say what you mean, then," Goronwy said. "It's easy enough for your lord to defer blame to a man whom we cannot reach. Is it not enough that a Bohun sought the life of the crowned Prince of Wales? Is it not enough that the Prince's brother and vassals plot against him? Humphrey should be in shackles, not smirking here in this office as if he's too young to know better!"

"Goronwy," I said.

"He was at Evesham!" Goronwy thundered. "He knows what's at stake!"

"I do know," Humphrey said. It was as if he was forcing the words past his teeth. "But I misjudged the nature of the threat, spending too much time with those who are discontented, thinking their lot my own. Owain and Dafydd think too small. They are concerned only with their little patch of Wales. I did lose my father at Evesham, and it was Edward himself who ensured his death. My mistake was in forgetting which side I was on."

"Other than your own, you mean," Goronwy said.

"The enemy of my enemy is my friend, eh?" Hywel asked, putting it into speech for the first time.

Humphrey ignored the others, staring at me, his face stony. "I apologize, my lord, for forgetting my nobility and yours."

"Good men died," I said. "You may ask their forgiveness when you see them. For now, you will remain in my household, as my guest, and we will continue as planned to Brecon."

"May I stay with him, then?" John asked.

I studied him. "Do you vouch for him, Humphrey?"

Humphrey's expression was one of a man who'd sipped some very sour wine. "I do, my lord. He is one of my grandfather's trusted servants."

Goronwy snorted.

I nodded. "So be it. We leave tomorrow. If needed, I expect you both to use your sword on our behalf."

Humphrey and John bowed, dismissed, and left the room, talking low in French. "I want them watched," I said.

"It is already done," Goronwy said, and closed the door behind them.

"That was quite an outburst, my friend," I said. "You were hard on the boy."

"At his age you ruled lands of your own in Gwynedd and had begun to gather men around you who followed your lead, even to death," Goronwy said. "Humphrey is the same age as Dafydd was when he challenged you at Bryn Derwin. If we had been harder on him, perhaps we wouldn't be where we are today, paying the price for his lack of restraint."

"Humphrey is a small problem," Hywel said. "I'm most concerned about Edward."

"That rutting son of a goat!" Goronwy said, his color rising again.

I allowed myself a smile, as the goat to whom he referred was the king of England himself.

"I've never met the man and I already hate him," Hywel said. "If we'd been at Evesham, we could have defeated him."

"We would not have won," I said. "I couldn't afford to risk my throne for a lost cause, not with all England and half the Marche arrayed against Montfort. He couldn't see it, but I didn't need Meg's soothsaying to know what would happen."

Goronwy harrumphed again. It was an old argument. Simon de Montfort, married to King Henry's sister, had brought the English crown to its knees, ruling for a time in Henry's stead. A parliament of barons, Humphrey's father and grandfather among them, resented Henry for his capriciousness, mismanagement of the realm and favoritism towards his French relatives who'd aided him. Montfort had recognized me as the Prince of Wales in 1265 and I'd held him a friend, but he'd been unlucky in battle, and in the end, the rising star of Prince Edward could not be stopped.

It had become clear to me before that final battle at Evesham that the tide had turned on Montfort. Bad luck was partly to blame for bringing him down, but also his own arrogance. He'd believed himself invincible. He thought that God rode at his side, an ancient failing for rulers of every stripe.

More immediately, as had happened to me more times than I could count, the allies who had supported him—Marcher lords and English barons—had switched sides, as inconstant as the wind in their allegiances. Edward had taken advantage of their weakness and pugnacity, and had known the exact moment when their desire for personal power trumped their sworn loyalties. At that moment he'd struck, convincing all but a very few to come over to his side, whether with cajolery, righteous anger, or outright bribes.

Edward was unlike his father, Henry, in every way imaginable. His power grew with every passing month. Humphrey's father had died at the head of the foot soldiers he commanded and refused to abandon. But honor meant something different to him than to Edward. To Edward, power was the only thing that mattered.

15

Meg

I was glad Elisa wasn't with me. She would have had dark words for me about being with Llywelyn. Mom, on the other hand, once she got over the existence of time travel and all that, would have been just as starry-eyed over Llywelyn as I was. *He's the Prince of Wales! Our beloved, lost Llywelyn!*

Elisa thought I should have gotten therapy after I left Trev. The idea that I'd married Llywelyn—at least in our own eyes—would have sent her running for the phone book. I could hear her in my head: "You've known him for *how* long?" or "You're on the rebound" or "He's too old for you. You're still trying to replace Dad." She was probably right. I didn't have any answers for her, other than that I loved Llywelyn. Back in Radnor that might not have been enough. Here in Wales, it most definitely was.

Nobody treated me any differently than before, but I felt different about myself. By the first week in March, I'd been with Llywelyn for over a month. Each day we woke, traveled a little further on our journey to Brecon, and went to bed at night, whether that was in a castle, a manor, or one time in a tent on the ground. None of this was worthy of notice or comment by anyone other than me. I was surprised, even, by how easily Llywelyn's men accepted me. I was Llywelyn's woman, always *there*, and that was enough to be going on with.

The difference was how I treated myself. I knew what it was to be Trev's wife, but it was a very different thing to be Llywelyn's wife. Llywelyn's wife was competent, thoughtful, and treated well by all. I never had to worry about Llywelyn hitting me, even when something happened over the course of the day to make him lose his temper. I didn't have to *manage* him—to walk on eggshells half the time and avoid him the other half. Llywelyn *told* me what he was thinking, and why, and what made him angry was that I hadn't expected it.

"I thought you told me that men and women were equal in your world," he said.

"They . . . are," I said. "They can be—even supposed to be, I guess. It's just that I wasn't when I was with Trev."

"Humph," Llywelyn said. That was generally his response every time Trev came into the conversation, which fortunately wasn't often. "Well, it's time you started being as equal as a thirteenth century woman, then. I don't have much patience for the twentieth century if there are still men like Trev in it. We have enough of his kind here."

By sheer necessity, I began to fit in.

I hadn't worn a watch the day I'd come to Wales, and I realized that I didn't miss it. I loved how time moved, slowly or quickly, but without being marked in small increments. There was more time for Anna. Each day had a natural rhythm. Things happened, and if something didn't get finished, tomorrow would come soon enough. In winter in particular, the days weren't very long, and people thought nothing of sitting over dinner for hours in the evening after a long day of riding or walking, because there was nowhere else to go and nothing better to do but listen to a forty-five minute tale sung by a bard.

One of the few nights we tented in the middle of a forest, I found myself sitting on a log, sandwiched between Goronwy and Llywelyn, with Anna curled onto my lap, dozing in the warmth of the fire. I'd put away my guitar for the evening, once my fingers got too cold to play. Marshmallows and hot chocolate would have made the moment perfect.

"You're happy here, aren't you?" Goronwy said.

A quick glance at Llywelyn showed him pretending to ignore us and focusing intently on a stick he'd stuck in the fire. "I am, Goronwy," I said. Llywelyn eased a touch closer to me. I hid my smile and kept talking. "I miss my mother and my sister, but I do love it here, even if it's not at all what I would have expected."

"What do you mean?"

"I don't know if I can explain," I said. "You know that the way we live in America is very different from Wales, right?"

Goronwy shrugged. "Prince Llywelyn has spoken with me of this."

"We dress differently, most people know how to read, people die of fewer diseases, though we have different ones too, and as a rule, women have a better lot in life. But people who live in that world don't realize what they've lost along the way."

"And that is?" Llywelyn said, proving his ears were as wide open as I'd suspected.

"People are more aware of how others feel and what they think. Everyone is adept at reading everyone else, and genuinely interested in figuring them out."

Neither man was impressed. "Of course," Llywelyn said. "We have to live together, don't we? That's not the case in your world?"

"No," I said, shaking my head at how obvious it was to him. "As a rule, you'd never look at or talk to a person you didn't already know—whether on the street, at a meal, or in a shop. Everybody behaves as if they are completely alone, even when—or especially when—surrounded by a crowd."

Both men gaped at me. Even in the flickering firelight, I was good enough now at reading people myself to see the disbelief reflected plainly in their faces. "Why?" Goronwy said. "How could that be?"

"Because chances are, you'll never see any of those people again. It isn't worth the time and effort invested." And then the real reason struck me. "It's because we don't depend on each other anymore."

Goronwy shook his head. "Every man depends on every other, from the lowliest serf who hoes the field, to the knight who rides into battle, to the monk who prays for our souls."

"And when a man dies, he has companions to remember and celebrate his life, and to mourn him," Llywelyn said. "I don't see how your people could imagine otherwise."

"Yes, well," I said, "that's another difference. People in my time don't think about death."

"That's just foolish," Llywelyn said. "People don't die in your time? You yourself said that your father and husband died."

I pulled the blanket tighter around myself and snuggled closer to Llywelyn. "They die but nobody talks about it. Death here is part of daily life in a way it isn't in the twentieth century, at least in America. Here, it's always at the table with you, like an uninvited guest who insists on staying for dinner. It doesn't matter if people die from disease, battle, or childbirth—death is always with us."

"Of course," Llywelyn said.

"You say 'of course'," I said, "but it's not 'of course' where I come from! Here, people don't shy away from talking about it and they don't pretty it up with phrases like 'He's moved on' or 'She passed away' which everyone in my town uses. For you, it's 'He's dead and I'm sorry (or not sorry) for it,' or 'Me mam died last winter. I miss her.' You just say it straight out."

I was unusual for a young woman in the twentieth century in that I *had* seen death, in both my husband and father. I didn't know a single classmate whose parent had died, or if they had, they didn't talk to me about it. Death was swept under the rug and you were supposed to get over it in whatever fashion you were able and get on with your life.

Here they did all get on with their lives, but nobody *forgot*. In fact, everything important to the Welsh I lived with revolved around people who'd died: they wove tapestries and rugs depicting past battles; most of the songs were about famous, dead people; and most of their mythological stories ended badly. You couldn't pay me to read a book that ended with the hero dying, but the people around me *assumed* that he would—and yet, they went about their lives with the quiet hope that this time, just once, he wouldn't. The entire country was full of optimistic pessimists.

* * * * *

We turned our horses off the road, following the men ahead for a brief stop. "Where are we?" I gazed at the fallen stones.

"This?" Llywelyn said. "It's a Roman fort. We often rest here." He lifted me from the saddle.

"Yes, but . . ." I stopped, trying to take it in. The fort had lost its roof, but the walls still stood fifteen feet high and each at least fifty feet wide, built in a square. I walked across the grass in the clearing and through the open front door, vacant now, and into the cavernous space on the other side, with trees and bushes growing where once a legion had lived. A shiver went down my spine as I touched the stones that men—born two thousand years before I—had chosen, and crafted, and placed here.

Lost in thought, I walked from room to room. I loved everything about history, and the best part was walking in the steps of people who'd come before me—which was good, given that I'd been *living* history these last months. I came out of my reverie, however, when I entered a small room, nestled in a building along the eastern wall. An altar sat in the center of the room, with words carved into the stone and a picture of a bull.

"What happened here?" I asked Llywelyn, who came to stand beside me.

"It's a chapel, though not to our God. Soldiers worshipped Mithras here. None of the men like to come this way."

I stood uncertainly in the doorway. "I won't either, then. Pagan gods or not, I'm a Welshwoman now. I can respect what they feel."

Llywelyn put his arm around my shoulder and turned me back the way we had come. "Goronwy told me when you first arrived here that he thought he'd call you 'Morgane'—that you saw the future not because you lived it, but in a scrying bowl."

"He didn't!" I said. "Besides, Morgane was Arthur's sister. I don't even *have* a brother."

Llywelyn laughed and pulled me to him. "You've bewitched *me*. I suppose that's all that matters."

*****

The night before we reached Brecon, we stayed at a castle set at the junction of the Usk and the Senni Rivers. It was a castle built by Llywelyn and one which he oversaw directly, through his castellan, Einion Sais. Einion had his own castles too, but this was one of the largest in the area, next to Brecon. It was also the most modern, since Llywelyn built it himself. I had to like that.

What I didn't like was the tension among Llywelyn's men. That first evening after dinner, as I rocked Anna to sleep in her cradle, Llywelyn explained.

"The closer we get to England, the worse it will get. Ten miles? Twenty miles? It's hard to know where Wales ends and the Marche begins. We've fought over this land for centuries, and we all can feel it."

No, I didn't really understand. Llywelyn shifted in his seat to lean forward, his words earnest and heartfelt, and elaborated further. "We've hallowed this ground with the blood of our ancestors. They lived here, plowed these fields, hunted in these mountains, all the way back to the time before the Romans came. Their remains are spread over every inch of this land, and for me to give that up, to negate their sacrifice because of some neglect on my part, means that I give up the very part of myself that is Welsh. It is impossible and unfathomable."

"The English don't understand this at all."

"Don't understand and don't care," Llywelyn said. "They themselves are newcomers to our shores. They conquered the Saxons, who came after Rome fell, but only after we'd already lost all but our small corner of this island. The English kings only care for the land because of the power and wealth it gives them, not because it gives them life."

"I'm English too, in that sense," I said. But I recognized the fervor in Llywelyn's voice and respected it, even if I couldn't share it. "That's what you're most afraid of, isn't it? Not dying for your own sake, but because of what Wales will lose if you do."

"Yes," Llywelyn said. "I don't want to die, of course, but you tell me that when I do die, Wales ceases to exist and that my people are subject to seven hundred years of English oppression. I can't comprehend that. I told Goronwy that you were from the future and he still doesn't believe me, but even he can see that the future you foretell is so frightening and devastating that it doesn't matter if it's true or not. What matters is that you've presented it as a possibility, and now that I've heard it, I must do everything in my power to ensure that it doesn't come to pass."

"I hope that you can, Llywelyn," I said. I rested a hand on his knee. "I hope that I haven't just given you foreknowledge of a future that you can't change."

"I think we've already changed your future, haven't we, Meg? If you were to return to your time, you wouldn't be the same woman who left."

"No," I said. "I wouldn't, but neither is Wales the same place with me in it. I still don't understand how so little of your daily life got written down."

"Didn't you tell me that history was written by the victors?" Llywelyn said. "Who wrote our history?"

"The English," I said. "I know. It would be helpful if more of your people were literate, because it's a lot harder to suppress a people when they have their own voice to pass on through the ages in books."

Llywelyn stared into the fire. "Your world is so far away, Meg. I can't comprehend the enormity of those years. I can't even begin to imagine the changes that have occurred." He transferred his gaze to me. "But then again, you're here, a young woman of Welsh descent who only invites comment because your Welsh is accented strangely. How is it that the world has changed, but the people in it have not?"

I shook my head. "I think the changes are mostly on the inside," I said, "just like we talked about before. Those changes don't show."

Llywelyn was right too, that fourteen years from now seemed a long way off—I'd be not quite thirty-five. Would I still be with him? Would he send me away like the other women who couldn't give him a child? Would I even be alive? Thirty-five was nothing to a twentieth century woman—I'd barely have started living. At thirty-five, women were often grandmothers, perhaps not ready for the grave, but *old*. I didn't want that to be me either.

*****

"You rutting bastard!"

I stopped short. My hand was out, ready to push open the door onto the battlements, Anna on my left hip.

After my conversation with Llywelyn the night before, I wanted to see the countryside, to feel what he felt. Too often these last weeks, my focus had been on keeping Anna happy or how sore my back and rear were, not on the land through which I was riding. It was always beautiful, but so densely packed with trees on every side that you couldn't see more than the road in front of you and occasionally a hill rising up ahead or behind.

Instead of going through it, I backed away from the door, uncertain if I should listen in case it was important, or leave because it was merely two men fighting over a woman.

"If our lord discovers your failure, he'll have both of our heads!"

"Then don't tell him," the second man said.

"You were supposed to have finished this already." It was the first man again.

"Well I haven't!"

"Young Humphrey . . ." the first man began, but his partner cut him off.

"Humphrey de Bohun is a bloody traitor! He turned his back on me. He had the nerve to say that though I'd been loyal through many battles, it was only because of that loyalty that he would pretend he hadn't heard my plea. He'll have none of this. I'm lucky he didn't turn me in to Prince Llywelyn."

Now I knew who the second man was at least: Humphrey's companion, John de Lacey, the man sent by Humphrey's grandfather. Then heavy footsteps sounded on the other side of the door, pounding along the battlements. Hywel's voice penetrated the stairwell. "You there!"

"Yes sir!" It was the first voice.

"What good is a guard who stands in one place? You know how close to England we are here!"

"Yes, sir," the man said.

I'd starting backing down the stairs at Hywel's speech, but now turned and fled. My breath came in short gasps as I followed the curve of the tower. I was out of sight of the door in a few steps. If one of the men opened it, however, they would know by the pounding of my feet that they'd been overheard.

With a rush, Anna and I burst out of the stairwell and onto the second floor landing—and ran full-on into Llywelyn.

"What is it?" he said, his hands grasping my forearms to stop my headlong rush.

"I've just heard . . ." I gasped, trying to catch my breath. "There were men talking on the battlements . . ."

"In here," he said, and pushed me into the room he was using for his office.

"Rutting bastard!" Anna said, her voice cheery. "Rutting bastard!"

"I gather you've been listening where you shouldn't, too, young lady," Llywelyn said, rubbing Anna under her chin. He turned to me. "Now tell me."

"I wanted to walk on the battlements, just to see the countryside," I said. "Before I could push through the door at the top of the stairs, I overheard angry voices. Two men, one of whom sounded like Humphrey's man-at-arms, arguing about something—a plot against you, I think."

Llywelyn's face darkened. "I misjudged him, then."

"No, you didn't," I said, hastening to redirect his thoughts. "They were angry because Humphrey refused to help them."

"Ah." Llywelyn stood in front of me, his hands on his hips, thinking. "Did you hear any of what they were planning?"

"No. I'm sorry. I ran because I was afraid John would come through the door and see me."

"Understandable."

"Hywel interrupted them, anyway. He saw them; he would know who the men were. Maybe he observed something else that would help."

"You have a tendency to end up right in the thick of things, don't you?" he said. "The solar would be safer."

"But not nearly as interesting," I said. "I don't want to bore you."

Llywelyn's mouth twitched. "No, we wouldn't want that, would we?" And then. "Let's find Hywel and see what he says."

I was pleased he was letting me come—he certainly didn't have to—so I passed Anna to Maud, her new nanny, who was darning stockings in the next room. She was a widow a few years older than I, whose two children and husband had died in a sickness two years before. The thought brought me to my knees, but she hadn't given up as she might have—as I can imagine I would have if I'd lost Anna—and was loving and fiercely protective of Anna, who in turn adored her.

Llywelyn and I mounted the stairs I'd just run down. This time we went through the door at the top. It was a gorgeous, spring day, with a scattering of white clouds in the blue sky. Flowers bloomed, particularly the early bulbs, and Llywelyn said that the farmers were already planting crops in the lands along the coast and the warmer, richer lands in southern Wales.

The guard who paced the four corners of the tower stiffened in salute as Llywelyn walked by him. I couldn't tell by looking at him if he was the same one who'd talked to John, so I trailed after Llywelyn. Hywel spied us from his post on the top of the gatehouse tower, thirty yards on, and met us half-way down the walkway.

The castle was roughly rectangular in shape, with the round gatehouse tower protruding from the southern wall and the square keep taking up another corner. Llywelyn had explained that the round tower was built first, purely as a defensive measure, before the keep was built for comfort.

"My lord," Hywel said, with a quick bow.

"Just now you encountered John de Lacey and another man arguing, did you not?" Llywelyn said. "Meg overheard them."

"Did she?" Hywel said, looking past Llywelyn to me. "I didn't see you, madam."

"I was behind the door."

"They were arguing about a plot they'd conceived," Llywelyn continued. "We were hoping you knew more than she."

"No," Hywel said shortly. "I sent my man, one Huw ap Cadoc, to his quarters. I was not pleased with his lapse in attention as it was."

"We'll need him now if we are to confront Lacey," Llywelyn said.

"Yes, my lord. I'll bring him to the hall." Hywel strode away, back towards the gatehouse tower, and Llywelyn and I backtracked to the stairs and the great hall.

We'd only just entered, however, when Hywel appeared through the great double doors to the keep.

"He's gone," Hywel said, without preamble, "along with John de Lacy."

Llywelyn swung around to stare at him. "You're sure?"

"I spoke to Humphrey who is with the squires in the bailey. Nobody saw them leave, but as the postern gate lies behind the stables . . ." his voice trailed off at the expression on Llywelyn's face.

"I know, dammit!" Llywelyn said. "I built the place." He strode to the entrance doors and stared out them.

"Should I order men to follow?" Hywel came up beside Llywelyn.

"Yes," Llywelyn said. "They're probably long gone—making for Huntingdon no doubt—but let's make sure of it."

"Yes, my lord," Hywel said. "And your plans? Have they changed?"

"No. We leave for Brecon tomorrow. Bohun will come for Humphrey and hopefully we will be rid of the lot of them."

I placed a hand on Llywelyn's arm. "Next time I'll listen longer."

"You certainly will not!" Llywelyn said. He wrapped an arm around my shoulders and pulled me to him in a tight squeeze. I put my arms around his waist and hugged him back.

"Women make good spies," I said. "Nobody ever suspects us."

"Not my woman," Llywelyn growled. It was exactly what I would have expected him to say. "It's bad enough to have plots and subterfuge every time I turn around without worrying about you too."

"Yes, my lord,"—and smiled to hear myself say it.

16

Llywelyn

At long last: Brecon.

I'd entered the keep earlier in the afternoon with Goronwy, pleased as always that I'd taken it from Bohun. Humphrey had been several steps behind us, escorting Meg and Anna, and he'd craned his neck to see what changes or improvements I'd made to his grandfather's domain. I'd had to rebuild some of the craftsmen's sheds in the bailey, damaged by fire when we took the castle, as well as make extensive repairs to the several of the walls. The latest problem was that the Honddu River slid by right under the southeastern castle walls and was undermining the stone foundation. The spring floods hadn't helped.

"I'm glad that you made it without mishap, my lord," Tudur said, striding up to Goronwy and me.

I clapped him on the shoulder. "I'm glad to see you too, friend. You have news for us?"

"I do," he said, "though your young man-at-arms, Bevyn, whom you sent ahead of you to warn of the traitor in our midst only adds to the uncertainties."

I glanced at Humphrey, who pulled out a chair for Meg at one of the tables and then sat across from her with a chess board. I'd watched him carefully since Lacey left, not wanting to give away the fact that I knew of Lacey's potential betrayal. It was a test of a sort. So far, he'd not passed it.

"Has he played the game of kings with her before?" Goronwy asked.

"Not that I'm aware," I said. "Maybe I'll stick around to sweep him off the floor when she's done with him."

Goronwy smirked. "You do that, my lord. I'll make sure the men are properly settled in their quarters." He paced away and I turned to Tudur.

"What did you find? Whose ring was it?"

"Owain confessed it was his, but he'd given it to Dafydd many years ago."

"As I feared," I said. "Dafydd sent a messenger out of Gwynedd."

"That is all we know, for now, my lord," Tudur said. "The question remains: to whom did Dafydd send him?"

"And did he reach his destination?"

"And why did he die? Because he was a loose end that needed tying?" Tudur said. "To destroy any link between Dafydd and our unknown man? Or to prevent him from reaching him."

"We'll think on it," I said. "Dafydd has much to answer for, even without this."

A commotion from the kitchen caught my attention. One of my new boarhound puppies burst through the doorway, followed by Anna. The puppy ran under a table and I scooped the girl into my arms.

"Careful, *cariad,*" I said. "He bites."

"He's nice," she said. "Can I have him, Papa?"

"He'll be bigger than you someday. Perhaps we'll find you a kitten instead."

Anna put her arms around my neck and squeezed. My heart melted. I carried her to Meg and sat down to watch the chess match. "Is everything in order?" Meg said, her eyes still on the board.

"Yes," I said, shifting Anna in my lap. "We should hear soon if Lacey reached your grandfather, Humphrey. Then you can go home."

Humphrey looked up, met my gaze, and looked down again.

I allowed a few heart beats to pass. "Do you have something to tell me, son?"

Meg's hand hovered above a pawn. Humphrey didn't answer, so she picked up the piece and gently moved it into position. Humphrey continued to stare at the board, not meeting my eyes. Then without warning, he upended the chess board, sending the pieces scattering across the table and floor.

"God damn them to the seventh level of a fiery hell!" Humphrey surged to his feet and I matched him, afraid of what he might damage next. Meg reached for Anna and I handed her over before moving to confront Humphrey.

"Control yourself," I said.

Humphrey sputtered. He fisted his right hand and slammed it into the wall behind him.

"Please believe that you are among friends, Humphrey," Meg said. "Just tell us."

Humphrey massaged his right hand with his left. "John asked that I aid him in some plot against you," he said through gritted teeth. "I didn't—" He stopped. "I sent him away."

"But didn't feel the need to tell me of it?" Llywelyn said.

"No! I did not!" Humphrey said. "Nor uncover the details, beyond that it was not for my grandfather that he was working."

"Not your grandfather?" Meg said. "Isn't John his man?"

"He is," Humphrey said.

"Was." Hywel strode across the hall towards us. "I followed him, as you requested, my lord. But instead of taking the turning to Huntingdon, he continued past it, on north."

"What did you say?" Humphrey spun around to face Hywel, his face draining of color. "Why would he go north?"

"I don't know," Hywel said. He turned to me. "My lord, I apologize, but I didn't want to risk my men by taking them further into England. We turned back and informed the Earl of Hereford of his grandson's imminent arrival at Brecon."

"Did you tell of him of his wayward servant?" Meg asked.

"I did," Hywel said, "and he claimed no knowledge of his destination. Lord Bohun said, however, that he would attempt to find out more and would report those findings to you, my lord."

"Did he?" I said. "A new spirit of cooperation indeed among the Bohuns. It is without precedent." Humphrey glared at me, but when I matched his gaze, he soon looked away. Once again he'd not comported himself as well as he might have, and he knew it. He bent his head and sagged onto his bench.

The others left, Anna crawled under the tables to find the wayward chess pieces, and Meg and Humphrey resumed their game, though neither player's attention was on it. Although I could have chastised Humphrey further, Meg was all he needed.

"Why didn't you tell us, Humphrey?" She moved a castle forward and didn't look at him.

"Where do my loyalties lie, my lady? I am your prisoner."

"Are you?" she said. "It looks to me the only prison you inhabit is one of your own making."

At her words, Humphrey abandoned any pretense of playing the game. "You're speaking of honor again."

"You knew the right thing to do," Meg said, "but you didn't do it. We are enemies, yes, but not in this and not today."

"It would serve my house if Lord Llywelyn were dead."

"And it is worth the loss of your soul to see that happen?"

"I have killed men," Humphrey said, "but only in battle. These machinations and subtle plotting are beyond me. I know that worries my grandfather, who is a master."

"All you have to worry about, Humphrey, is your own actions," Meg said. "It may be your destiny to lead men in war, perhaps even against my lord. But it's not your nature to sneak around in the dark. Prince Llywelyn has been open in his dealings with you, and as you yourself are a knight, he expects the same in return."

"I know it. It was not clear to me that stopping a plot perpetrated against him by another was also my duty."

"And now?"

He held her gaze. "I still don't know that it is."

Meg nodded. "That's honest anyway."

Humphrey tipped his chin in my direction. "Your prince knows subterfuge well. My grandfather has told me."

Meg glanced at me and her eyes twinkled. "I believe it. He'll tell you that the ends justify the means at times, but he'd also say that he accepts responsibility for his actions. A lord must understand himself and his motives, whether for good or ill."

"I can do that," Humphrey said. "I will do that."

"Then you will be a man of whom your grandfather can be proud," I said.

Humphrey gazed at Meg for another count of ten, then stood, bowed, to both her and me, and left the room.

"You think that of me, do you?" I caught a stray hair that had come loose from Meg's wimple and tucked it behind her ear.

"I know it."

* * * * *

Bohun made Humphrey cool his heels with us for more than a week, so it was actually Gruffydd ap Gwenwynwyn who was the first of the conspirators I confronted. He strode into Brecon's great hall as if he owned the place, which he, of all my barons, allies, and enemies, never had. I found his attitude irritating so got straight to the point.

"Where is your son?" I asked him. Gruffydd halted before me, made the proper obeisance, even if the bow wasn't quite as deep as it should have been, and seated himself across from me. A servant brought a trencher of food and a carafe of wine.

"In England, with Prince Edward," Gruffydd said.

"That tells me everything and nothing," I said. "I've not spoken with Humphrey de Bohun himself, but his grandson is with us here at Brecon and he confirms Owain's involvement in an attack on me at the forest of Coed y Brenin. What do you say to that?"

Gruffydd turned beet red and sputtered, but didn't reply.

Tudur leaned in. "You didn't think our lord would charge you with this outright? Did you think that he would dance around you, anxious to appease you and your heir?"

Gruffydd's hands clenched and unclenched. Finally he seemed to master himself. He straightened in his chair and came out with the truth. "I have dealt with him, my lord. I assure you that I had no part in his misadventure."

"I didn't think you did," I said. "You've never been a fool. Your son, however, doesn't appear to share your strengths."

"My son," Gruffydd said through gritted teeth, "was led astray by your brother. When Dafydd came to him with a plan to attack you, he felt that he couldn't turn away such a powerful overlord."

I let the silence draw out as I studied Gruffydd. He held my gaze, defiant. Again it was Tudur who spoke. "If you really believe this explanation is a proper justification for his actions, I wonder that you've held onto your lands as long as you have. Would not the proper course for Owain have been to inform Prince Llywelyn—or you at the very least—of Dafydd's plans? Loyalty to the Prince of Wales surely trumps loyalty to a traitorous brother, whether or not he is a prince."

This was the same conversation Meg had just had with Humphrey. I wondered why this appeared to be such a difficult concept for everyone to grasp. Meg told me I was much loved by my people's descendants. But maybe it would be better to be feared by those who lived now.

Goronwy stood behind me, tapping his foot in an uneven staccato. I was tempted to put a hand on his leg to stop him, but refrained. I too was impatient with Gruffydd. I couldn't trust him and I couldn't ignore his son's blatant rebellion. He would have to bend or I couldn't let him leave Brecon.

Gruffydd took a long gulp of wine and set down his cup. He scrubbed his hair with both hands, sending the graying curls sticking up every which way, and then to my relief, capitulated.

"You have my apologies, my lord. I dragged the story from him when he returned to Powys. He claims the plan was entirely

Dafydd's, but I can hardly credit it. It was Owain himself who convinced the Bohun lad to join them; he who paid a village headman to empty his village; he who aided Dafydd in his kidnapping of your woman. When and if Owain finds himself under my roof again, be sure that I will keep him on a tight rein. I will also send a report to Prince Edward of his deeds. He will be no more pleased at Owain's activities than you are."

I wasn't too sure of that but let it go. I had what I wanted from Gruffydd, for now.

* * * * *

We were nearly into April before a man shouted from the top of the battlements that the Hereford delegation was coming, the elder Humphrey de Bohun at its head, as evidenced by his personal shield—six red lions *en passant* on a gold background.

Humphrey de Bohun was a lion of a man himself, with a mane of white hair and beard, in the fashion commonly worn among the English.

"My lord Prince," Bohun came to a halt in front of me, back straight, jaw firm, and tipped forward in a slight bow, an exact replica of Gruffydd's posture a week earlier. Except in his case, the Bohuns *had* owned Brecon. Clare had taken it from him early in the Baron's War, and then I took it from Clare. The Bohuns and I had been allies then, though our alliance hadn't gone so far as to inspire me to give the castle back to them.

"Lord Bohun," I said.

I seated him on my right hand and had Goronwy on my left. Meg sat demurely with Anna at the head of the closest side table. I was sure her ears were as wide-open as they could be. Humphrey entered the room a moment later and made a bee-line for his grandfather, who didn't stand to greet him.

"Find yourself a seat, boy," Bohun said. "I'll speak with you later." His words pulled Humphrey up short, though he was becoming quite good at the stone-faced look.

"Yes, sir." He turned to seat himself across from Meg. I didn't say anything. Among the English, a man could be twenty-one before he came into his inheritance. It was ridiculous to leave it so late, with half a man's life gone already. Perhaps that was this younger Humphrey's problem: his grandfather still treated him as a child when he had the mind to be a man. He resented that treatment and his anger was manifested in foolish behavior.

"You'll release him to me, then," Bohun said between bites of chicken. He tossed an empty bone into the dish set in front of us and speared an onion with his belt knife.

"Yes," I said. "I told you I would."

"And no hard feelings, eh?"

"I wouldn't say that," I said. "I lost good men because three noble boys—and I don't care that Owain and Dafydd are nearly thirty—had men-at-arms to command and thought to end my life for a lark."

"Huh." Bohun grunted. "If a Bohun seeks your death from now on, it will be on a field of battle, not an ambush."

"Before we captured your grandson, I would have thought that the case anyway," I said.

Bohun rumbled deep in his chest and his eyes narrowed at Humphrey who didn't notice as he was conversing with Meg. "I hear you have a new woman."

I paused, a wine goblet half-way to my lips. "Yes. I would hardly have thought such news would invite comment."

"Everything you do invites comment, especially when it's out of the ordinary. I hear she warned you of the ambush too, though I confess, rumors that she is a witch are surely grossly exaggerated, if that is the woman there with the child on her lap."

"That is she. What of Lacey?" Meg and Anna were none of Bohun's business.

"No word," Bohun said. "I sent out riders, but he has disappeared."

"And Edward?"

"Ah." Bohun looked squarely at me for the first time. "We come to the meat of it. You know he intends a Crusade?"

"Yes."

"He cannot go until he accumulates funds he does not yet have," Bohun said.

"Always the plight of princes."

"And earls." Bohun snorted. "Be that as it may, he seeks the security of his father's kingdom while he is away; I believe he sees you as a threat to that."

"His father still lives," I said.

"A figurehead," Bohun said. "You know that. We all face the ambitions of the younger generation, and I am one generation older than you. Any man who has seen his son die for an ideal has faced his own mortality. My grandson must grow stronger before I die. It is now, with Edward on the verge of leaving for the Holy Land, that I must take those steps that will secure my lands for him."

"Surely Edward wouldn't deny your grandson his inheritance?" I said. "He forgave you for fighting on the losing side."

"It was my son at Evesham, not me," Bohun said. "I paid the fines. On top of which, I am Edward's godfather and he knows me well. He'd prefer that every one of the barons of the Marche were at each other's throats, as that will mean they won't be at his or his father's while he's away. For him to refuse me my lands would only bring instability to the region in his absence. He knows that. Edward is a calculating bastard if there ever was one."

"You speak frankly," I said. "I'm surprised."

"You expected me to pay you for my grandson in gold?"

"No," I said. "You are correct in thinking it was information I wanted. Do you have more to tell me?"

"I can speak to you of Clare," Bohun said, "and Mortimer."

Christ! "The both of them chafe at me like pebbles in my shoe," I said. "News of Clare's building plans is what brought me south in the first place, but it is Roger Mortimer who's been much in my thoughts of late."

"You don't have to worry about Clare as yet." Bohun waved his hand dismissively. "He's not done more than dropped a few stones on the ground so far. No, his plans are to bring you south and bring you down."

"How?"

"That I don't know. Gilbert de Clare was my ward four years ago when he inherited his lands, and fought alongside my son until he betrayed us for Edward. Does Edward trust him? I don't think he trusts anyone. Does Mortimer? I only know that you have done something to garner Mortimer's ire and rumor has it that he hates you with an inspired passion."

I put down my cup to study Bohun who chewed avidly on a piece of parsley. "I supported Montfort against the King," I said. "Mortimer was the king's staunchest ally through loss and triumph. He carries a grudge against me three years on, but not against you?"

"You're the easier target," Bohun said. "And you have no heir to your lands."

"Do you suppose they think to use Clare as their weapon?"

"That is exactly what I think," Bohun said. "And Clare is young enough still to seek to please them as proof of his allegiance."

"And despite *your* allegiance to the English crown, you can't abide Clare."

"The whoreson burned Montfort's boats and the bridge across the Severn at Gloucester! I'm surrounded by men whose honor is a thin sheen through which they manipulate the world, easily swept aside at the first hint that it might serve them better to be without it!"

"I have always been constant," I said. "I've only bowed to necessity."

"Well, there is that. I can only say the same."

We both lifted our glasses, thinking of all the times we'd had to bend our knees, our necks, and the honor we had left, despite Meg's staunch admiration, to an English king or to necessity in order to hold onto our lands, lands we only held at the king's pleasure. I, at least, had Wales and the Welsh people as a patrimony. Bohun's right to his lands was more ephemeral. His family had carved their estates out of lands that had once belonged to others and could again. He'd lost his son at Evesham. Even if Humphrey didn't realize it today, he was Bohun's most precious possession.

*****

"We must see now, to Clare," I said to Meg. We stood on the battlements above the gate and watched the Bohuns exit through the northern castle gate and follow the road east to England. They rode side by side at the head of Bohun's men. The elder Bohun hadn't castigated his grandson in public, but I wouldn't have wanted to be in Humphrey's shoes when his grandfather admonished him in private. *That* would be a tongue lashing to remember.

The scouts I'd sent south had returned an hour earlier. "It is as you suspected, my lord," Bevyn had reported. He was the youngest of the group but the other men respected his intelligence and ability and allowed him to speak for them all. "A few stakes in the ground are all that Clare has placed. However, of more significance are the preparation for defensive dams and moats."

"We spoke with people in a village nearby," Rhodri continued. "They claim it will be the largest castle ever built—even in the whole of England!"

"So the Red Earl has plans, does he?" I said. "We'll see about that."

"King Henry will support you, surely," Goronwy had said. "It's your land."

Tudur snorted. "Not likely. The King won't be pleased to know that Clare is playing fast and loose with our treaty, within only a few months of its confirmation, but within the Marche, the King has tied his own hands long since."

"Marcher lords are allowed to wage war on one another without royal interference," Goronwy said. "But Prince Llywelyn is not included in that understanding."

"So *we* say," said Tudur. "Clare doesn't seem to be paying attention."

"Then I will make him," I said.

Even as I dictated the letter to King Henry objecting to Clare's actions, the Earl of Hereford's parting words stayed with me, hovering in the back of my mind like the warning they were: "You have a warrior at your threshold in Mortimer. Don't allow the Red Earl to distract you such that you lose this castle. It is *my* castle, remember, and I expect it back in good condition, when you're done with it."

And that night, I lay awake thinking of battle, unable to sleep, even as I wrapped my arms around Meg to hold off the coming challenge:

May twenty-second, in the year of our Lord, twelve hundred and sixty-six. I pace across the great hall of my castle at Brecon. Although it belonged originally to the Bohuns, I took it from Clare in 1265. Mortimer thought it should have been his. He cannot forgive me.

The men are waiting; they've been waiting for days as we've watched the progress of Mortimer and his men across the plains, up and down the ridges and valleys that lead to Brecon. They crossed into Wales at the great Dyke, and I wish every day of my life that it still stood as it once did, a barrier between my people and those who seek to conquer us.

I mount Glewdra and she tosses her head in expectation. Battles don't scare her. She's fought in many, carrying me through all of them with a surety that makes her one of my staunchest friends. I pat her side.

"Another chance, cariad."

She whinnies and trots forward, head up and proud, for she knows that it is her place to ride at the head of any host of men. I'm joined by Goronwy and Hywel.

We cross the drawbridge and take the main road out of Brecon. Once past the village, however, we head across the fields, making for the heights above Felinfach, the last major ford before Mortimer can reach us.

"You are prepared," I say to Goronwy, not as a question, but a statement of fact.

"Yes, my lord," he says. "They will crowd the ford. It is the best place to hit them, and the farthest they will reach into Wales, now and perhaps forever."

"You are that confident?"

"Do you remember Cymarau?"

"I could never forget such a victory," I say.

"It will be like that," Goronwy says.

I nod, sure in his assurance, and turn my attention to the road ahead and the task that lies before us. We will turn Mortimer back, and he will not raise another army for many a year.

The sun rises over our heads as we climb the ridge, a hundred feet above the ford, but sloping down to it over less than a quarter mile. Goronwy has spent some time thinking about his plan of attack and has prepared the ground accordingly. Trees blocking our view of the river have been cut down and hauled away, and now the archers crouch behind a stone wall he built over the course of three days, a perfect one hundred yards from the ford. At Goronwy's signal, they will stand and fire.

As horseman, we wait just inside the stand of trees at the top of the ridge. Mortimer doesn't know we're here, hasn't realized that our scouts have been following his progress throughout the last three days. Mortimer's stronghold at Wigmore Castle in Herfordshire is not far away, but this is a foreign land and he doesn't know the terrain.

I suspect, though I do not know, that Mortimer's attempt at Brecon is actually an attack on Clare, whom he despises, even as he welcomes him back into the royal fold. King Henry gave Brecon to Clare, if he could take it from me, that is. As he cannot, Mortimer sees it as fair game.

A mistake.

"They're coming, my lord! They've reached the ford of the Dulas!"

Goronwy's hand rises and then falls, loosing the arrows the archers have been holding. The arrows fly, arcing through the morning light, the sun glinting off their metal heads. They hit, and the carnage begins at the ford. Another flight of arrows flies, and then another. Underneath the cover of the last, Goronwy releases the cavalry. They race forward, screaming to the heavens, a lance headed straight for the heart of Mortimer's men.

For once, Goronwy has convinced me to stand with the rear guard, to watch as a sentinel on the hill.

Under normal circumstances, it is my role to lead my men, but today, there is something he wants me to see.

And there it is. On the left flank of Mortimer's army is the man himself. He has led a host of men and horses away from the ford and is attempting to cross at a more southerly point. Yet, the horses flounder in the current. I could have told them that the Dulas runs deep there. Any Welshman could have. But he is of the Marche, and has received some bad advice.

With a shout, I urge the men with me into a gallop. We race down the slope to the point where Mortimer will come across, if he makes it. He sees us coming and even from this distance I see him shake his head. Almost at the same moment, another flight of arrows passes over our heads and slams into the hapless riders on the opposite bank. The archers have moved east so as to not hit us, and have found better ground from which to kill.

Mortimer glances left then right. He shouts at me words I can't hear properly over the rush of the water and the screams of dying men and horses. He brandishes his sword, but then turns his horse's head and retreats up the bank. His men follow.

Soon the defeat becomes a rout. Mortimer's army is decimated; defeated so entirely that only a handful of knights and men-at-arms are able to flee to the woods on the other side of the Dulas.

The archers fire at their backs and more men go down. The horsemen outpace the foot soldiers, who are racing away, but still not fast enough because Goronwy gives the order for our cavalry to cross the river after them. They splash through the river shoulder to shoulder and give chase, running Mortimer's men down from behind, one by one. In the final count, Mortimer loses a hundred and fifty foot and twenty horse at the ford of Felinfach. We lose less than a tenth of that.

Death is everywhere, but yet again, has not come for me.

17

Meg

I slipped out of bed and pulled the extra blanket that lay at its foot around my shoulders, careful not to wake Llywelyn. For the third night in a row I was having trouble sleeping. Now, here it was at nearly dawn and I'd slept no more than a few hours. I knew why, knew not sleeping wasn't going to help me deal with what I was facing. But telling myself over and over to relax was helping no more this night than it had the one before.

I hopped onto the window seat the Bohuns had so generously built under the only window in the castle of any size at all, and pulled the curtain half-way across to hide the light from the open shutter.

Brecon was a fortress, built on a rise at the confluence of the Usk and Honddu Rivers. The Honddu River rushed by in the moonlight thirty feet below my feet. The view was so spectacular I imagined I could see London from where I sat, though mountains rose between us and the plains of England. The water in the river was high from yesterday's heavy rain, muddy and full of debris washing in from the banks and tributaries. The snow had long since melted away and the spring rains had come.

I glanced at the curtain that separated our room from the one adjacent, but no noise came from behind it. Although reluctant, I'd bowed to the inevitable pressure and moved Anna out of our room to one where she now slept with her nanny.

After more than two months in Wales, I didn't know if she even remembered what home had been like. I imagined that if she were to see it again, it would come back to her, but she'd adapted well to the day-to-day life of the castle. I didn't know how I felt about that. She would grow up as a thirteenth century woman, and despite what Llywelyn had said about not seeing much difference between how people were on the inside, it worried me. At least I would ensure she could read, write, and do math. But she wasn't ever going to understand about dinosaurs.

The rushing water tempted me to dangle my feet as if sitting on a dock, but I resisted. Even I could see that it wasn't seemly behavior for the companion to the Prince of Wales, even when no one else was looking.

And then someone was looking.

Llywelyn slipped his arm around my waist, lifting me slightly so he could slide in behind me, his back to the wooden wall that formed the box of the window seat, and one leg braced against the stone of the window frame. I rested against his chest,.

"Not sleeping again?" He shoved the curtain wide to let more light from the bright moon into the room and then pulled me closer.

I bent my knees and pulled my nightgown over them so it formed a tent over my legs and covered my feet. "What do you mean, again?"

"Tonight, last night, the one before. Did you think I wouldn't notice you were gone when I rolled over?"

"You seemed to be sleeping deeply."

"My hope was that you would share your concerns with me, and then we could both sleep, but clearly that hasn't happened."

"Oh, Llywelyn," I said. "I—"

A *snick* came from the door to the room as the latch lifted. We froze and watched, unmoving, as a crack appeared between the frame and the door. A hand clenched the edge of the door, silently opening it further to give room to an object that pointed at the bed.

A crossbow!

My breath caught in my throat. The sound I made was slight, but carried loudly enough in the silent room for the assassin to swing the point of his arrow from the bed, where he thought we'd be, to the window seat.

He hesitated, perhaps unbelieving, and then shot—but Llywelyn had already moved. Between one breath and the next, he pulled me with him into a dive out the window, headfirst towards the Honddu River. Somehow, he was able to turn us in a complete flip so we hit the water with a mighty splash, feet first, before I even had a chance to catch my breath.

Cold! The shock forced all the air from my lungs and caused Llywelyn to release me. Our combined weight had pulled us well under and I struggled to the surface, fighting for air and against the current that pulled us downstream, away from the castle. I bobbed to the surface.

"Meg!"

"Here!" I said. He was five yards from me, moving in a faster current and I spun in a complete circle, my legs working furiously, before I managed to angle myself more towards him. He reached for me and I grasped his fingers, allowing him to pull me to him. I stopped fighting the current and began floating with it, thankful to be alive.

"What is it about water in this country! What in the hell am I doing in a river again?"

Llywelyn sputtered with laughter, understanding my resentment. At least it wasn't February and the water wasn't *quite* as cold as before.

We followed the Honddu under the bridge that led from the castle to the town, and then for the short distance it ran before reaching the Usk. The water was frighteningly choppy now, as it swung us into the main current of the larger river. Llywelyn tried to stop us at the ford across the Usk, but even his long legs couldn't resist the force of the high water.

We sailed a hundred yards before we passed a rocky outcrop in the river that had created a sandy spit on the western bank. I kicked off for it. My sluggish limbs could barely move and my teeth chattered.

Llywelyn grabbed my arm. "No!"

"Why?" I swung around, uncertain. He got an arm around my waist and we slid past the spit.

"They will look for us there first. There is another place, a half a mile downstream."

"Are you sure?"

"The river curves east," he said. "We'll find safety there."

A log floated by to our left and he grasped it, swinging it in front of us so I could hold it too. Another three minutes, and Llywelyn was able to push us toward the southern bank. The riverbed had widened and grown more shallow as it swung east, and consequently slowed. My feet hit bottom and we stumbled onto a sandy spit on the southern side of the Usk, formed as the river curved. I fell to my knees and crawled out of the water, and then turned onto my back. Llywelyn threw himself onto his stomach, his arms and legs sprawled wide.

"I'm clearly too old for this kind of exercise," he said.

I coughed, choking on the mix of water and laughter. "You're only forty-something, you silly man. You'd better not be too old. We've a long road ahead of us."

"We're only a half a mile from the castle. Admittedly, I don't spend much time walking, but I don't think that distance will task me greatly."

"That's not what I meant." I lay flat on my back, my hand resting on my belly.

Llywelyn rolled onto his side and pushed up on one hand so he could see my face. "What do you mean?"

I turned my head to look at him and didn't speak. Couldn't speak. He must have seen something in my look because his eyes narrowed. "Speak plainly, madam."

"I'm going to have your baby," I said. "That's why I haven't been sleeping."

"What?" Llywelyn loomed over me so he blocked the moonlight. He patted me up and down. "Are you all right? Mary, mother of God! I can't believe I just threw you into the river!"

"I'm fine, Llywelyn. Honest. A little cold water can't hurt the child."

"How late are you?"

"Ten days," I said. "I've never been this late before except pregnant."

"I can't believe it!"

"So you're happy?" I was suddenly a little worried. He *had* to be happy.

Llywelyn laughed. "By all the Saints in the Heavens! I hadn't a hope it would come this soon!" He laughed again and pulled me into his arms. I'd never seen him laugh like this, but it wasn't the same for me.

"I'm scared, Llywelyn," I said.

"You'll be fine. I know it."

"It's just—" I couldn't articulate everything I was feeling: I was afraid of dying in childbirth, of what a sibling would mean to

Anna, of raising a child in the thirteenth century. Not for the first time, I longed to see my mother.

Llywelyn squeezed me more tightly. "If you hadn't been pregnant and stewing about it these last three nights, you wouldn't have been sitting on that window sill. And if you hadn't been sitting there, I wouldn't have gotten out of bed, and we'd both be dead."

"There is that." I wrapped my arms around his neck. "I love you."

"I love you too," he said, "but I think we ought to get moving."

"I don't feel very good," I said, starting to shake.

He checked the location of the moon to gauge the hour. "I'm in a rather telling state of undress, your wet nightgown reveals more than I want another man to see, and it's too cold for us to be outside and wet. We need to find some clothes quickly."

"I can rip my gown," I said. "You can tie the scrap around your waist."

"Good idea," he said.

We scuttled forward into the brush at the edge of the sand bar and I worked at the lower section of my gown, starting at just above my knees. My hands were stiff but Llywelyn held the ends of the gown tight and I found a loose thread and ripped it. Llywelyn wrapped the scrap around his waist and I tied it in a sarong-type knot.

"Very dashing," I said, as he crouched down again behind our bush to check the area for any signs of human activity.

Llywelyn took my hand and began to lead us west through the trees, back towards the castle. It was very dark under the trees, but there was a hint of grayness to the murk that told me dawn was not far off.

"Do you have a plan?" I asked.

"Not much of one," Llywelyn said. "It begins and ends with clothing."

Fortunately, we didn't have to walk more than a hundred yards before we came upon a hut, centered in a patch of dirt scraped bare of vegetation. It stood under a shaft of moonlight that filtered through the trees.

"You or me?" Llywelyn said. We inspected each other. He certainly *looked* better than I did. His shoulder length black hair was thrown back from his face and I loved that he'd not grown that mustache he'd threatened me with. He was tall and muscled; I knew he was laughing at me as I studied him because of the way his eyes were twinkling, even if he wasn't smiling.

"Me," I said. "I'm not threatening. I may look bedraggled, but *you* are completely unacceptable."

Llywelyn smirked at what he viewed as a compliment. "I'll wait here."

Wincing on the stubby grass, rocks, and sticks that poked my feet, I tiptoed across the yard to the hut, took a moment to gather my thoughts, and knocked. A woman opened the door. She was much older than I, with gray hair pulled tight in a bun at the nape of her neck. She wore a dress that was patched, but clean. I was glad to see that the floor of the hut behind her was well-swept and the room ordered.

"Yes," she said, looking me up and down. "What is it?"

"My man and I fell in the river," I said. "Do you have a spare change of clothes we could borrow?"

"Borrow, is it?" she said. "You mean take."

"We would leave you ours in exchange. When we are safe again, we can return your clothing to you."

"Humph," the woman said. "Where's your man?"

"Waiting in the bushes," I said. "He's wearing fewer clothes than I am."

"And that's not much," the woman said. She looked past me and I waved a hand towards where Llywelyn crouched. He stepped out from the trees. The woman sighed. "You might as well come in."

"Thank you," I said.

Llywelyn minced his way across the uneven ground. At his approach, the woman's eyes widened. "My lord!"

"Indeed," Llywelyn said, coming to a halt on her threshold. "Have you seen any English nearby?"

"I haven't, my lord," she said, "but others from the village have spoken of it. Little groups of them, poking their nose in where they don't belong. Coming from the south, they are."

"Is it Clare's men, do you think?" I asked Llywelyn.

"I don't know," he said. "It was a bold move indeed to get past my guards and into our room with a crossbow. We've had traitors up and down Wales apparently, about whom I've been completely unaware."

"That's always the way of it, my lord," the woman said. She'd gone to a box set in a corner of the room and removed a small stack of clothing from it.

"We must get back into the castle," Llywelyn said.

"Anna's there, Llywelyn." I grabbed his arm, the panic rising as it hadn't before, even in the river. "They won't hurt her will they?"

"I'm sure she's fine, Meg," Llywelyn said. "They won't bother with her. She's not my natural child and they know it." He turned back to the woman. "I need another way inside the castle, other than through the front gate. Has the river flooded the undercroft gate, do you know? My engineers have been concerned about the Honddu side of the castle for the past year."

"Not that I've heard," she said. "One of my neighbor boys and my nephew got into it just the other day."

"What undercroft gate?" I said.

"Clare arranged a way to provision the castle from the river, just in case it was ever attacked—by me," Llywelyn said.

"Can we use it?" I said. "I need Anna, Llywelyn. We need to go now."

"I know, *cariad*," he said, drawing me closer. "We're already there."

"I can tell you the way," the woman said. "Straight out the back door and across the clearing is a trail between two matched trees. It leads directly to the gate that guards the Usk. If you follow the river west you'll see the ford, though with the flood, you'll be hard pressed to cross before noon."

"Thank you," Llywelyn said.

We dressed quickly in the clothes she provided, the fabric well worn from use, but not by her. I glanced at the woman out of the corner of my eye, acknowledging the loss she must have suffered to have these clothes to spare. I didn't know that I could ever get used to it.

"The boots are a little tight," Llywelyn said, tugging them on and cursing under his breath. His toes were well scrunched at the tip.

"At least they're well-worn," I said. "The leather is soft. Can you walk?"

Llywelyn gingerly put a foot on the ground and hobbled forward. "Well enough," he said. Llywelyn tugged my hand and I followed him out the door.

18

Llywelyn

A lightness and joy filled me that even the troubles of the day couldn't suppress. The emotion augmented the sharpness of my vision; I couldn't explain it otherwise, either by the brightening day or the clearness of the air.

Meg carries my child!

With effort, I restrained myself from punching the air every time I thought about it and tried to focus on the task at hand.

While we were in the hut, the sky had lightened. Soon the sun would push over the horizon. Early spring flowers poked through the damp ground, and it reminded me again of my incredible luck. *I am alive. And Meg carries my child.*

I checked Meg beside me. She was caught up in the baby too, more so even than I, and I didn't think it had sunk in fully that someone had wanted to kill us. The anger that I'd been keeping in check for the last hour began rising in my throat again and I tamped it down. It would do me no good.

It was the kind of thing my grandfather had cautioned me against, on one of those rare instances when we were alone and he'd a moment to spare for one of his many grandsons: "It is not the actions of a man when he is sober and clear-eyed that are his measure, but when he is pressed hard, his back against a wall. At those times, fear and anger will be his undoing, and it is a rare man who can put aside those feelings and do what must be done. Be one of those men."

Meg trudged beside me through the woods, her hand clasped tightly in mine. "So who betrayed you this time?"

"Hard to say."

"Not Goronwy," she said.

"I trust him with my life," I said. "If he's betrayed me, I could never trust my own judgment again."

"He loves Anna."

"And love for your daughter is a proper test of a man's character?"

"It ought to be one," she said, "though many tyrants through the ages have loved their children and yet despoiled their country. It seems contradictory to me."

"Men are nothing if not contradictory," I said. "That's one of the first things you learn when you begin to lead them. Plenty of people are perfectly capable of holding two entirely opposite opinions at the same time, and arguing vehemently for each in turn."

Meg laughed. "So young, and yet so cynical."

We walked on, our silence drowned out by the rushing of the river. We gazed across it at the castle.

"Now what?" Meg said.

We'd come out of the woods to the south of the castle, but the Usk was still in full flood, so we had no way to cross, except over the bridge to the castle. I studied the battlements and the gate. I couldn't see the other gate from where we stood as it faced east, reached by a bridge across the Honddu. That's the one we'd gone under. This one was even larger and better fortified.

Except today.

The portcullis was up and the drawbridge down. "I don't like this," I said. "Where is everybody? The guards?"

"We look like peasants in these clothes," Meg said. "I can't wait any longer. I have to go in there. Anna's going to wake soon and if I'm not there, she'll cry." She glanced at me and I shrugged. *Into the lion's den.* We ran to the bridge across the Usk, our footsteps thudding across its length. At any second, I expected to hear a shout from within the gatehouse, but no one called to us.

Just past the portcullis, I tugged Meg through a left-hand door into the gatehouse. Then I stopped short, surprising Meg who bumped into me and caught my arm. The two guards who should have been protecting the entrance to the castle sprawled unconscious on the ground. I bent to check the breathing of one of the men while Meg felt for his pulse. She looked at me and nodded. "It's faint, but there."

The other man was alive too.

I slid the first man's sword from its sheath and hefted it. It was hardly my grandfather's sword, but it would do for now. Then I tugged the belt knife out of the spot on the man's waist where he carried it and handed it to Meg. "Here." She was too small to hold a long sword, but in a pinch, a knife might do.

"What's happened to them?" Meg whispered, though there clearly was no need for quiet as anyone else in the guard room was unconscious. "Were they dosed, or poisoned?"

I cast my mind back to the night before. Anna, Meg and I had shared the meal with everyone else.

"You pushed your mead away last night," I said. "Why?"

"Pregnant women shouldn't drink alcohol," Meg said. "It's bad for the baby." She glanced at me. "You didn't drink it either, though. Was that just because of me?"

"The well at Brecon is deep and the water always good," I said. "I wanted a clear head."

"Maybe that's it, then," she said. "That's what they used. But it doesn't matter now. We should get moving."

"This way." I took her hand and with her at my heels, knife and sword out to counter any threat, we poked our heads out of the guard room. *Nothing*. How could there be nothing? Where were my men? Or the assassin and his men, if he had them? "No one's awake."

"We should close the portcullis," Meg said.

The mechanism was designed to release with the push of a lever. I hit it with my boot and it let go, falling to the ground with a rattling crash.

"If anyone awake doesn't know something's up, they do now," I said. Grunting at the effort, Meg helped me push the great double doors closed and dropped the bars across them. "It takes three men to winch the drawbridge closed. We'll leave it as it is for now."

We moved into the bailey, hugging the gray stone wall that fronted the Honddu River, into which we'd fallen. Brecon's great hall was in the bailey, at the base of the motte where a circular keep of last resort and the oldest part of the castle shot up against the sky. The Bohuns had greatly expanded the castle during their reign. The outer wall of the great hall, above which housed the room where we'd slept and Anna still lay, was worked into the curtain wall. This fortification projected out from either side of the hall and formed a complete circle around the motte.

Last night, the great hall had been full of men, the stables full of animals, and the bailey busy with craft workers. Many of the people who worked in the castle lived in the little village outside it, so I wasn't surprised at their absence. With the dawn, however, people should be starting to stir. Now, the silence was eerie, only broken by the sound of our boots scuffling on the rocky ground.

The vast expanse of Brecon before us was daunting. I glanced up the hill at the keep. What might await us there? Most of my men had actually slept in its old hall that had been the center of the castle before Bohun built his new one.

Control what you can; let go of what you can't. It would take too much time to explore all of Brecon on our own, and the continuing silence made me worry that our assassin had resources we didn't yet know about. Where was the spy who'd shot at us waiting? Someone had left the castle open to attack, but for whom?

Meg released my hand and darted toward the second gatehouse that guarded the crossing of the Honddu. She entered the gatehouse before I could catch her and dropped the portcullis with another loud crash. Meg reappeared and had the gall to look contrite. "Sorry. Someone left the castle wide open on purpose."

"Next time, warn me first," I said. "I'm going to keep you on a tighter rein than before."

She made a face at me, but I took her hand again and we cat-walked up the steps to the great hall. As in the gatehouse, the scene that faced us in the hall brought us to a halt. My men had fallen where they sat at the end of dinner. At the time, I'd noticed that the meal had been less raucous than usual, but I'd attributed it to some hard riding during the day.

"Anna," Meg said, and took off toward the staircase. She hiked her skirts and went up them two at a time. I caught her by the time she entered the hallway and we pushed open the door to our room together.

Our bed lay as we'd left it. The window to the right of the bed was still open, but with an arrow lodged at head height in the frame. That pulled me up short, but Meg pulled aside the curtain blocking Anna's room and looked in.

She sighed. "Anna and Maud are asleep. I can see them breathing."

I let out a breath I hadn't realized I was holding, and then spun towards the open window at the echo of pounding hooves. The wall of the castle curved west, away from the river, and I stretched out the window to see around it. A man appeared beneath the castle wall where it abutted the river and ran toward a dozen men on horses who rode towards Brecon from the north.

"Stay here!" I ordered Meg. Without waiting to see if she obeyed me, but thinking that with Anna close she would, I raced out of the room, down the first flight of stairs to the great hall, and then continued down the second flight to the kitchen. Like the rest of the castle, it was deserted, and I hurried across the floor to the pantry and the postern gate.

A curtain separated the kitchen from the pantry but once through it, I braked at the sight of a man standing in front of me. He'd been facing the other way, towards the vaulted undercroft that led to the postern gate. My footsteps had given me away and the man did a double take as he recognized me, and I him. "You!" Lacey said. He reached for his sword but mine was already in my hand.

I ran him through.

I pushed and shoved Lacey's body past the doorway and onto the stairs beyond. With a final kick, I rolled him down it, and then slammed the door to the passage. I dropped the locking bar across the door. Fearing that I didn't have time for this but had to take the time nonetheless, I wrestled one of the big chopping tables from the kitchen, through the pantry, and laid it sideways across the door. If someone had an axe, they could chop through the sturdy oak, but otherwise, they were going to have a tough time getting through it.

I raced back to the great hall and nearly collided with Meg in the doorway. "Where's Anna?"

"With Maud," she said. "She's awake and well. Those men, whoever they are, are milling about in the field to the north. They've discovered that both gates are closed and don't seem to know what to do."

"Their man intended that they'd walk in unhindered. Come with me." I led Meg through the great hall with its unmoving men, across the bailey, and into the armory in the back of the main gatehouse. "Can you shoot a bow?"

"No," she said. "Are you kidding? Those things are so huge I don't know if I can even stretch it six inches."

"It needs to not just be me up there, so I'm going to dress you like a soldier and we can see who this is and what he has to say." I fitted her into a mail shirt and dropped a helmet on her head. It had a hideous-looking feather on the top of it and I hoped whoever was out there would be so distracted by the bizarre presentation that he wouldn't realize my companion was shorter than average—and certainly not Goronwy.

"Maybe there's a box I can stand on," Meg said, tugging a tunic with my colors on it over her head.

"Excellent idea." I grabbed a wooden crate in which arrowheads had been stored and dumped its contents on the ground. "Let's go."

We climbed the circular staircase up to the top of the gatehouse tower, Meg laboring a bit behind me under the unaccustomed weight of the armor. We popped out on the top of the battlements and I put the box on the ground so that Meg could see between the crenellations which were at chest height for me.

I didn't like what lay before us.

"Who is it?" Meg said.

"My cousin, Roger Mortimer," I said. "He's one of the few Marcher lords who remained faithful to the crown throughout the Baron's war. Humphrey de Bohun the elder spoke of him to me just the other day."

"So we've got Bohun, who's gone home; Clare, who's defying you in Senghennydd, and now Mortimer, here in Brecon. I thought the Bohuns had owned Brecon?" Meg said. "Or at the very least, Clare, from whom you took it. Have the Mortimers ever had it?"

"No," I said. "Though Roger appears to be putting in a claim. I defeated his men two years ago before he could reach this far into Wales. The battle became such a rout that I'd heard he's been unable to raise another army."

"It seems he's trying stealth instead."

"Coward."

"And it's his sons who kill you," she said.

"Have a heart, Meg!" I said. "I'm not dead yet."

"No, no! I didn't mean that! You're just taking this so well."

"He can't touch us up here," I said. "No archers."

"What are you going to do?"

"Have a little chat," I said. I lifted my chin and raised my voice. "Cousin! What brings you to Brecon so early in the morning?"

Roger pushed his helmet to the back of his head. "So it is you. I shouldn't be surprised. You always did have the devil's own luck."

"Life is full of surprises," I said. "I live, no thanks to you, it seems."

Roger tsked through his front teeth. "It was you, then, who entered not long ago through the southern gate?"

"You saw us?"

"From a distance," he said. "Apparently, our efforts here were for naught." Roger spun his horse around, effectively ending our conversation. I'd expected more.

He called words to the other men-at-arms who rode with him, words in English that I didn't understand, and pulled his sword from his sheath. He spurred his horse and galloped towards his men. As he approached the lone man standing, the one who'd run out of the passage to greet him, he swung his sword and severed his head from his body. The man hadn't a chance. His body fell and Roger continued on without looking back.

Meg stepped away from the wall, ripped her helmet from her head, and vomited on the stones at her feet.

"*Cariad.*" I wrapped my arms around her waist. "It's all right."

"It isn't." Tears streamed down her face. "How can it be?"

I scooped her up and carried her down the stairs and across the bailey to the hall. As we entered, several of my men stirred. Some had even gotten so far as to stagger onto a bench in order to rest their heads in their forearms on the table. I put Meg in my chair and crouched in front of her. Her face was wet from tears.

"Is this what it's going to be like for our child if we have a son?"

I studied her, not completely sure what she was asking, but knowing at the same time there was only one answer. "Yes."

"I love you, Llywelyn," she said. "I want to have a child with you, but I'm afraid to raise a son here. I don't want him to grow up to be like Roger Mortimer."

"What if he were like me?"

She gazed at me, tears still leaking out of the corner of her eyes. "You are who you are because of a childhood that is not one I would wish on any boy. What you have done—what others have asked of you—is not what I want for my son."

"He will be what God makes him," I said.

Meg shook her head. "He will be what we make him, and what the world makes him. Look at Humphrey de Bohun. He's struggling to find his way in a world in which the rules keep changing and he's not strong enough inside to withstand pressure from men like your brother."

I think I finally understood what she was saying, and had an answer for her. "Our son will be what he needs to be because you will make him that. He will be smart and strong, loving and courageous, because you are all those things. Our son will be the Prince of Wales, and they will call him *Fawr*, just like my grandfather."

"Everyone will ask too much of him." Her tears had dried and her gaze was steady on my face. "And so much of me. They already ask too much of you."

"Only because I am what they need," I said. "I can think of no one I would rather have as the mother of my son. If anyone will be capable of facing down Edward and England at my side, it's our son."

19

Meg

"**M**y tongue feels like the backside of a dog," Goronwy said. I mopped his brow with a warm washcloth. He'd woken, ill as all the men were, and now lay sprawled on his back on one of the benches in the hall. He'd vomited when he'd tried to lift his head earlier, and both of us were loathe for him to try again.

"I believe it was the mead," Llywelyn said.

"I did not over-drink last night!" Goronwy said, conscious enough now to work up the energy to thwart any aspersions on his character.

"I didn't say you did," Llywelyn said. "The healer believes it was poppy juice, which can cause deep sleep—sometimes too deep, but thankfully not in this case."

"By the Saints! Who's the witch who poisoned us?" he said.

"No witch, Goronwy," Llywelyn said. "Merely a man who worked for Roger Mortimer against me. He has paid for his mistakes with his life."

"You caught him, my lord?" Goronwy said. "Do we know him?"

"Mortimer removed his head from his body to show his displeasure at the outcome of the plot," Llywelyn said.

"The whole thing wasn't very well planned anyway," I said. "Why did the man keep the gates open, when Roger Mortimer rode in from the north? He couldn't even get into the castle from the north because both the towers are built to block access to the gatehouses from any direction but the drawbridges."

"He could, actually," said Llywelyn. "The ford of Rhyd Bernard is just upstream of the confluence of the Usk and Honddu. He didn't think he needed it, though."

"Because he had the gate in the undercroft."

"Well, yes, but was he going to lead those horses through there one by one?" Llywelyn said.

"Okay, you're right," I said. "I was surprised at all those stairs for horses to navigate at Castell y Bere, but here—were they going to get up from the kitchen to the hall?"

"That's the point, of course," Goronwy said. "The stairs leading down to the postern gate at Castell y Bere are behind the stables as an added protection in case someone decides to enter that way. I confess, I never thought of putting the door in the kitchen."

"Anyway," Llywelyn said, "Mortimer said that his scouts saw Meg and me enter through the southern gate. They may have been close behind us when we went in, but as soon as we closed the portcullis, were forced to ride west to the nearest ford across the Usk."

"A long way as it's in flood," Goronwy said.

"That they rode around is the reason we had enough time to do what we did," Llywelyn said. "Luck, as Roger said."

"Luck serves those who are best prepared, my lord," Goronwy said. Llywelyn and I exchanged a look. Llywelyn settled himself on the bench at Goronwy's feet and Goronwy lay back, his hand across his eyes. "It isn't as if it hasn't worked before."

"Taking a castle by stealth, you mean," Llywelyn said.

"You mean like the Trojan horse?" I asked.

Llywelyn smiled, his eyes alight. "You've read Homer?"

"Not in the original, but yes."

"But you know the story," he said, "how the Greeks built a giant horse to hold their men. The Trojans, thinking the offering a gift to their gods, brought it inside their city."

"They had to tear down their own gates to do it, I believe," Goronwy said. "Certainly a lesson to us all."

I touched Llywelyn's arm and spoke in a low voice. "They found the city. Six hundred years from now they uncovered the walls and the gold—much as Homer described."

Goronwy and Llywelyn gaped at me.

"Sorry," I said.

Llywelyn took in a deep breath. "Don't be sorry, Meg. It's disorienting to have you speak thus. At times, I don't know what's real and what's not."

"I know what's real," Goronwy said, "and it has to do with a man trying to assassinate you. It's convenient for Mortimer, isn't it, that the conspirators are all dead?"

"Mortimer knew what he was doing," Llywelyn said. "What else does he have in store for us?"

"You really think there was only the one?"

"Two," Llywelyn said. "Lacey's body is in the kitchen. He must have gone north to Wigmore Castle to meet Mortimer, and then returned with a companion to implement their plot. I killed Lacey before I blocked the door to the passage."

"Oh." I looked away, unable to ask him how he felt about that—how he could take a life and then shrug it off—or appear to shrug it off. Was that what he was going to teach our son?

Goronwy read my thoughts. "You think it doesn't bother him, Meg? You've never heard him talking in his sleep, words you might not understand? Shouting sometimes, even?"

"Goronwy," Llywelyn said, a warning in his voice.

I kept my eyes on Goronwy. "I've heard him."

Goronwy nodded. "Don't let the bluff talk and the bravado fool you. If you think that our prince will not relive the moment he killed Lacey, or forget the light fading from his eyes, then you don't know him, or any of us. We live with it every day. Too many men allow the drink to take them rather than admit how much they care; and it's then that they cease to be Welshmen and become something less than human, which is of no use to me, in battle or otherwise."

"Yes, Goronwy." He was right. I'd chafed at Llywelyn earlier about the fate of our son, but I should have known better who Llywelyn was. I *had* heard him in the night.

I'd also seen the young men, pale and stammering after the skirmish at the Gap, and seen the vomit mixed with blood on the road. What scared me was how human they all still seemed, even though their daily lives were full of what no man should have to bear—and what he couldn't bear and remain the person he was before the killing. That's what I feared for my son, and didn't know how to deal with, despite Llywelyn's reassurance.

I'd had a friend who'd joined the National Guard in college and was sent to Kuwait during the Gulf War. His tank was one of the first to cross into Kuwait City. Seven hundred years later, men talked about war in the same way men did here: in public, bravado and beer; in private, hollowness in their voices and vacancy in their eyes when the emotion they held tight inside their chests threatened to overwhelm them.

Too often in the twentieth century, we thought of war as not unlike playing a video game. Killing was mostly from a distance, with our bombs and our long-range mortars. But not my friend. His tank had killed hundreds of men, he said, and there were nights he lay awake, reliving the deaths of every single one of them. *Just like Llywelyn.*

Goronwy was still looking at me and I met his gaze. He nodded. "If you really are who you say you are, Meg, I can't imagine what your world must be like."

"I almost can't either, anymore," I said.

"What else might be in store for us?" he asked. "Can you tell me?"

"I don't know of any coming battles. Not for a long while, but I've been wrong before."

"That history of yours, Meg," Goronwy said, fingering his lip. "I'm not sure that very much of it is right."

"Quite honestly, I don't either," I said.

"Are you sure about what happens at Cilmeri?"

"Yes," I said. "That I'm sure of."

Then Llywelyn put a hand on Goronwy's shoulder. "By the way, Meg and I have some good news, my friend."

"Do you now?" Goronwy looked from Llywelyn to me. A grin had split Llywelyn's face and he punched the air. I tried hard not to smile, but I couldn't keep it suppressed in the face of Llywelyn's joy.

"Really? Do you mean . . . a baby?"

"Yes!" Llywelyn clapped a hand on Goronwy's shoulder.

It was a bit different from Trev's reaction when I'd told him I was pregnant with Anna. He'd been mad at first—understandable in retrospect, given how young we both were, me especially at not even eighteen. We'd gone for a walk in a park—the best way I could see to tell him—and he'd driven off without me after I told him. I'd walked home, crying. I'd already told Mom, and when I'd informed her of Trev's reaction, her face had taken on a calm expression, instead of anger.

"Well then," she'd said. "We're on our own."

But then Trev had called and apologized and I'd forgiven him. Mom said that if someone had told her what he'd become after Anna was born, she wouldn't have been surprised. But we hadn't known, either of us.

Llywelyn, however, was having a hard time containing himself. "We aren't going to tell anyone else, not for a while, not until it becomes obvious," he said, bouncing up and down on his toes. The two men grinned at each other and I wouldn't have been surprised if their heads had come off and floated around in the great hall all by themselves.

"Your brother won't be happy," Goronwy said.

"Ha!" Llywelyn said. "You have the right of it!

"I hate to rain on your parade," I said, "but it's going to be an impossible secret to keep. Do you imagine Maud doesn't know already? Or the maidservant? Everyone within a hundred mile radius of Brecon is counting the days until they're sure I'm late."

"At least there won't be any questions about paternity," Goronwy added, "not with as close as you've kept her."

I narrowed my eyes at him for speaking of it so openly. *Men.*

*****

We were half-way through May when King Henry of England responded to Llywelyn's letter in which he requested that either King Henry intervene in the dispute with Clare, or he allow Llywelyn to go in himself. Henry's response was one of placation and equivocation. Llywelyn read me the letter, and then mocked it.

"*Oh me, oh my! What's to be done with that Clare fellow?* The man writes as if he didn't rule the most powerful kingdom on earth!" Llywelyn said. "It's his fault this is happening in the first place, since he was the one who told Clare during the Baron's War that he could keep whatever lands he took from me. It set a bad precedent."

Llywelyn swung around to me as I sat on a cushion on the window seat in his office. I set down the guitar I'd been playing, trying to work out the melody for one of the Welsh ballads, and paid attention.

"The King has always been weak. Such was the complaint of the barons in the first place," said Tudur, who'd brought Llywelyn the letter.

"And Clare's letter?" I said.

"Now there's a piece of subtlety," Tudur said. With my pregnancy, he'd softened towards me somewhat, but didn't trust me.

Llywelyn picked up Clare's letter and waved it at me.

"I don't understand," I said, peering at the paper. Clare hadn't written anything on it.

"It is of the finest parchment," Llywelyn said, "but it says that he doesn't care about diplomacy; he's not even going to bother with appeasement or carefully crafted lies. The page is *blank*."

"He's saying," Goronwy said, "that he doesn't care to talk to us. He's going to continue with his building project and the devil take us, damn that whoreson to hell."

"Goronwy," Llywelyn said.

"It's okay," I said. "I've heard it before."

"When do we move?" Goronwy said.

"I'd like to be in Senghennydd by mid-June," Llywelyn said. "No foot soldier is going to want to leave his planted fields or herd animals, but I can't allow the work at Caerphilly to continue without a show of force."

"I'll send out the word," Goronwy said. "It's going to be a long summer."

* * * * *

So Llywelyn left Brecon with an army. For the first time in my months in Wales, I was alone, with just Anna. At first, I didn't know what to make of myself. There seemed everything and nothing to do. Anna and I could entertain ourselves well, and a certain part of every afternoon required a nap for both of us, but the absence of Llywelyn in my bed left me with an ache in my heart I couldn't assuage. More than one evening, I found myself sobbing after I put Anna to bed, sure I would never see Llywelyn again and I would be forever lost in the thirteenth century.

Anna, at least, was a delight. She would be three years old in August and time was passing more quickly than I could have imagined. We played in the kitchen garden, walked along the river, and tried not to get underfoot. Because Llywelyn and I weren't officially married, I was not the mistress of the castle—that role belonged to Tudur and a man named Madoc who ran things when Llywelyn was somewhere else. That left me at loose ends, with no real tasks.

The castle was also on the edge of a war zone, so few women and families lived there, as at Castell y Bere. The good part of that was I didn't have to spend time in the women's solar, sewing. The bad part was there wasn't anyone to talk to. Not that I had anything in common with thirteenth century women anyway.

Well, that wasn't entirely true. I was pregnant, and that fact alone was enough to prompt comment from everyone at every turn. I found it strange to *be* pregnant, and yet have no ultrasounds, no blood work, no monthly visits to the doctor. I just lived as I had before, but with a growing life inside me.

What made me the most uncomfortable was the idea of having the child without a doctor handy. Anna's had been a natural birth in a birthing center with no drugs, but the hospital had been only seconds away and I'd felt safe. Here, it was up to me to make sure everyone washed their hands and boiled whatever instruments they might want to use. I'd talked to the midwife, Alys, already. She'd raised her eyebrows at what I'd said, but not disagreed. Carrying the future Prince of Wales had it uses, after all.

A c-section, though, was not going to be possible. Whenever I thought of it my mind shied away. I'd brought it up with Llywelyn, though, before he left.

"I'm scared," I said, flatly. "Scared for you, right now, scared for me later."

We lay in bed together and he'd pulled me to him and tucked me under his chin. "I'm scared too, not so much for me. This adventure with Clare isn't without peril, but not of great concern to me. But you . . ." he stopped.

"The birth with Anna went well. I've no reason to think I'll have a problem, and yet . . ." I stopped too, as afraid to articulate our fears as he was.

"You're afraid you'll lose the baby," he said, his voice barely above a whisper. "You're afraid you'll die and leave me and Anna alone."

"Yes," I said, releasing a breath. "It isn't so much dying itself that worries me, though I surely don't want to. I don't want her and you to have to go on living without me. I've left too much undone."

"Every man feels that way," he said. "When I raise my sword and order my men to charge, my last coherent thought before the fire of battle overtakes me will be of you, and what I lose if either of us doesn't survive the year."

"And as always, in your case especially, what Wales loses," I said.

"Yes. Always that." He paused. "The priests tell us that we should pray for the Will of God. That's hard to do, when so often what comes out is, 'Please Lord, I need to live.'"

*****

As my pregnancy became more obvious, which it did far sooner than when I was pregnant with Anna, I received more and more attention for it. On one hand, I was protected at every moment, most especially when I left the castle, which only happened when Anna and I walked across the drawbridge into the town for the weekly fair. On the other hand, every person I passed wanted to touch my belly (for luck it seemed) since I was carrying a child that the Prince—and all of Wales—never thought they'd see.

Llywelyn and his army had been gone two weeks and should have reached his lands in Senghennydd, when Dafydd appeared on the doorstep. He arrived just as the evening meal was finishing, striding up the hall as if he owned it.

"My lady," he said, bowing. He straightened, his eyes blatantly traveling from my face, to my breasts, to my not quite protruding belly.

From his place beside me, Tudur leaned toward him over the table. Llywelyn's chair, on my right, was empty.

"Dafydd," he said, not according him any title, least of all 'prince'. "Why are you here?"

Tudur and I still weren't getting along that well, but I'd never been happier to have him by my side. From his tone, he at least preferred me to Dafydd. I might be a witch or a spy who'd captivated his Prince, but Dafydd was a traitor and a killer, and not to be tolerated.

"I've come to throw my full support behind my brother," he said. "We seek shelter for the night, and then we'll be off south."

Tudur leaned back in his chair and gestured toward a seat to the left of him at the high table. "Of course. Sit yourself. We would have news from the north."

Dafydd signaled to his captain, who'd waited in the doorway of the hall for approval. Within minutes, Dafydd's men began finding seats next to the twenty or so men that were all that was left of the Brecon garrison. Madoc exchanged glances with two of his men and they got to their feet, ostensibly to offer their seats to another, but I didn't think that was it.

It looked like they were quartering the room with their eyes, determining sight lines and defensible positions. They ended up in opposing corners of the hall. Madoc leaned casually against the wall to the left of the fireplace. Another man stood by the great front doors, and the third propped his shoulder near the spiral stair up to our apartments, his eyes only half on the game of dice being played by the men closest to him.

"I don't like this," I said, keeping my voice low.

"Nor I," Tudur said. "We're vulnerable and outnumbered, and having Dafydd and his men here is like inviting a wolf to dinner."

"Surely his men are loyal to Llywelyn?"

Tudur gave me a pitying look. "Who pays them?" Then he answered his own question. "Prince Dafydd. They will do his bidding, just as did the men who attacked our lord at Coedwig Gap."

I realized how insensitive I'd been to one of the sources of Tudur's animosity towards Dafydd—it was Dafydd who'd indirectly caused Geraint's death. *How could I have forgotten that?* I put a hand on his arm. "I'm sorry."

Tudur nodded, his eyes watchful. Dafydd took his seat and helped himself to the remains of the meal. Tudur signaled to a servant, who cleared our places and brought several fresher dishes for Dafydd.

"You look well, my lady," Dafydd said. "Certainly no worse for having gone for a swim in the best waters Wales has to offer."

I stared at him, shocked that he would bring up his attempt to abduct me and kill his brother—and brazen out his criminal behavior. I leaned forward so I could see past Tudur to answer him, but Tudur put his hand on my arm to shush me. I sat back, not knowing what else to do. I wanted to berate him, but was afraid of him too, and afraid to make things worse or say something that Llywelyn wouldn't want. Tudur must have felt the same thing because we sat together in silence.

As it grew longer, Dafydd's amusement became palpable. "I hold the best interests of Wales always in my heart," he said.

Tudur couldn't hold back a snort and I couldn't hold my tongue. "Dafydd, dear," I said, trying for a sickening sweetness that he couldn't mistake, "you certainly have an odd way of showing it."

"Oh, that," he said, waving a hand dismissively. "All in fun. You made it clear at Criccieth that you belonged to Llywelyn. I was merely having a joke with him, like we did when we were boys. It was an amusing game, that's all."

"You know what they say about men and jests." I stood to leave, unable to sit one second longer at the same table with him.

"What do they say?" Dafydd said, as I hoped he would.

"Jests are the last recourse of a man with a small dick." Tudur was in the middle of taking a swallow of wine, which he proceeded to spew onto the table in front of him. I patted him on the back. "If you'll excuse me." I walked away, shaking so badly by now that I was sure they could see it.

Tudur followed right on my heels.

"My lady!" He wiped his face with a handkerchief as we rounded the corner into the stairwell. "I haven't laughed so hard in a long time. Well done."

"I had to do it," I said. "I don't want to rile him, but I hate that self-satisfied smirk he always wears."

"Our lord has expressed a similar sentiment. My concern now is that you have angered and humiliated him in front of others." He glanced back at the high table, and then raked his eyes around the hall. "Hywel is worried too. Our men ceased to drink the moment Dafydd and his men entered the hall, and none will sleep tonight." Tudur took my elbow and escorted me to my room.

"Bar the door and don't open it until you see Dafydd's banners, riding away from us south."

"I will," I said. "And thank you. I trust that even if you don't like me, you seek to serve Llywelyn."

Tudur's gaze was measuring. "I distrust everyone. In truth, you less than most." And with that, he turned on his heel and disappeared down the stairs.

Well. That was unexpected. But Tudur was right. What I'd said was funny, but not smart.

20

Llywelyn

The pungent smoke from the campfire spiraled upward with that peculiar tang that filled the air only before a battle. I didn't know why, but when we traveled in times of peace, as we had from Criccieth to Brecon, the scent was never quite the same. I breathed it in, taking it for what it was—a sign that war was at hand and I would have to face it, yet again.

"Your brother, Dafydd, arrives."

"The foolish bastard dares show his face here?" Hywel said, incredulity evident in his face as well as his voice.

"Thanks to King Henry, we appear to be stuck with him," Goronwy said.

Dafydd meandered through the camp, raising a hand in greeting to one man and then another. I met Goronwy's eyes and he nodded. I didn't have to tell him what I was thinking: *Make a note, Goronwy, of those to whom he speaks. It may serve us well to know who among my men he views as allies.*

"I have so many enemies, I can hardly keep track," I said. "A reduction by one, even temporarily, is a blessing."

By the time Dafydd reached us, I'd tamed my expression. The grimace was gone. To know that I was angry would only serve as ammunition against me later. Better to swallow my pride and temper, and treat him as if I was glad to see him.

Dafydd dismounted and bowed, scrupulous in his obeisance. "My lord brother," he said. "I bring you letters from both Tudur and Meg."

I took the letters, glad to see them, though the thought of Dafydd in the same room as Meg brought the taste of acid to my mouth. I would not want her here; would never want to risk her, but it stuck in my craw that my absence left her vulnerable to my brother. "Thank you." I unclenched my jaw to let the words through.

"Your woman is in blooming health," Dafydd added. "But she has quite a mouth on her. I wouldn't want her in my bed."

"That's good to hear," I said, "since she's in mine."

I knew if I said anything more, I would have reproached him with the events of the winter, and now was not the time. The men were preparing for battle and it would do me no good to divide them before we started.

Goronwy came to my rescue. "How many men have you brought?"

"Thirty horse," Dafydd said. "I know you have a plan. What is it?" In an instant, Dafydd slipped into his on-again-off-again role as counselor and confidant. Instead of back-handing him across the face, I replied in the same tone.

"Gilbert de Clare builds. He laid the foundation stone on the 11th of April. He has dozens of craft workers. He has masons, ditch diggers, and camp followers. They're building him the finest castle in the realm."

"And what are you going to do about it?" Dafydd said.

"I'm going to burn it to the ground," I said. "I was going to wait until there was a little more to burn, but Goronwy convinced me we must attack immediately, before Clare gets wind of the size of our force."

"Surely he must know you're here."

"He has few soldiers stationed in this region, surprisingly. I've had scouts make a fifteen mile circuit around Caerphilly. He has no standing army. His knights are spread thin across the whole of his lands. My fifty horse, plus your thirty, and our two hundred foot should carry the day."

"If he's not gotten very far in the building, it won't take long," Dafydd said. "One night. But then, he can rebuild it in a day too."

I shook my head. "I have no intention of giving him that chance. I will strengthen the garrisons at my castles in the region and prevent him from moving into the area again."

"When is this to begin?"

"Tonight," I said. "You're just in time."

"Good," Dafydd said. "I'll inform my men."

"I want you on the right flank," I said. "Hywel on the left."

"And Goronwy?" Dafydd asked. "Where will he be?"

I realized that the question he was really asking was, "Does Goronwy watch over me? Do you trust me to do my part?" I wasn't sure if I could really trust my brother, but the odds of him being friendly with Clare were slim.

"He and Gruffydd ap Rhys lead the foot soldiers to Morcraig," I said. "All should be under my control by morning."

*****

It isn't that I enjoy battle, but I would say that the fire that lights in my belly at the start of every fight acts as a potion, a poison some would say. All I know is that it goes to my head. Goronwy was correct when he told Meg that I see every man I've ever killed in my dreams, but he's wrong if he thinks I've never enjoyed killing. When the fury of battle takes you, there is a savage joy to it, as if your true self is finally let loose, and all notions of chivalry, stateliness, and civilized behavior are stripped away. What is revealed then, is the raw coil of a man, the essence of him that only cares about surviving, as if we were barbarians from the north who ate our meat raw. There are times when I understand why they do.

Just as dusk fell, the men gathered at the edge of the forest of Llanbradach, two miles north of Caerphilly. I'd already sent Goronwy, Gruffydd, and the men to their task. The people of the region and my scouts had reported that Clare had abandoned

Morcraig when he started work on Caerphilly. Clare might not see the advantage in the half-built castle, but I wanted the heights.

Morcraig was built on a ridge on the south edge of the Glamorgan uplands. From the castle, a man was afforded uninterrupted views south across the coastal plain to Cardiff. Gruffydd ap Rhys, my vassal, would find himself reinstalled by morning. From his seat, he could control all his lands and keep an eye on Clare for me.

The foot soldiers were his men. While my knights were a formidable force, it was right that he was taking most of the risk in this endeavor. He had the most to gain, and as he'd already lost everything, there was an urgency in him that I'd not seen before Clare had driven him from his lands. He'd not realized what it meant, before, to be a lord without a castle.

For our part, the guards at Caerphilly would not be enough to stop our force. The addition of Dafydd's thirty men was, in fact, most welcome. I preferred overwhelming odds whenever possible. My only fear, in truth, was that we'd fired up the men for battle and would arrive at Caerphilly to find none on offer. It was at such times that men become difficult to control.

"We're getting close, my lord," Hywel said. The outlines of the castle, still less than head high, were just visible through the darkening sky a hundred yards ahead. "Clare has cleared the forest for some distance all around. We'll soon be exposed."

We rode to the top of a small hill that gave us a slight vantage point. "Mother of God!" I said at the sight of the construction.

"It appears to be as they promised," Hywel said. "It will be the largest castle in the whole of Wales."

"Not if I have any say in the matter," I said. I pulled out my sword and held it above my head; then stood in the stirrups and signaled to the twenty-five men in my company to form up.

"Ride, men of Wales!" Dafydd called, a distant figure to my right. He urged his horse forward and led the charge. I let him.

My men surged forward, flowing down the slope and across the clearing to the burgeoning castle. Every third man held a torch. Although it made us targets for archers, a fire-lit cavalry charge inspired fear in the most hardened of men and I counted the risk worth it. To the men in the craft houses surrounding the site, it must have seemed like a dragon had descended among them.

I trotted Glewdra across the clearing in front of what Clare had meant to be the front gate and met Hywel near what looked to be the beginnings of a dam for the castle moat. One of several.

"What hubris Clare has to build such a colossus!" Hywel said as he greeted me. Unlike mine, his sword had blood on it.

"I need you to see to the men, Boots," I said. "I didn't want more than a skirmish, but this is less of a fight than I hoped it would be."

Hywel nodded and headed towards the mass of men who'd collected towards the eastern edge of the building site. They milled about, looking for targets, but none presented themselves. The builders and masons weren't our enemy and my men herded them into the middle of the building site and set them to work piling wood and brush on the stones and half-walls. Burning them would destroy them and leave Clare with only wreckage.

Goronwy circled the perimeter of the grounds on the far side of the field, looking for riders or men on foot who might be trying to escape to warn Clare. I turned Glewdra in the opposite direction, intending the same. As I came around the corner of a stone block—this one soon to form the base of one of the castle towers—a boy stepped from behind it, brandishing a long stick as his only weapon.

"Don't be a fool," I said. I leaned down and with my left hand, yanked the stick from his hand.

"I'll fight you to the death," the boy shouted, now raising his fists, as if that would hold off a sword. I reined in fully, studying him in the flickering light of the fire from the buildings which my men had set on fire.

"Now, why would you do that?"

He blinked. "You are thieves and barbarians from the north!"

"You should speak respectfully when you talk to a Prince of Wales," a voice spoke from behind me. I turned to see my brother riding up beside me.

The boy crouched, and then dashed to one side. Dafydd urged his horse after him and in an easy motion, leaned down and scooped him up. I followed, wanting to make sure Dafydd wouldn't harm him, though I saw no anger in him tonight. "A man knows when to fight and when to save his energy for another day," Dafydd said.

The boy didn't answer.

Then, Dafydd slowed his horse. "But you aren't a man, are you?" Even in the gloaming darkness, his quick grin was evident.

"Please let me go," the girl said, and her voice came out sounding so much like Meg's that first night at Criccieth that my heart twisted at the memory.

"I won't hurt you, *cariad*," Dafydd said.

The girl gazed at Dafydd, wide-eyed, but no longer cowering. Between one heartbeat and the next, Dafydd had transformed himself into the being that attracted women like flies to a pot of honey.

"My lord," Dafydd said, bowing his head slightly in my direction. I nodded and let him ride away with his prize. Enough women had told me, such that I assumed it to be true, that Dafydd was an accomplished lover. Despite his obvious failings, he would not mistreat the girl, no more than I had Meg.

I returned to the center of activity.

As I expected, Hywel had set up a perimeter of guards around the castle. "No one got away, as far as I know," he said. "Though in the dark, it's difficult to say."

"Good," I said.

Hywel looked ruefully at the devastation. "It won't hold Clare up for long," he said. "It's just going to make him angry."

"Clare is a twenty-five-year old boy. I could not let him build unchallenged. The precedent such an act sets is unthinkable."

"He will go to the King," Hywel said.

"No. I don't think he will. He doesn't want King Henry to interfere in Wales any more than I; less so, in fact, because the rights of the Marcher lords are so much more tenuous than mine. He will attempt to settle this himself."

"Shall we press on to Cardiff?" Bevyn, my young man-at-arms, pulled up beside us. He was breathing hard. He'd been in the forefront of the battle—just where he liked to be.

I looked south, to the sea I couldn't see from where I sat, and pictured Clare's castle on its hill overlooking the Severn Estuary. "I have neither the men nor the inclination for a long siege. We came to teach Clare a lesson. I'll give Gruffydd my support until July, and then I must return north. I have a woman and child to see to."

"Best wishes on his birth, my lord," Bevyn said.

"Thank you," I said. "I'll be counting on you to teach him as he grows."

Bevyn's eyes brightened. "It'll be my pleasure, my lord. It surely will."

* * * * *

"Damn the man!" I said as I burst through the door into the kitchen garden. "Why can't he be predictable?"

"What is it?" Meg sat against one wall, soaking up the last heat of the mid-October day. We'd had rain every day for a week, and the bright sunlight that spilled through the branches above her head was very welcome. Her hand rested comfortingly on her belly, while Anna sang from the other side of a bush as she dug in the dirt with her little shovel. I came to a halt and drank Meg in. Since Caerphilly, I'd been more absent than not, seeing to my lands and marshalling every man I could to my side. But for the first time in my life, I resented my responsibilities.

"It's Clare again. Apparently our meeting a month ago wasn't enough. Now he wants to meet me south of here."

"Where?"

"The old Roman road follows the Usk to the standing stone at Bwlch. Remote."

"I thought you'd resolved your dispute for now?" she asked. "I thought you agreed that you would rule the north of Senghennydd and he would control the south and wouldn't build further on his castle at Caerphilly."

"That's what I thought too."

"So what changed?"

"I don't know." I sat, stretched out my legs to their full length, and crossed my ankles, leaning back against the garden wall.

"What do you think he wants?"

"He wants me out of Senghennydd," I said. "It's that simple. Barring that, he wants to start building his castle at Caerphilly again. What I wonder is to whom he has spoken in the weeks since Tudur hammered out the latest agreement. Why does he need to see me face to face?"

"There hasn't been any fighting, has there?"

"Not that I know of. I would have thought that Gruffydd would have sent me word if there had."

"If he were free to do so," Meg said.

I turned my head to look at her. "You have a point. And before you say it, I can see a trap opening between my feet too."

"I'm afraid to say it at all," Meg said. "You need to meet him in person? You just saw him at Castell Dinas; and your emissaries will meet again in the new year. Why this meeting? Why now?"

"Because he wants it resolved sooner and requests me, face to face, to hammer out our differences."

"Is that usual?"

I shrugged. "I've met King Henry at the Ford of Montgomery. I would meet Edward, if need be. I can speak to Clare again."

"Okay, I'll say it," Meg said. "Cilmeri."

"It's a long time from now," I said. "I've no reason to believe Clare treacherous."

Meg pursed her lips. "Send Clare a letter and say you've urgent business in the north and wish to proceed with the arbitration as planned."

"He would know I wasn't telling the truth."

"Would he? Why? And why does it matter? You rule in Wales and can do as you please."

"I wish it were that simple. I do have the right to defend my lands and have done so against the Marcher lords, but everything I do has consequences." I studied her. "You recall that Bohun says Mortimer hates me?"

"I do," Meg said. "I also recall that he tried to take Brecon from you—and kill you—not long ago."

"And failed on both counts," I said. "Do you think his ire has faded? Can you see how his failure this year might fester within him such that fourteen years from now his sons lure me to Cilmeri and kill me?"

"Gilbert de Clare is not Roger Mortimer."

"But he could be," I said, "given time. Besides, this wasn't the first time I've defeated Mortimer. I've decimated his army *twice*. The first time was in 1262 at Cenfylls, and the second was only two years ago when he marched on Brecon and we stopped him at the ford, just to the northeast of the castle. The man has reason for a grudge."

"And if you can avoid making Clare into another Mortimer, it is worth the effort," Meg said.

"Yes," I said. "That is it exactly."

"How far is it? Can I come?"

I looked at her for a heartbeat and a half. "Meg."

"All right, all right," she said. "You don't need to tell me why I shouldn't."

"It's day's ride. No more. I've a castle close by and we'll make our base there before our meeting with Clare."

"Why Bwlch?"

"Clare's new mistress, since his marriage to Alice de Lusignan ended last year, is a Picard of Tretower Castle, located only a few miles away."

"That's just great," Meg said. "And what happened to his first wife? I thought you couldn't get a divorce in England."

I smiled. "I think he's going for an annulment, which might be hard to prove given that they have two daughters. You do have to pay a lot for it, and convince the Pope of your utter sincerity—though the fact that she has had a relationship with Prince Edward for many years may eventually aid Clare's cause."

Meg stared at me, aghast. She shook her head. "I don't understand that."

"That's not surprising," I said, "since nobody else does either. But as you may have observed, when a Prince wants something, he tends to get it."

"I had noticed that." She wrapped her arms around her belly as the baby kicked again.

"Don't be like that," I said. I put my arm across her shoulders and pulled her in to kiss her. "Am I really such an ogre?"

"I just don't want you to go away again, not so close to the baby's birth. I hate worrying about you."

"I'll take extra precautions," I said. "There will be no Cilmeri at Bwlch. Don't worry."

21

Meg

Llywelyn left with a host of men-at-arms and I tried not to worry, as he asked. I had other things to occupy my mind. I hadn't told him before he left, but I was having some contractions, every now and then. It was nothing serious, but similar to what had happened with Anna when I'd had contractions for three solid weeks before her birth. They would go on and on, reaching a crescendo toward early evening, only to die down around bedtime. Then they'd start over the next day at nine in the morning. Not fun.

And today was Halloween (though they didn't call it that—it was All Hallow's Eve), the day before All Saints Day. The celebrations were already beginning in the village, where the weekly fair was in full swing. I held Anna's hand as we walked across the drawbridge and down the road to the market square. It had rained in the night, but not so much that the road was muddy.

Little puddles pocked the road, and I tugged Anna away from them, not wanting her to get wet on the way there. I'd let her get wet on the walk home and then change her clothes.

Normally, as Llywelyn's woman, I rode into the village, even for the short distance from the castle to the market, but at nearly nine months pregnant, I wasn't allowed near a horse, much less on top of one. Beside us, two of Llywelyn's men-at-arms walked —Bevyn again, undoubtedly irritated at being left to mind me, though Llywelyn had tried to appease him by implying that this was a grave responsibility and he'd better not screw it up, and Rhodri, the young man who'd befriended Anna at the Gap, a lifetime ago now.

To understand what a medieval village fair was like, you first had to do away with anything you'd ever learned from movies, and particularly, focus not on what things looked like, but how they *smelled.* I'd gotten used to it in large part, but the sensitivities of early pregnancy had reasserted themselves at this late stage and I had to close my nose as I entered the village. The smell was a nauseating concoction of frying food, tanning leather, smoke, urine, decomposing organic matter of every variety, and manure.

The village was closely compacted due to the town wall that surrounded it. This protected it, but it also contained it and made the townsfolk 'in-fill' rather than spread their houses out as was more usual in Welsh communities. Very often, villages in Wales consisted only a few huts in which an extended family lived:

uncles and aunts, grandparents, cousins, and various distant relations.

At the most, these were in groups of five or six; the family worked together communally in the fields or in the raising of sheep, goats, and cattle. Many Welsh were also nomadic, splitting their time between the pastures of the lowlands in the winter, and the mountain meadows in the summer. The market fair, then, was an exciting event for everybody, and because of the imminent holiday, the Brecon fair had brought in revelers from miles around.

Anna swung between Rhodri and me. We lifted her over a particularly noxious clod of refuse. He and I exchanged a glance of understanding, and he swung her onto his hip.

"Let's see what trouble we can get into, shall we?" he said to her.

She smiled and touched a finger to his burgeoning mustache. Fashions were changing in Wales and more and more of the men sported them. I hoped Llywelyn would refrain from growing one, but Bevyn looked at Rhodri with something bordering on envy. I wanted to tell him that he'd grow up—and acquire the ability to grow one—
soon enough.

Rhodri and Anna stopped at a display of finger whistles. The proprietor took one out and handed it to her—a classic tactic which meant that if I didn't pay for it, I would either have an irate seller or a crying daughter. Sighing, I opened my purse. Bevyn leaned in, took out an appropriate amount, and began to bargain with the man. He and Rhodri had evidently decided, as had been the case in the past, that they still didn't trust my Welsh enough to allow me to bargain all by myself. They were probably right. Anna's Welsh was coming along so well she might do better than I.

The stalls circled the village green and lined the road on both sides into the village. Players had set up their tent in the middle of the green—I wondered what we'd get this time. All Hallow's Eve, so far, was showing itself *not* to be my favorite holiday in Wales. I didn't like all the ghosts and witch talk, especially if any of that talk was going to be directed at *me*, and I wasn't sure that some of it hadn't been.

"Did you hear she knew about the ambush at Coedwig Gap before it happened?"

"Did you know that only she and the Prince were spared when the entire castle was poisoned?"

"Had you heard that she can read?"

"Don't you worry, my lady," Bevyn said, gesturing to the costumes and strange decorations. "No one will harm you today."

"Why is that, Bevyn?" I asked. "Because they think I'm a witch and will cast a spell on them?"

"Not at all!" Bevyn said. "Where did you get that idea? Nobody's saying that!"

"I'm sorry, Bevyn," I said. "I must have misunderstood some of the gossip I overheard."

"It's true that you confuse people, but you've brought nothing but luck to the Prince. And now you will give him a son!"

Oh don't say that! What if it's a girl?

Then he put his hand on my arm, and the boyish exuberance was gone. "Your lord will be fine. Gilbert de Clare is a knight. His father was a force to be reckoned with in the Marche and he will not betray that memory."

"I don't know about that, Bevyn," I said. "That's probably why he's so belligerent. He feels like he has large boots to fill and he's worried he won't be able to."

"It's every son's fear," Bevyn said.

"I don't want to think about it."

"It's right before you," Bevyn said, and he didn't have to gesture towards my belly for me to know what he meant. "Every man is haunted by his father's expectations—it's a jumble of hatred, fear, loyalty, and love."

"I loved my father," I said.

Bevyn snorted. "You're a girl. It's different with you."

I was offended, but I also thought he was wrong and told him so. "It's different but not as much as you think. It isn't that he expected me to ever fight a battle, or lord my authority over anyone, but he had expectations for me that I failed to live up to, even as I knew my failure would sadden him." I glanced at Bevyn, not sure he was capable of understanding.

"I would like to see Anna grown," Bevyn said. "I'd like to know that she's like you."

"And this child," I said, resting a hand on my stomach.

"Your son is going to be a great man. He'll put us all to shame."

"He'll have to learn Latin," I said. "Poor boy."

Bevyn grinned.

We passed several huts whose occupants had left out pitchers of drink and plates of food to distract and satisfy the dead, so they wouldn't bother the living. I hoped Bevyn was right. Maybe I'd misunderstood the glances and stares—that they were admiring, rather than fearful.

With the Christian Church overtaking Wales, Halloween was becoming incorporated into All Saints' Day, a day set aside to honor all the Saints in the Christian calendar. Quite frankly, I was dreading having to sit in church for half the day tomorrow and was already planning my escape, pleading an antsy Anna or the onset of labor, even if it wasn't true.

The drama the players had begun in the center of the green was one I'd seen before, depicting the life of St. David, the patron Saint of Wales. As he was conceived through the rape of a nun, and the players embellished his life with rather dramatic exorcisms of various exotic creatures, it was definitely rated R and I pulled Anna away before she could see more than a minute of it. She was only three, but the masks they wore were scary even for me.

On the other side of the green, I found my favorite stall—the one that made scented soaps. I wasn't allowed lavender anymore, since it could induce miscarriage, but many other scents attracted me and it was a heady mix to stand under the tent and block out the rest of the market. I knew the soap-maker well, so I was surprised to see a new person, a young man, turn to me today.

"Madam," he said.

"Good morning." I looked hard at him, recognizing his voice but not sure from where. Then he tugged his hood back so I could see his face and put one finger to his lips.

"How may I help you today?" he said, in a loud voice

I stepped closer and lowered mine. "Humphrey! What are you doing here? Why are you disguised?"

"Where is the Prince?" he asked, tense and urgent.

"He left us four days ago for Bwlch, to meet Clare. The conference is set for this afternoon."

Humphrey swore. "My grandfather believes that Clare will betray him."

I sucked in a breath. "Why? How do you know?"

"We've had word," he said grimly.

"I warned him myself," I said. "It wasn't that he didn't listen, but he thinks everything is a trap and said he would take the usual precautions."

"He may need more than the usual," Humphrey said, "if my grandfather is right. It's possible Clare brings an army against him."

Feeling faint, I looked for Bevyn. Spying him, I gestured him closer and then turned back to Humphrey. "Why are you hiding? You could have walked into the hall to tell me this."

"The tension among my grandfather's allies in the Marche is such that he would rather nobody knew of our involvement."

"And yet you came to warn us?"

Humphrey gazed at me, his eyes like flint, looking far older than his years. "You expected otherwise from me?"

"I didn't know," I said. "When you left us, you didn't know yourself."

"What is it?" Bevyn said. Then he recognized Humphrey and his face reddened. "What are you doing here?"

"The Prince is in danger," Humphrey said.

"Someone must ride to warn Llywelyn." I tugged on Bevyn's sleeve. "Humphrey says that an entire army might wait for him in Bwlch."

Bevyn studied Humphrey. "I don't trust you."

"You don't have to trust me," Humphrey said, "but you must ride for Bwlch immediately."

"Bevyn, please," I said. "We have few men in the garrison, but they could leave within the hour. I would go to him, but I can't, not—"

"I can," Humphrey said. "I have men waiting for me on the hills above Felinfach. The Prince will need them."

Bevyn came alive at that. "No Bohun is going to lead the rescue of my prince. Leave the soaps and come to the castle. Tudur needs to hear of this and he can decide who rides and who doesn't."

Humphrey tugged his hood over his face again. Bevyn hustled him down the road toward the castle, swerving in and among the other revelers until they were lost from view.

"Where's Bevyn going?" Rhodri's head was turned toward the spot Humphrey and Bevyn had been, and he now made his way to my side, still carrying Anna.

"To the castle. The Prince is walking into an ambush," I said. "We need to get back. Tudur is going to need you."

22

Llywelyn

The standing stones that peppered the countryside in Wales had always drawn my interest. Gwynedd had its share. Some of my people were afraid of them, but when I touched them, felt the stone underneath my fingers, I remembered my ancestors who'd placed them there, for reasons they'd not passed down to us. Only one standing stone stood on the hill at Bwlch, a forlorn thing, left to itself in a meadow, half way up a hill that was hidden by trees on every side.

Goronwy and I bent over a map, spread out on the table in the hall at our borrowed castle. The sun hadn't yet risen, but he'd already sent out scouts to quarter the area. Tretower Castle was another ten miles on, and that was the direction, we presumed, from which Clare would come.

"It's the mountains behind that worry me," Goronwy said. "His men could hide in the miles of forest and rock up there."

"Which will make the going rough," I said. "We will take the proper precautions, listen to what Clare has to say, and be on our way."

Goronwy grunted. "We can always take to the river," he said. "The Usk is just on the other side of the road. We can follow it all the way home if need be."

"So be it," I said. "We've done what we can. I can hear Meg's warnings in my ears, but this is a chance I feel we must take."

We rode out an hour later at the head of a column of men, just as the sun peered over the tops of the peaks behind us. The trees grew more thickly on both sides of the road the further south and west we progressed. At Bwlch, we would leave the road, though it continued ahead to an old fort the Romans abandoned long ago another mile on. I hoped that my men had not been afraid to enter it, because it would be a perfect place to hide, if Clare had betrayal on his mind. *Too late to tell them now.*

As we approached the field which Clare had indicated we would meet, Goronwy reined in. Together we looked through the trees, up the slope to the meadow where the stone stood sentinel, guarding its meadow since before Christ was born.

"I don't like it," he said.

"You never do." I spurred Glewdra up the hill. The thirty men behind us followed, milling around the stone uncertainly when we realized we were all alone.

Goronwy urged his horse closer. "What now?"

I shrugged. "We wait, I guess. I don't—"

"My lord!" One of my men shrieked the words, an instant before a hail of arrows poured out of the trees above us. I flung up my shield instinctively and arrow hit it, just in the place my head had been a moment before. I spun Glewdra around to call to my men but they'd already broken apart and reformed around me, protecting me at the same time they made to charge towards the line of archers. Goronwy rode on my left, cursing steadily as he struggled to keep close to my side.

Another hail of arrows hit us and three horses went down, causing the men behind them to swerve out of the way. Then a third barrage. By that time, however, we'd reached the crest of the hill and the archers broke ranks at our approach. I urged Glewdra to leap over the stakes they'd placed in front of their lines, intending to run the archers down, but as the fastest of them disappeared behind a thick screen of trees, a company of cavalry took their place, charging out of the woods directly at us.

"May God protect us!" Hywel said. He too had an arrow in his shield. He spurred his horse to the side and wove between the men, determined to position himself properly to stave off the first assault.

Then I lost sight of him as our enemies hit us, as unstoppable a force as a boulder rolling down hill. They tore into our lines—tore them apart—with their momentum and numbers. Goronwy disappeared in the roiling mass of men and horses and I yanked Glewdra sideways to avoid a fallen log that blocked my retreat. Another horse fell in front of me and a pike caught Glewdra's leg. She stumbled and couldn't right herself. I tugged my feet out of the stirrups and jumped free before she crushed me beneath her. She struggled and twisted, but her legs had failed her, probably forever.

I'd lost my shield somewhere in the fray and wielded my sword with both hands, the sweat dripping in my eyes beneath my helmet. I tried to maneuver away from the main force of English soldiers, keeping to the high ground as I searched for men wearing my colors in the blur around me. I confronted a man equal in height to me, made all the taller by his high-plumed helmet. We struggled to find our footing on the grassy slope.

Then suddenly Goronwy appeared and hacked at the man from behind. As soon as he'd killed that man, he backed towards me as he tried to fend off the relentless attack. Hardly a man remained on horseback this far up the hill. A sea of red tunics surrounded us. As I slashed at the soldiers in front of me, a voice in my head cursed my stupidity more loudly with every second that passed. *I should never have come. Dear God, how many men have we lost? I should have known better.*

My strength waned, even as Goronwy and I stood back to back, fending off one attacker after another. My chest heaved with the effort and I flailed out with my sword, no longer under control. Beyond our immediate assailants, ten of Clare's men formed a perimeter around us, having ceased to fight. Finally, the closet of Clare's men took a long pace away from us. I still held them off with my sword, but no one challenged me. Goronwy and I had lost and had no place to run.

One of the men held up his sword, in mock salute, and pulled off his helmet. Gilbert de Clare stood in front of me, unmistakable with his mane of red hair turning prematurely gray.

He bared his teeth. “Now, the negotiations begin.”

I lowered my sword, speechless. Why didn’t he run me through and be done with it?

Then another man joined Clare, strolling out from under the trees into which the archers had run. “A Prince does not kill a Prince, cousin.” Edward pulled off his own helmet. “I just wanted your undivided attention.”

At his approach, I raised my sword again, needing to keep him, of all my enemies, at bay. “Does your father know of this escapade? We are at peace, are we not, with a treaty signed with your own hand?”

“Treaties are made to be broken.” Edward gestured at the carnage around us. “A few men is a small price to pay for a kingdom, is it not?”

“A few men,” Goronwy whispered from behind me in Welsh. “Good men.”

“What do you want?” I said.

Clare spread his hands wide. “My lands back. Castle Morcraig abandoned, Gruffydd ap Rhys back where he belongs, in Ireland where I put him, and the ability to build my castle at Caerphilly unhindered by you.”

“That is my land, not yours. The people support me and I claim it by right of treaty with England and through my grandfather, who won it at the point of a sword.”

"You forget your place," Edward said.

I glared at him. "It is my land."

Now Edward laughed. "Whose men are dying at his feet? Whose own life hangs in the balance? I assure you it isn't mine. The moment you die, all Wales will fall to me."

That was terrifyingly prophetic, but I firmed my chin and answered. "I am the Prince of Wales. Your father called me thus and what you do now violates every principle of God and man."

"That's where you're wrong," Edward said. "That is what you don't appear to understand. You and your line are of the past. What is principle when the rule of a nation is at stake?"

"You have no honor," I said.

Edward coughed and laughed at the same time. "Honor! I see now that you cling to the past. I am the Prince of England. I will rule my country and yours; you will bow to me. I am of the future and I tell you now, an independent Wales has no place in that future."

I stared at him, finding it impossible to voice my horror at his words. He was a madman, and yet the most powerful man in my world. "Your father—"

"My father is not long for this world," Edward said. "When I return from Crusade, I will take your country. God wills it."

I shook my head.

"Give me Senghennydd," Clare said, keeping to his main point, though he glanced at Edward, nearly as horrified as I. If there was no Wales, there might be no Marche. *Is it only now that he realizes he is in bed with a viper?*

"No," I said. "We have the King's peace."

"You have no army; I see one man beside you, the rest are dead or wounded on the ground. Who's to say how you die this day? I could kill you and no one would be the wiser. Why should I wait for all Wales to fall to me?"

"My brother, Dafydd, would fight you."

"Your brother is a weak man, vain and full of bluster. He leagues with you, he leagues with me. Has he shifted in the wind again?" Edward shrugged. "So he would fight, but he's not strong enough to withstand my wrath."

"My brother plots with you?"

"You are mighty slow, old man." Edward said. "Your brother sent a report to me of a plan to ambush you in Gwynedd. I believe the Bohun whelp was in on it, along with Gruffydd ap Gwenwynwyn's son. Obviously, they failed and your brother fears my response."

"You've not heard from him since the spring?"

"Why do you harp on this issue? Do you not understand that before long I will bring the full force of my power to Wales? You stand here thinking yourself noble, but it will not last, not when I am King."

Goronwy cleared his throat. "A Prince does not kill a Prince, you said."

Edward smiled, a similar smirk to the one my brother often used, but backed up with eyes that glinted like steel, and a backbone to match. "Made to be broken," Edward whispered. He raised his sword as did the men in the circle that surrounded us.

I raised mine. All was lost. I had a thought for Meg and the child she carried, and a hollow fear that they wouldn't live out the day, if either Edward, or Dafydd, caught her. What was honor, when my life was lost? Perhaps Meg could answer me that, but I had no answers for her.

"Cymry!" The chorus echoed across the hills and no sound could ever have been more beautiful.

I couldn't see them from where I stood, but Edward and Clare's response told me all I needed to know. Fifty at least, I reasoned, pounding toward us down the road from Brecon. Edward and Clare glanced at each other. Edward saluted me with his sword, sheathed it, and walked to his horse which cropped the grass, so well trained that the smell of fear and sweat and blood of battle hadn't discomforted it. By the time he was mounted, Clare and his men had melted into the trees, leaving Goronwy and me all alone on the hill.

I turned as my men rode up to us.

"Bohun. Tudur."

Tudur was off his horse before he'd fully stopped to grab my shoulders. I hadn't realized I was weaving on my feet. He eased me to the ground and I rested my arms on my knees and my head in my hands.

"You were just in time," Goronwy said.

"Or far too late, depending," I said, surveying the wounded and the dead. "Where's Boots?"

"Here, my lord!" Bevyn crouched over a man half-way down the hill and raised his hand. "He's alive but wounded."

I turned to Tudur. "And Meg? Rhodri and Bevyn were to guard her."

"It was she who sent us, my lord, upon Bohun's news."

"That's the last time I assign the job of guarding Meg to Bevyn, as he's abandoned his post both times," I said, but I couldn't be angry at him. I turned to Humphrey. "Thank you."

"Are we even now?" Humphrey gazed down at me.

"Did you know that Prince Edward was going to accompany Clare?"

Humphrey gaped at me for a heartbeat before mastering himself. "Your lady spoke of honor and she was right to do so, but it comes to me that there's very little of it left in this world. Very soon, honor will be replaced with expediency. You might want to make sure you're not on the losing side when it does." He bowed, more deeply than he ever had, and turned away to join Bevyn in caring for the wounded.

"That one bears watching," Tudur said.

23

Meg

I paced the battlements at Brecon, looking east. I felt like a seaman's wife, watching and waiting on a widow's walk for the ship that would bring her husband home. I waited through All Saints' Day, and the next, for Llywelyn's return. And he did come, he and Goronwy, leading a much diminished company of men. Humphrey was not among them.

I met him at the entrance to the hall; he didn't speak, just put his arms around me and rested his head on my shoulder. I looked past him to Goronwy, who met my eyes, just briefly, before looking down.

"Tell me," I said.

"We lost half our men," Goronwy said, "and the other half wounded. Those who could ride, or for whom we had horses are here. The rest we left at our borrowed castle to await aid and their women."

"From one moment to the next, the world ended, Meg. It's only because of our young Bohun that I live."

"Prince Edward was behind this," Goronwy said.

"Edward!" I said.

Goronwy heaved a sigh and lowered himself to a bench near the fire. "He's spreading his wings. This was only the beginning of his plans for Wales, and he made it clear that nothing—no treaty, no sense of honor, no right—will hinder him."

Llywelyn leaned heavily on me and we walked together to sit beside Goronwy. "Are you injured?" I asked him.

"No," he said. "My pride is bruised. A paltry thing, considering the number of men I lost because I expected better of Clare. He took me completely by surprise."

I looked down, not answering. He glanced at me. "Yes, I know you expected it, because of Cilmeri. But that was a rare thing, you know. How could any treaty ever be signed if the men coming to the meeting feared for their lives? It is a terrible precedent that Edward sets."

"He doesn't care," I said. "He feels that he is a law unto himself."

"He wears the right of God like a crown," Goronwy agreed. "We face much danger from him in the coming years. Maybe he'll be killed by the Saracens during his Crusade and we'll be saved from facing him again."

"No," Llywelyn said. "Wales has never been that lucky."

*****

Some days later we lay side by side in bed, our hands clasped beneath the blanket. Then Llywelyn rolled over and put a hand on my belly. "I spoke of luck," he said, "and our lack thereof."

"Yes."

"But you are more than lucky for me. You give me the hope that God has seen our plight and seeks to aid us in our time of need."

I put my hand on his. "I hope so, Llywelyn, but I'm scared."

"Of the birth?"

"Of everything," I said. "I'm scared of loving you so much and not deserving that love. I'm scared of losing you. It was a near thing. How many more chances do you get?"

"Fourteen years you gave me, Meg. I plan to use every single one of them."

"Did you think of that, there on the hill?"

"No," he said. "I was so damn scared that all I could think about was dying and leaving you and our son unprotected, with only Dafydd standing between Wales and England—Dafydd and his loathsome designs on you."

"But you want to name our baby Dafydd, if it's a boy?" We'd talked about names over the last months, and he'd always come back to that one.

"It was my uncle's name, and the name of the patron saint of Wales. What name could I give him that wasn't that of an enemy or one who has betrayed me? Owain? Gruffydd? Rhys? I think not."

"Okay," I said, laughing at his predicament. "But your brother is going to think he's named for him."

"Let him think that," Llywelyn said. "We know the truth." He rolled onto his back and soon was breathing gently, easing into sleep. I was glad and gently rubbed the top of his shoulder. He was going to need his sleep, because I was feeling an ache in my back that meant *baby, and soon! It's early though, if my dates are right.*

I awoke some time later to a cry from the next room. Feeling the need to use the guarderobe, I swung my legs over the bed, heaved myself to my feet, and walked to the curtain that separated our room from Anna's. I pulled it back and found Anna sitting up in bed, but no nurse beside her.

"Where's Maud, sweetie?"

"I don't know," she said. "I need to pee."

"Okay," I said and held out my hand. Anna clambered out of bed and toddled toward me, staggering slightly on sleepy feet. I eased open the latch to the door, not wanting to wake Llywelyn, and left it ajar. Anna and I walked down the hall to the toilet. I opened the door and stuck in my head. The room was empty, and the smell wasn't too bad. Llywelyn had ordered the toilet cleaned daily because I had a tendency to lose my lunch if the stench got too bad.

I hiked up Anna's nightgown and lifted her onto the seat. She leaned forward into my belly, clearly very sleepy, and I crouched in front of her so she could rest her head on my shoulder. As I shifted to find a more comfortable position, the room shifted with me.

Pop!

I clutched Anna to me. She gasped, and I gasped, and then we were gone.

* * * * *

The blackness took me. It was an abyss opening before my feet and I choked as we fell into it. Then my feet hit the ground and I fell over, my arms still wrapped around Anna. My mouth was open in a scream but nothing was coming out.

"Mammy!" Anna found her voice. "Look!"

I lifted my head and stared at the lights on the house in front of me. Electric lights. I sat up, supporting myself on one hand, and Anna stood next to me, her hand on my shoulder. I couldn't think. My brain whirred but processed no thoughts. Then the front door slammed and a woman came out the door, wiping her hands on her flowered dress. She trotted down the front steps toward us, slowed, then stopped, her breath coming in gasps.

"Mom," I said. I reached for her. She fell to her knees in front of me, touched a trembling hand to my face, and we both began to sob.

"Meg, my darling Meg," she said, wrapping her arms around me, the wetness on her cheeks mixing with my own tears.

"Gramma, Gramma, Gramma," Anna said, bouncing up and down. In the back of my head, I was surprised that Anna remembered her, and then I realized that she was saying 'Gramma' in Welsh: "*Mam-gu*."

"The baby's coming, Mom," I said, breathless. "Now."

"Let's get you into the house," she said, wiping at the tears on her cheeks with the backs of her hands and not asking me any questions I couldn't answer.

I stumbled with her to the front door, clutching her hand. I was bent over in pain from the child that was coming but still lost in the thirteenth century. I found myself crying in relief at being home, and at the same time for Llywelyn, for the man who'd died in every version of history we knew, on that snowy hill at Cilmeri.

Mom kept repeating *cariad* over and over again, which only made me sob all the more. "We'll get you to the hospital, Meg," she said, helping me up the steps. "How long have you been contracting?"

"Days," I said. "But it's too early. The baby's not due yet, or so I thought."

"I'll get the ambulance," she said. "You sit."

While she made the phone call, Mom put me on the couch next to the door, the very same couch I'd sat on with Anna the day we'd driven to Wales. Anna climbed onto the couch and snuggled beside me. The contractions were coming strongly by the time the ambulance came, and then the hours blurred together in a midst of pain and anxiety, and finally joy.

Llywelyn and I had a son.

* * * * *

I stared out the window, David in my arms, watching the lights come on as evening progressed. I marveled at the brightness and color, but couldn't help *missing, missing, missing* my life in Wales. *Until time do us part*, Llywelyn had feared, and he'd been right to. We would probably never know what had caused me to come to him after Trev died—at the very spot where he died. Or why. Only that I did.

"Can you tell me, *cariad*?" Mom said the next morning. "I missed you."

I shifted my head to get a better view of her in the chair beside the bed, and adjusted David on my breast. "I'm sorry, Mom," I said. "I spent the last nine months explaining where I'm from, and now I must explain to you where I've been, and you aren't going to believe me any more than they did."

"Meg," Mom said. "I'm your mother. What won't I believe?"

"That I traveled to thirteenth century Wales. That David's father is Llywelyn ap Gruffydd, the Prince of Wales."

I held Mom's eyes, though her face showed no expression, but then she smiled. She stood, came to sit on the side of the bed, and took my hand. "I know," she said.

"You *know?* I said. "How do you know?

"Anna," she said. "She's told me all about her Papa, and horses, and a man named Goronwy who made her laugh. She spoke in Welsh. You've done wonderful things with her, Meg."

"You believe me!"

"You are my darling daughter," Mom said. "There's nothing you could tell me that I wouldn't believe, if you believed it to be true."

When David grew old enough to travel, we flew to Wales—against my mother's better judgment. I begged her for help, for I didn't want to go alone, and eventually she consented to come with me.

"He's not there, *cariad*," she said, even as she booked the tickets and then paid for them. "The castles are gone or empty shells. It will be nothing like you remember them. Keep your dreams. Cold reality will only dash them."

Mom was right, and yet she wasn't.

We went first to Criccieth, since it was there that I'd started—we'd started—though I'd only stayed there for a day. It was as I remembered, a mighty fortress built on rock on a promontory in the sea. But the walls had mostly crumbled, and I confused the lady at the visitor center who speculated on its successive construction, postulating that it was Edward who had built the outer curtain wall. *I think not!*

I stood on the edge of the cliff, as the battlements were gone, and looked out over the sea. Then I turned to the town below. The mountain loomed behind it, as it always had, but the village had spread along the seashore, thriving and modern, having long since filled in the marsh in which my car lay buried. Power poles lined the beach instead of trees, but if I closed my eyes and *breathed*, it smelled the same. It was my Wales, but still, without Llywelyn in it.

Everywhere we went, I collected stories about Llywelyn. *He lived* here. *He fought* there. Two different abbeys claimed his body as his final resting place, but none could produce his grave. Throughout, I restrained myself from pointing to the baby in my arms and saying: "Look! This is his son! The true Prince of Wales! Open your eyes and see!"

We reached Brecon in the driving rain. Anna had held Mom's hand as we walked across the parking lot, but she stopped as soon as she saw the castle and refused to go any further. I could understand, for it shocked me too. The castle had a giant, white house attached to it.

"What is that?" I asked.

"It says on the information sheet, 'Brecon Castle Hotel'," Mom said. "That's where we're supposed to be staying."

"What have they done to it?" I breathed.

Mom scooped up Anna and we walked across the castle grounds, or what had been the castle grounds and into the front entrance of the house. Mom checked us in as I blindly wandered the reception room, following my nose, until I reached the garden and the last standing stones of the old castle. Mom and Anna followed me outside and we stood in the center of what had been the outer courtyard.

"Papa's not here, is he?" Anna said.

"No, honey." My eyes filled with tears. "He's not."

That was the last of the Welsh castle tours. We visited Roman ruins and the massive and well-preserved English castles that Edward had built to subjugate Wales, but I didn't want Anna to wonder where Llywelyn was when she was too young to understand my grief or cope with her own.

I did go without them, just once, with only David in his sling, to Cilmeri, a small town just a few miles west of Builth Wells. A farmer had put up a memorial stone—really just a big, jagged piece of granite—to mark the spot where Llywelyn died. Every year on the 11th of December, patriots held a ceremony to mark the day and the spot where he fell. I couldn't bear the thought of that, and was glad that it was March and I was alone with only the flowers people who still thought of him had left. I read the death poems and songs to his memory with which people littered the meadow, and knew that I wouldn't come back.

The fire in his hearth has gone out,
Its light lost in the murk of the hall.
No one is left to tend it.
A great warrior, a king,
our Prince of Wales
Llywelyn
Has fallen in the snow.

He is quiet now, asleep under the mantle of peace.
The peace he reached for all his life,
But could never find and we could not give him,
Is his at last.

The fire in his heart has gone out.
His heat can no longer warm us.
But still we dream, we live
The morning sun wakes us.
In our hearts, he stays with us,
Dreams with us,
And will rise to walk in better days.

Mom and Anna had understood what I hadn't. Llywelyn wasn't there.

*****

"I hear you're leaving us?" My professor leaned across his desk and passed me the final paper that completed my senior requirements for graduation. "What did they offer you out there in Oregon that we didn't?"

I looked down at my paper. It was called *The Mythologization of Llywelyn ap Gruffydd: An Historical Perspective.*

"Space," I said. I knew my professor well enough to tell him the truth.

"Ah," Dr. Bill said, folding his hands and putting his fingers to his lips. "A Ph.D. is a long row to hoe, but that paper is a good start. Just make sure you don't stray too far into the realm of speculation. Then you'll have something that should be in the literature department, instead of history."

"I think I can handle it," I said, "though I confess there were times while writing this that I wasn't sure what was real and what wasn't."

"If we didn't love history so much, none of us would be here. We all get our heads so far into the past that sometimes we forget where we are. Don't let graduate school take over your life. Don't forget that you live in the here and now."

"Yes, Dr. Bill," I said.

Could he read my mind or what? It was four years since I'd returned to the twentieth century: four years of love and tears, and an enormous amount of work. Mom had pushed me towards getting back in school. That first quarter, I signed up at the local community college to continue those classes I'd started on before we'd driven to Wales. I'd found evening classes, early morning classes, independent study classes, and ones that coincided with the kids' naps. Over the years we'd bumped along pretty well, and with David in preschool and Anna in second grade, this last semester at the university had been a much more stable proposition for me.

If only Elisa could have been part of it too. My sister had been more stubborn than either Mom or I had thought possible. She flat-out refused to accept that I'd been to Wales, and that

David was not Trev's child. That she'd been distracted and harassed preparing for her own marriage during Christmas break four years ago, I could understand, but as the years had passed, we'd slid into a mutual non-discussion pact. I didn't mention Wales, and she didn't close her ears to my voice. And I'd sworn on a stack of Bibles never to mention it to Ted, her husband.

But the reason I was leaving Pennsylvania was that I no longer could live so close to the place where Wales started. At first, I drove to the spot every day, maybe multiple times a day, as long as I had both Anna and David in the car with me. Yet, in snow, rain, or sun, the road never became what it had been. Often, I'd park beside the road, get out of the car, and walk all over the hill, poking into the dirt and sometimes even shouting Llywelyn's name. But he never answered, and the road never opened for me into that black abyss that had brought us to Wales in the first place.

What I could never come to terms with was *why* it had happened. If I was *meant*, as Llywelyn thought, to come to Wales, to save his life and bear his child, why was I back in Pennsylvania? If I was *meant* to save Llywelyn's life and his dynasty, why did he still die on that snowy hillside in 1282? None of it made sense.

Except for the very real existence of David, I wouldn't have believed it had happened at all—as if it was a year-long dream which I only awoke from in my mother's garden. I hoped that by leaving Pennsylvania, Llywelyn would haunt me less. I intended to continue my research on Wales, to become an historian, but I needed to stop *living* in the past. I needed to get away to an entirely different place, and face the fact that this was the only life I was going to get.

As I watched David grow, I could see his father in him. Even at four, he was a driven child, a perfectionist, always wanting to climb higher, run faster—push himself harder than any child I knew—and most adults, for that matter. And maybe that's where the answer lay—maybe I needed to raise my son to be the man *he* needed to be, and hope that who he was would transcend space and time, if that *time* ever came.

But I couldn't tell David who his father was. It wouldn't do to raise a boy who thought he was the Prince of Wales. In the twentieth century, that job belonged to another man, in another country, a world and a lifetime away. Even Anna appeared to have no memory of Wales at all. Now that she was in school, she refused to speak a word of Welsh, as if punishing me for taking her away from all that she loved.

No. It's best that we leave.

And yet, I still lay in bed at night, and wept for him. Wales lost him, I lost him, at the very point when his triumph was within his grasp. Still, I heard the hope under the despair, and dreamed of what might have been and what could still be. Someday. Hope for me; hope for him.

Walk with me, under star-strewn skies,,
Your hand warm in mine.
Until the dawn, I'll dream of you,
Good night, my love. Good night.

Until that sun wakes you, and you turn to find me beside you once again, I wish you dreams of peace. Good night, my love. Good night.

The End

The story of Meg, Anna, and David is continued in the next book in the *After Cilmeri* series, *Footsteps in Time.*

Excerpt: *Footsteps in Time: A Time Travel Fantasy*

Chapter One

"**D**o you want me to come with you?"

Anna looked back at her brother. He'd followed her to the door, his coat in his hand.

"Okay," she said, trying not to sound relieved. "You can hold the map."

The clouds were so low they blended into the trees around the house and Anna tipped her head to the sky, feeling a few gentle snowflakes hit her face. They walked across the driveway, the first to leave tracks in the new snow.

"You're sure you can handle this?" David asked, eyeing the van. It faced the house so Anna would have to back it out.

"Christopher's waiting," Anna said. "It's not like I have a choice."

"If you say so," David said.

Their aunt had asked Anna to pick up her cousin at a friend's house, since she had a late meeting and wouldn't make it. Ignoring David's skeptical expression, Anna tugged open the door, threw her purse on the floor between the seats, and got in the driver's side. David plopped himself beside her with a mischievous grin.

"And don't you dare say anything!" she said, wagging her finger in his face before he could open his mouth. He was three years younger than she, having just turned fourteen in November, unbearably pompous at times, and good at everything. Except for his handwriting, which was atrocious. Sometimes a girl had to hold onto the small things.

"Which way?" Anna asked, once they reached the main road. The windshield wipers flicked away the new snow, barely keeping up. Anna peered through the white for oncoming cars and waited for David to say something.

David studied the map, disconcertingly turning it this way and that, and then finally settled back in his seat with it upside down. "Uh . . . right," he said.

Anna took a right, and then a left, and within three minutes they were thoroughly lost. "This is so unlike you," she said.

"I'm trying!" he said, "but look at this—" he held out the map and Anna glanced at it. One of the reasons she'd accepted his offer, however, was because maps confused her under the best of circumstances. "The roads wander at random and they all look the same. Half of them don't even have signs."

Anna had to agree, especially in December, with the leafless trees and rugged terrain. She drove up one hill and down another, winding back and forth around rocky outcroppings and spectacular, yet similar, mansions. As the minutes ticked by, Anna clenched the wheel more tightly. They sat unspeaking in their heated, all-wheel drive cocoon, while the snow fell harder and the sky outside the windows darkened with the waning of the day. Then, just as they crested a small rise and were taking a downhill curve to the left, David hissed and reached for the handhold above his door.

"What?" Anna asked. She took a quick look at him. His mouth was open, but no sound came out and he pointed straight ahead.

Anna returned her gaze to the windscreen. Ten feet in front of them, a wall of snow blocked the road, like a massive, opaque picture window. She had no time to respond, think, or press the brake, before they hit it.

Whuf!

They powered through the wall and for a long three seconds a vast black space surrounded them. Then they burst through to the other side to find themselves bouncing down a snow-covered hill, much like the one they'd been driving on, but with grass beneath their wheels instead of asphalt. During the first few seconds as Anna fought to bring the van under control, they rumbled into a clearing situated halfway down the hill. She gaped through the windshield at the three men on horseback who appeared out of nowhere. They stared back at her, frozen as if in a photograph, oblivious now to the fourth man on the ground whom they'd surrounded.

All four men held swords.

"Anna!" David said, finally finding his voice.

Anna stood on the brakes, but couldn't get any traction in the snow. All three horses reared, catapulting their riders out of the saddle. Anna careened into two of the men who fell under the wheels with a sickening crunching thud. Still unable to stop the van, she plowed right over them and the snow-covered grass, into the underside of a rearing horse.

By then, the van was starting to slide sideways and its nose slewed under the horse's front hooves, which were high in the air, and hit its midsection full on. The windshield shattered from the impact of the hooves, the horse fell backwards, pinning its rider beneath it, and the airbags exploded. By then, the van's momentum had spun it completely around, carried it across the clearing to its edge, and over it.

It slid another twenty feet down the hill before connecting with a tree at the bottom of the slope. Breathless, chained by the seatbelt, Anna sat stunned. David fumbled with the door handle.

"Come on," he said. He shoved at her shoulder. When she didn't move, he grasped her chin to turn her head to look at him. "The gas tank could explode."

Her heart catching in her throat, Anna wrenched the door open and tumbled into the snow. She and David ran toward a small stand of trees thirty feet to their left, and stopped there, breathing hard. The van remained as they'd left it, sad and crumpled against the tree at the base of the hill. David had a line of blood on his cheek. Anna put her hand to her forehead and it came away with blood, marring her brown glove.

"What—" Anna said, swallowed hard, and tried again. "How did we go from lost to totaled in two point four seconds?" She found a tissue in her pocket, wiped at the blood on her glove, and began dabbing at her forehead.

David followed the van tracks with his eyes. "Can you walk up the hill with me and see what's up there?"

"Shouldn't we call Mom first?" Their mother was giving a talk at a medieval history conference in Philadelphia, which is why she'd parked her children at her sister's house in Bryn Mawr in the first place.

"Let's find out where we are before we call her," David said.

Anna was starting to shake, whether from cold or shock it didn't really matter. David saw it and took her hand for perhaps the first time in ten years. He tugged her up the hill to the clearing. They came to a stop at the top, unable to take another step. Two dozen men lay dead on the ground. They sprawled in every possible position. A man close to Anna was missing an arm and his blood stained the snow around him. Anna's stomach heaved and she turned away, but there was no place to look where a dead man didn't lie.

But even as she looked away, it registered that the men weren't dressed normally. They wore mail and helmets, and many still had their swords in their hands. Then David left at a run, heading along the path the van had followed. Anna watched him, trying not to see anyone else. He crouched next to a body.

"Over here!" he said, waving an arm.

Anna followed David's snowy footprints, weaving among the dead men—every one butchered. By the time she came to a halt beside David, tears streamed down her cheeks.

"My God, David," she said, choking on the words, her voice a whisper. "Where are we?" Heedless of the snow, Anna fell to her knees beside the man David was helping to sit upright. She was still breathing hard. She'd never been in a car accident before, much less one that landed her in the middle of a clearing full of dead men.

"I don't know," David said. He'd gotten his arm under the man's shoulder and now braced his back. The man didn't appear to have any blood on him, although it was obvious from his quiet moans that he was hurt.

The man grunted and put his hands to his helmet, struggling to pull it from his head. Anna leaned forward, helped him remove it, and then set it on the ground beside him. The man looked old to have been in a battle. He had a dark head of hair, with touches of white at his temples, but his mustache was mostly grey and his face lined. At the moment it was also streaked with sweat and dirt—and very pale.

"Diolch," he said.

Anna blinked. That was *thank you* in Welsh, which she knew because of her mother's near-continual efforts to teach them the language, although Anna had never thought she'd actually need to know it. She met the man's eyes. They were deep blue but bloodshot from his exertions. To her surprise, instead of finding them full of fear and pain, they held amusement. Anna couldn't credit it, and decided she must be mistaken.

The man turned to David. "Beth yw'ch enw chi?" he asked. *What is your name?*

"Dafydd dw i," David said. *My name is David.* David gestured towards Anna and continued in Welsh. "This is my sister, Anna."

The man's eyes tracked back to Anna and a twitch of a smile flickered at the corner of his mouth. "We need to find safety before night falls," he said, still all in Welsh. "I must find my men."

Now *that* was equally ridiculous and impossible.

Pause.

Anna was trying to think what to say to him, anything to say to him, when someone shouted. She swung around. A dozen men on horses rode out of the trees near the van. David settled the man back on the ground and stood up. At the sight of him, the lead rider reined his horse. The others crowded up behind him.

They all stared at each other, or rather, the men stared at David. They seemed frozen to their horses and Anna looked up at David, trying to see what they saw. He had turned fourteen in November, but his voice hadn't yet changed so he hadn't grown as tall as many of his friends. At 5' 6", he was still four inches taller than she, however. David had sandy blonde hair, cut short, and an athletic build, thanks to his continuous efforts in soccer and karate. Anna's friends at school considered him cute, in a geeky sort of way.

"What is it?" she whispered.

"I don't know," David said. "Is it our clothes? Your hair?"

Anna touched her head, feeling the clip that held her hair back from her face. The bun had come lose and her hair cascaded down her back in a tangled, curly mass.

"They're looking at *you*, David, not me."

The man they'd helped moaned and David crouched again beside him. His movement broke the spell holding the horsemen. They shouted, something like "move!" and "now!"

and their lead rider climbed the hill and dismounted. He elbowed Anna out of the way, knocking her on her rear in the snow, and knelt beside the wounded man. This newcomer was about David's height, but fit the description Anna had always attributed to the word 'grizzled.' Like all these men, he wore mail and a helmet and bore a sword. He had bracers on his arms—*where had I learned that word?*—and a surcoat over his chain mail.

He and the man held a conversation while David and Anna looked at each other across the six feet of space that separated them. Despite her comprehension earlier, Anna couldn't understand a word. Maybe the man had spoken slower for their benefit, or in a different dialect from what he spoke now. The men must have decided something, because after more shouting, other men hurried up the hill, surrounded the downed man, and lifted him to his feet. He walked away—actually walked—suspended between two men who supported him on either side.

David and Anna sat in the snow, forgotten. Anna's jeans were soaking wet, but stiff from the cold, and her hands were frozen, even in her gloves.

"What do we do now?" David asked, his eyes tracking the progress of the soldiers.

"Let's go back up the hill," Anna said. "We didn't drive that far. There must be a road at the top."

David gave her a speaking look, which she ignored. Anna took a few steps, trying not to look at the dead men whom she'd managed to forget for a few minutes, and then found herself running away across the meadow. She veered into the wheel tracks of the van. David pounded along beside her until she had to slow down. They'd reached the upward slope at the far side of the meadow. The snow was deeper here because men and horses hadn't packed it down; her feet lost their purchase on the steep slope and she put out a hand to keep from falling.

Anna looked up the hill. Only a dozen yards away, the van tracks began. Beyond them, smooth fresh snow stretched as far as she could see. It was as if they'd dropped out of the sky.

More shouts interrupted her astonishment and Anna turned to find horsemen bearing down on them. She looked around wildly but there was nowhere to run. One man leaned down and in a smooth movement, caught her around the waist. Before she could think, he pulled her in front of him. She struggled to free herself but the man tightened his grip and growled something she didn't catch, but could easily have been *sit still, dammit!*

"David!" Anna said, her voice going high.

"I'm here, Anna," he called. The man holding her turned the horse and they passed David, just getting comfortable on his own horse. Dumbstruck, Anna twisted in her seat to look back at him.

All he did was shrug, and Anna faced forward again. They rode across the meadow and down the hill, reaching the bottom just as the wounded man got a boost onto a horse. He gathered the reins while glancing at the van. Anna followed his gaze. It sat where she'd left it. It was hopeless to think of driving it, even if they had somewhere to go.

The company followed a trail through the trees. A litany of complaints—about her wet clothes and hair, about her aching neck and back from the car crash, and most of all, her inability to understand what was happening—cycled through Anna's head as they rode.

Fortunately, after a mile or two (it was hard to tell in the growing darkness and her misery) they trotted off the trail into a camp. Three fire rings burned brightly and the twenty men who'd ridden in doubled the number of people in the small space. The man behind Anna dismounted and pulled her after him. Although she tried to stand, her knees buckled and he scooped her up, carried her to a fallen log near one of the fires, and set her down on it.

"Thanks," Anna said automatically, forgetting he probably couldn't understand English. Fighting tears, she pulled her hood up to hide her face, and then David materialized beside her.

"Tell me you have an explanation for all this," Anna said, the moment he sat down.

He crossed his arms and shook his head. "Not one I'm ready to share, even with you."

Great. They sat unspeaking as men walked back and forth around the fire. Some cooked, some tended the horses staked near the trees on the edges of the clearing. Three men emerged from a tent thirty feet away. Their chain mail didn't clank like Anna imagined plate mail would, but it creaked a little as they walked. Someone somewhere roasted meat and despite her queasiness, Anna's stomach growled.

Nobody approached them, and it seemed to Anna that whenever one of the men looked at them, his gaze immediately slid away. She wasn't confused enough to imagine they couldn't see her, but maybe they didn't want to see her or know what to make of her. Anna pulled her coat over her knees, trying to make herself as small as possible. The sky grew darker and still she and David sat silent.

"Do you think we've stumbled upon a Welsh extremist group that prefers the medieval period to the present day?" Anna finally asked.

"Twenty miles from Philadelphia?" he said. "Bryn Mawr isn't that rural. Somehow, I just can't see it."

"Maybe we aren't in Pennsylvania anymore, David." Anna had been thinking those words for the last half an hour and couldn't hold them in any longer.

He sighed. "No, perhaps not."

"Mom's going to be worried sick," she said, choking on the words. "She was supposed to call us at 8 o'clock. I can't imagine what Aunt Elisa is going to tell her." Then Anna thought, *stupid!* She whipped out her phone.

"It says 'searching for service'," David said. "I already tried it."

Anna doubled over and put her head into David's chest. Her lungs felt squeezed and her throat was tight with unshed tears. He patted her back in a 'there, there' motion, like he wasn't really paying attention, but when she tried to pull away, he tightened his grip and hugged her to him.

Eventually, Anna wiped her face and straightened to look into his face. He met her eyes and tried to smile, but his eyes were reddened and his heart wasn't in it. Looking at him, Anna resolved not to pretend that all was well. They needed to talk about what had happened even if David didn't want to. *How many books have we all read where the heroine refuses to face reality? How many times have I thrown the book across the room in disgust at her stupidity?*

"What are you thinking?" she asked him.

He shook his head.

"We could leave right now, follow the trail back to the van," Anna said. "It couldn't be more than a few miles from here."

David cleared his throat. "No."

"Why not?" she said.

"What for?"

"I want to climb to the top of the hill we came down and see what's up there," she said. "I know the tracks of the van disappeared, but we had to have driven down that hill from somewhere. We couldn't have appeared out of nowhere."

"Couldn't we?" David said. He sat with his elbows resting on his knees and his chin in his hands. When Anna didn't respond, he canted his head to the side to look at her. "Do you really think we'll find the road home at the top of that hill?"

Anna looked away from him and into the fire. *No . . . No more than you do.* "You're thinking time travel, aren't you?" she said.

"Time travel is impossible."

"Why do you say that?"

Anna's abrupt question made David hunch. Then he straightened. "Okay," he said. "If time travel is possible, why don't we have people from the future stopping by all the time? If time travel is possible, all of *time* itself has to have already happened. It would need to be one big pre-existent event."

"That doesn't work for me," Anna said.

"Not for me either," said David. "It's pretty arrogant for us to think that 2010 is as far as time has gotten, but these people's lives have already happened, else how could we travel back and relive it with them?"

"So you're saying the same argument could hold for people traveling from 3010 to 2010. To them, we've already lived our lives because *they* are living theirs."

"Exactly," David agreed.

"Then where are we? Is this real?"

"Of course it's *real*," he said, "but maybe not the same reality we knew at home."

"I'm not following you," Anna said.

"What if the wall of snow led us to a parallel universe?" he said.

"A parallel universe that has only gotten to the Middle Ages instead of 2010?"

"Sure."

"You've read too much science fiction," she said.

David actually smiled. "Now, *that's* not possible," he said.

Anna put her head in her hands, not wanting to believe it. David picked up a stick and begin digging in the dirt at his feet. He stabbed the stick into the ground between them again and again, twisting it around until it stuck there, upright. Anna studied it, then reached over, pulled it out, and threw it into the fire in front of them.

"Hey!" David said.

Anna turned on him. "Are we ever going to be able to go home again?" she asked. "How could this have happened to us?

Why has this happened to us? Do you even realize how appalling this all is?"

David opened his mouth to speak, perhaps to protest that she shouldn't be angry at *him*, but at that moment, a man came out of the far tent and approached them. Instead of addressing them, however, he looked over their heads to someone behind them and spoke. At his words, two men grasped David and Anna by their upper arms and lifted them to their feet. The first man turned back to the tent and their captors hustled them after him. At the entrance, the man indicated they should enter. David put his hand on the small of Anna's back and urged her forward.

She ducked through the entrance, worried about what she might find, but it was only the wounded man from the meadow, reclining among blankets on the ground. He no longer wore his armor, but had on a cream colored shirt. A blanket covered him to his waist. Several candles, guttering in shallow dishes, lit the tent, and the remains of a meal sat on a plate beside him. He took a sip from a small cup, and looked at them over the top of it.

The tent held one other man, this one still in full armor, and he gestured them closer. They walked to the wounded man and knelt by his side. He gave them a long look, set down his cup, and then pointed to himself.

"Llywelyn ap Gruffydd," he said.

Anna knew she looked blank, but she simply couldn't accept his words. He tried again, thinking they hadn't understood. "Llywelyn—ap—Gruffydd."

"Llywelyn ap Gruffydd," David and Anna said together, the words passing Anna's lips as if they belonged to someone else.

Llywelyn nodded. "You understand who I am?" he asked, again in Welsh. Anna's neck was having a hard time bending forward and she barely got her chin to bob in acknowledgement. She was frozen in a nightmare that wouldn't let her go.

David recovered more quickly. "You are the Prince of Wales," he said. "Thank you, my lord, for bringing us with you. We would be lost without your assistance."

"It is I who should be thanking you," he said.

Anna had allowed them to continue speaking, growing colder and colder with every sentence. Llywelyn eyes flicked to her face and she could read the concern in them. Finally, she took in a deep breath, accepting for now what she couldn't deny.

"My lord," she said, "Could you please tell us the date?"

"Certainly," he said. "It is the day of Damasus the Pope, Friday, the 11th of December."

David's face paled as he realized the importance of the question, but Anna was determined to get the whole truth out and wasn't going to stop pressing because he was finally having the same heart attack she was. "And the year?" Anna asked.

"The year of our Lord twelve hundred and eighty-two," Llywelyn said.

Anna nodded. "You remember the story now, don't you, David?" she said in English, her voice a whisper because to speak her thoughts more loudly would give them greater credence. David couldn't have forgotten it any more readily than she could. Their mother had told them stories about medieval Wales since before they could walk—and tales of this man in particular.

"Llywelyn ap Gruffydd was lured into a trap by some English lords and killed on December 11, 1282 near a place called Cilmeri. Except . . ." Anna kept her eyes fixed on Llywelyn's.

"Except we just saved his life," David said.

Footsteps in Time is available now wherever books are sold.

Acknowledgments

I have many people to thank, not only for their assistance with Daughter of Time, but who have helped make my books better and my life sane for the last five years.

First and foremost, thank you to my family: my husband Dan, who five years ago told me to give it five years and see if I still loved it. I still do. Thank you for your infinite patience with having a writer as a wife. To my four children, Brynne, Carew, Gareth, and Taran, who have been nothing but encouraging, despite the fact that their mother spends half her life in medieval Wales. Thank you to my parents, for passing along their love of history, and particularly to my father, who died in 2011 but was one of my most ardent fans.

Thanks to my beautiful writing partner, Anna Elliott, who has made this journey with me from nearly the beginning. And thank you to my readers, without whom, none of this would be possible.

About the Author

With two historian parents, Sarah couldn't help but develop an interest in the past. She went on to get more than enough education herself (in anthropology) and began writing fiction when the stories in her head overflowed and demanded she let them out. Her interest in Wales stems from her own ancestry and the year she lived in England when she fell in love with the country, language, and people. She even convinced her husband to give all four of their children Welsh names.

She makes her home in Oregon.

www.sarahwoodbury.com

Made in the USA
Lexington, KY
22 August 2012